The Girl who Left the Village

An African Woman's Journey - Book 1

Eileen K. Omosa

Copyright

The Girl who Left the Village: An African Woman's Journey ~ Book 2

Same story, previously titled, Ignited by Education ISBN 978-09959908-7-6

Each of the books can be read as a standalone or part of a series. Some of the characters in one book are found in earlier or future books in the series.

Thank you in advance for telling your family, friends, and colleagues about this book.

The Girl who Left the Village
First Published in 2017
Eileen K. Omosa/We Grow Ideas
Canada

ISBN: 978-1-990124-04-4

www.eileenomosa.com

Acknowledgements

I am grateful to every individual I met as I went about creating *The Girl who Left the Village*

The following made a professional contribution:

Editor: Robert 'Babu' Wagner

Proof-reader: Mark Schultz at Wordrefiner.com

Wardrobe editor: Darleen Masakhwe

Cover designer: Sarah @ forcoverservices

Logistics: Eugene Wambongo

Book design template by BookDesignTemplates.com

DEDICATION

To all girls and women making decisions and choices during unpredictable times. Through sheer effort, you prove to society that positive change is possible.

And the Chase Began

She's the most educated girl in the village, but her parents are worried she read the wrong books. Will they ever reach a common understanding?

By sheer luck, Sophia Mariko has completed university education through grants for students from poor families. She's focused on building her career and to pay fees for her siblings when her father summons her to the village to get married.

Sophia could resist and stay in the city, but her job is insecure. Richie floods her work desk with red roses and proposes to marry her. She turns down his overtures but becomes desperate on learning he's the son of her employer.

How will Sophia choose? Can she shun marriage, yet her upbringing prepared her for the role of a wife and mother? Or will she abandon her job and drop back into the poverty she has worked so hard to overcome?

The Girl who Left the Village is book one in the series **An African Women's Journey**. Sophia's story starts continues in *The Secret he Never told Her* and concludes in *The Woman She Became*. A trilogy where education, culture, ambition, and love intertwine.

CONTENTS

Chapter 1

The matatu raced down the steep Valley Road. The high speed forced Sophia to open her eyes and be ready this time, in case of another accident.

In desperation, and without realizing it, she heard words escape from her mouth. "I will go for the interview. If they turn me down, at least I would have tried." To the dismay of the passenger seated next to her. Sophia realized her folly and retreated to her internal thoughts.

Since Sophia boarded the matatu, a public transport minibus, about forty minutes ago, she had been agonizing over the early morning accident.

She also wondered what would happen if she did not attend the job interview. She was already convinced that without a job, life would get worse, not only for her, but for her two brothers in secondary school, and another two in primary school and her sister in university.

The matatu was now full of passengers, though Sophia could not recall when the vehicle stopped to pick them up. Preoccupied with her thoughts, she promised herself that if she got the job, she would perform her tasks like no employee before her. She would set impressive standards, the same way she had done while in school and university.

Thinking about the poverty she was born into, she shook her head vigorously, to dispel the scary thought of her family falling deeper into debt. Her action compelled the passenger seated next to her to move further out into the passageway of the vehicle. Sophia noticed the reaction and promised herself not to drift into deep thoughts again and miss her bus stop in town. In no way would she arrive late for the 9:00am appointment.

~ ~ ~ ~ ~ ~

Annabel, one of the ladies at the hair salon, waved to Sophia. "You made it girl, a first at our premises. Go girl."

Sophia smiled back in gratitude. She straightened her now dry skirt as she quickened her steps towards Akoth Towers, one of Nairobi's most prominent office buildings.

Stopping to touch her skirt one more time, Sophia turned her head upwards, towards the tip of the 54-storey tower. She immediately looked away from the glare of the early morning sun. The view of the skyscraper, literally piercing the sky made her feel like a dwarf, at her above-average height of five-foot eight inches.

With each silent thump of her three-inch block-heeled shoes, she gained resolve in her gratitude that she was still alive. She was glad that most of the physical evidence of her early morning brush with death was gone, except for the pain in her shoulder and knees, which she would ignore until after the interview.

She approached the entrance into a new world. Stepping into the Akoth Towers, she pushed her chest out and shoulders back. Her act allowed the tailoring of her black boyfriend style blazer to accentuate her figure. The jacket elegantly offset the three quarter-sleeve lace detail, and the high neck of her blouse. A mismatch of a few different fashion seasons whose juxtaposition left her looking smart, though a little too geeky and proper.

Assured that her week-long practiced posture showed confidence, she walked on.

"I am here for a reason," Sophia thought to herself as she looked the receptionist in the eye, noticing the name Jasmine on the golden badge on her chest. "Good morning. My name is Sophia…"

Before she could complete her nervous introduction, a smile from Jasmine brought her some relief. "How can I help you today?"

Without breaking eye contact, Sophia said, "I am here to interview for the Personal Assis-tant position. Can you direct me to the interview room?"

Sophia watched as Jasmine walked out of the reception area, opening a side door, then beckoned her to follow.

Normally timid looking, partly a result of the poverty she was born into, Sophia knew that for the next two to three hours, she would need to perform the role of brave upstart, as if she was trying to win a BAFTA award.

How believable she would be, rested on the duration of the interview.

Pushing her fears aside, she noticed that she was being guided to the sixth floor. Jasmine pointed her towards some cushioned chairs, next to a heavy oak door. It was by the door that Sophia took a seat, facing the other corner of the vast waiting room.

Being alone, she took in the details of the space surrounding her. One side had no wall but a six-panel glass window running from wall to wall and ceiling to three-quarter way to the floor. She took in the beauty of faraway evergreen trees in the direction of the Nairobi National Park.

Her eyes shifted to face a line of black leather chairs on the opposite side of the room. She looked over her shoulder and saw a large abstract painting, just like on the opposite wall. The artwork helped break the monotony of black visitor chairs into sets of threes.

After five minutes of reflection, she heard, "Sophia Mariko." She at once abandoned her thoughts, picked up her courage and closely followed the smartly dressed woman who called her name, rolling out Mariko, her family name, like it was that important.

A stop of the click click sound of the woman's five-inch pumps announced their arrival at the boardroom.

Without warning, the words from the matatu attendant resounded in Sophia's head. "*Siste*, never forget today is a fresh start, your second chance in life." She mumbled, "Amen," as she was directed to the only empty chair in the room, located at the front of an expansive oval table.

The table was occupied with men in dark suits, some with light grey pinstripes etched in-to the fabric. Others in navy-blue hues all tailored and pressed to perfection.

She took note of the few women at the table, dressed in blazers so well cut they suggested that one's net worth sat on the cross-stitched lapels.

Sophia felt about one dozen pairs of eyes weigh down her shoulders. This reminded her that she was supposed to be committed to her confident posture. A posture which she had practiced since the letter inviting her to the job interview arrived.

She straightened her shoulders back with a push of the chest forward. Immediately, she felt awkward on realizing seconds too late, that the adjustment should have happened before stepping into the room. She was concerned that she may have thrust her chest out suggestively. She was mortified, a new fear that she at once suppressed. She had no time to ponder, as she heard questions directed at her.

"Tell me about yourself."

"..............................."

Why did you apply for the PA post?"

"..........................."

"What do you consider to be your biggest weakness and strength?"

".."

"How would your references describe you when I contact them?"

"................................"

With each response, she remembered to look at the person asking the question. She took glances at the many faces around the table as she answered each question.

"How do you plan to perform duties of a PA without prior work experience?"

"...................................."

"If you are given the job, when would you be available to start?"

".."

"Do you have any questions for us?"

There was an involuntary smile on her face upon hearing that question, a sign that the one-hour interview session had ended. She still responded with the seriousness the question deserved.

Though she could not recall details of the questions asked of her, she remembered that her mouth moved, and words formed to answer the questions thrown at her from various sides of the table.

She had done enough research to prepare for the interview. And, answering questions correctly had been her lifelong specialty since the time she first set foot in school and realized that being at the top of her class kept many problems at bay.

She was guided out of the boardroom, into another room located two doors down the long corridor, for the written part of the job interview.

While doing the computer exam, a broad smile formed on her face with the thought that this is an easy exam. It then occurred to her that the exam felt better than landing on concrete, right in front of a matatu.

She completed the exam and was guided out of the sixth floor. While downstairs, she took one look around the lobby and it left her silent and questioning. The entire first floor of the Tower seemed endless, due to the open concept and soaring architecture.

There was a row of elevators to her left, each with doors opening and closing, just as silently as they glided to the floors above. She wished the place could be her daily destination. For now, her thoughts were focused on boarding a matatu to get back to her house. She needed some privacy to nurse her bruised shoulder and knee.

Chapter 2

Under the subtle ceiling white lights that criss-crossed, Sophia saw a face that resembled Richie's. All too much not be Richie.

On recognizing one another, Sophia was instantly very aware that they were never in the same league during their years of university.

She, an intelligent student who could outperform anyone, had a starkly different ranking where money was concerned. She did not need endless bookshelves and classrooms to remind her that she was at the highest learning institution, to get an education, a degree, the key to a respectable job.

Subsequently, she spent her university years with a laser-sharp focus on her studies. She paid no attention to the men around her, or the difference in attire and activities that her female classmates partook.

Richie, a comparably quiet student, kept a considerable number of rowdy friends. Some of the friends made it their task to share their notes whenever he missed a class, which perplexed Sophia. She could not understand what kept people in Richie's orbit, since he was not flashy about his luck where money was concerned. Therefore, she tried to limit their meeting in the lobby of Akoth Towers to a brisk handshake and small talk about the weather.

To Sophia's astonishment, Richie's approach was different, almost implying that they had walked hand-in-hand in the last three years.

"Hello Sunshine." Richie called out, prompting Sophia to look over her shoulder, to see who Richie was addressing as he approached her.

Fearing that Richie would try the sort of hugs he gave to some of the smartly dressed ladies at university, Sophia extended her hand with a barely audible, "Good morning Richie."

When Richie's eyes fell on Sophia, all he saw was the girl he had always admired but was too scared to ask out.

While at university, he had found Sophia hard to approach. She always appeared serious, focused on her studies, talking only when asked a question.

He smiled again, more at seeing her oval-shaped eyes, befitting her heart-shaped face. Though he was used to seeing ladies with long hair or braids, he was attracted to Sophia's short, well-trimmed black hair. "Nice to see you, seems like years, yet it was only six months ago when we looked respectable in those graduation gowns."

Richie wished his words would get Sophia to smile, reveal her two lovely dimples, a feature that had always attracted him. To his disappointment, she did not smile.

How Sophia wished she could pour out her struggles in the last six months. How she wished to let the world know, that with her first-class degree in Finance & Business Management, all she had done was to slip deeper into poverty. She had become an expert at job applications, attended a few interviews, though nothing positive had come of her effort.

In no way would she voice her desperation while in the lobby of Akoth Towers. What if they gave her the PA job, how would she behave henceforth?

As Richie talked, Sophia was aware of how the toebox of her shoe was as constricting as the people around her. Right in front of her, Richie looked perfectly comfortable in his Armani suit and smart phone in hand.

She felt sweat begin to bead on her upper lip just as a wave of tiredness hit her. She feared that if Richie was on his way to the interview for the PA position, then she had serious competition.

"You are smartly dressed, are you headed to the interview?" she asked, licking her medium sized lips. She wanted to have an idea where she stood in getting the job.

"No. I happen to work here." Richie replied casually, with his signature smile, revealing a perfect set of white teeth, lighting up his dark chocolate-coloured, round face.

Richie was easy to single out in a crowd at six-foot one, with squinty eyes made brighter by black lashes, black hair trimmed to one inch.

Relief flooding her with new energy, Sophia chuckled at his reply, like his working at the prestigious building was a normal and well-known fact.

They parted ways, with Richie surprising Sophia with what she had feared, a hug, a side hug, to close out their encounter.

Sophia felt warmth rise to her neck as her stomach did a flip-flip into a feeling she'd never experienced before. She stole a quick glance at the reception desk, needing to see if anyone noticed the one-sided hug from Richie. She hurried out of the building.

Richie marched to the elevators located on the left side of the reception desk.

The subtle etched markings on the elevators announced they only served floors 25 to 52.

He scanned a card, and two doors parted to invite him in. He pressed 52nd on the wall pad and stood in one corner of the elevator, as if it was full of people, though he was the only one. Always careful with his time, he made effective use of his elevator ride. He checked his email messages, followed by news on the stock exchange.

Richie had learned over time that Mwasimba, his father, liked to have details of the stock exchange, but never enjoyed the online search for such information. Richie had since made a name within his family and the company as the source of up-to-date information on money and world markets. He was on the path to becoming a director at the Mwasimba Group of Companies.

The fourth born in a family of five children, Richie had never lacked anything in life. Patience, his mother, gave love to all the children, while Oliver Mwasimba provided money that paid the many workers within the expansive estate, they called home, in the city suburbs.

The workers laid tables with the finest food, cleaned, and chauffeured the children to private schools, playgrounds, and exclusive members' clubs.

Richie, like Michael, James and Bill, his older brothers, and Nick, his sixteen-year-old brother, grew up to not only love their mother, but freely share information that many would consider secrets.

Michael, now thirty-nine, had been married for fourteen years since completion of his university education in England.

Michael felt proud of the long hours he put in at the company, seeing project after project move from idea to launch. On the other hand, all that Beauta, his wife, wanted, was to enjoy the finer things in life.

She scanned her limitless black Amex card without hesitation. The card strained, but never drained Michael's bank accounts and the vast inheritance she brought into the marriage. Richie, who had been watching and learning from his oldest brother, had made one promise to himself, that when his time to get a wife came, he would find someone who was not only loving, but worked hard for her money.

While in the elevator, Richie recalled the warm feeling in his heart the moment his eyes landed on Sophia.

While at university, he had always admired her as a smart student, ready to help others to understand difficult concepts.

Though equally smart, Richie was cautious, not wanting to let his peers know how brainy he was. He preferred to divide his time between attending classes and volunteering at his father's company, with an occasional getaway for a family holiday.

Richie had learned at an early age to mask some of his endowments, which went beyond the titanium Amex card he had been using from the age of twelve.

Though endowed with a photographic memory, he preferred to feign normalcy, much to the chagrin of his tutors. He'd disappointed his parents when he insisted on attending the local national university, and not Oxford in the United Kingdom, their first choice.

"If Sophia gets a job here, there is no way she will fail my brother, or the company, as a top-level employee." These thoughts flashed through Richie's mind as the elevator rushed up-wards to the top floor.

A knowing smile engulfed his face with the thought that people at the Towers would need patience for Sophia to fit into their type of society. But he also acknowledged that Sophia, being an A-student, always ready to learn, would catch on amazingly fast.

Lost in thought, the elevator chimed `52nd floor' alerting him to his arrival.

He walked out, and instead of turning left to the South wing where his office was located, he turned right. He walked past Liz, the floor receptionist without acknowledging her, causing her to retract the smile on her face.

Richie stopped at the door to Michael's office and opened the door, forgetting that courtesy called for one to always knock before opening a closed door.

He paused at the door on seeing Michael talking with Elvin, the company's longest serving driver.

Richie had known Elvin as far back as he could remember. So, it was easy to spot many new wrinkles on Elvin's face that day.

Elvin had chauffeured Richie to many places as a child; with his parents, and later as a student to school, where strangers sometimes mistook him for Richie's father. This happened whenever Elvin parked at Richie's primary school, waiting for the young boy to appear from the school building, to be driven home.

Elvin, though a senior company employee, continued to work more as a family than a company driver.

~ ~ ~ ~ ~ ~

Barely ten minutes before Richie burst into the office, Michael had entered his office with renewed energy after the line of morning interviews. Compared to when he arrived at work early in the morning, Michael felt total relief, after the third interviewee of the day walked into the boardroom.

As Director of Marketing in need of a PA, Michael had asked his mandatory questions. Yet he spent the better part of the interview looking at Sophia, until he was convinced, she was the same girl almost killed by his car during his morning drive to the office.

Michael had called Elvin to his office to give him the news. Elvin had entered the office very scared, walking at a slower than normal pace, looking down at the wooden office floor.

On entry, Michael could tell that Elvin was confused by the smile on Michael's face. Maybe Elvin wondered if Michael was laughing at his predicament. To help Elvin, Michael said, "No need to give a statement at the police station, the girl survived. I have the evidence to prove that."

As Elvin composed himself, Michael continued. "For now, go park that Mercedes at the far end of the basement garage, and bring out the Volvo for future use."

The driver exhaled loudly in relief. Hitting a slender girl with the huge Mercedes car was no small matter.

Elvin's hands involuntarily left his sides, where they had been hanging all that time. His left hand went into his pocket, retrieved a well-folded brown handkerchief, wiped his forehead, and put the handkerchief back.

As Elvin turned to go implement Michael's orders about the car, Michael added, "One more thing, try not to use that road again. I know there are many other routes to get here from Karen. Understood?"

Richie entered the office to hear the last word uttered by Michael. The sudden entry gave Elvin a chance to escape from the room, to go do as instructed.

With a wide grin, Richie deposited himself on one of the two leather chairs in front of Michael's mahogany desk.

Michael took one look at his younger brother, then back to the papers on his desk. His first thought being that was not the right time for happy talk.

"How did the interviewees for the PA position perform?" Richie's words brought Michael to full attention.

"Why are you so concerned Richie? It's not like any of them lasts around here."

Richie, with a slight grin, said, "Well, to be frank, I believe that a former classmate of mine interviewed today, by the name of Sophia M-something. Your top choice perhaps?"

"Sophia." Michael repeated the name as he shuffled through the papers on his desk, happy to oblige his brother, whom he was currently mentoring into company management.

The name Sophia matched the same on the CV he had put a checkmark on. Holding the CV, he asked. "How did you know that she came out on top of the five interviewees? She got it."

Richie, looking down at his shoes, responded without looking up. "Sophia led the rest of us all through university, she never let any professor down, so I assumed the same with the interview."

Right across the desk from Richie, Michael was buried in his own world. The images running through his head were far from grade A intelligence and being able to perform PA tasks. Yes, Sophia performed well during the interview, leading the rest in the written section, but on realizing that the girl he thought Elvin had injured that morning was not only alive, but made it to the interview, Michael chose to give her the job as the least price he could pay her.

Michael's only wish was that Sophia did not recognize Elvin. Thanks to the tinted car windows, Michael knew he would remain incognito, from the back-left seat of the car. Michael also knew that by hiding the Mercedes long enough, Sophia would hopefully never connect her boss to the accident that almost took her life.

Chapter 3

It was past midday when Sophia boarded a matatu out of the city center, as there was no queue at that time of day. She decided to go check on competitors in her second-hand clothes business.

She had always wanted to tour the nearby open market like a buyer but had not yet done that since she always visited the market to sell her merchandize.

She also needed time to reflect on the morning accident and come up with a way to tell her younger sister, Joy, about it without putting too much fear into her.

Sophia alighted two bus stops after her usual stop. She walked to a nearby open-air market where she spent three hours, walking slowly, admiring clothes while noting the displays that attracted her eye, and the range of pricing for comparable items. On her walk to her residence, she hurried to avoid the evening crowds returning from work.

When Sophia opened the squeaky door into the one-room she rented in Kawangware, a low-income residential area in the city outskirts, Joy was already home, from her afternoon class at university.

The room was one of thirty, one-roomed houses in the rental compound. The rooms were built in two rows of fifteen houses on either side, with an open walkway separating them.

At the entrance to the house, Sophia had an unobstructed view of the kerosene stove they used for cooking, and their three aluminum cooking pots. Running along the adjoining wall to the back of the door was an old three-sitter sofa, with few remnants of the original lime-green and brown fabric.

Across the room, directly opposite the sofa, was a bed, the sleeping quarters for the two girls. The metal bed, covered by an attractive lime-flowered bed cover, brought some life to the room.

Two metal boxes were hidden under the bed, holding valued clothes and the personal items for Sophia and Joy.

The fourth side of the wall was filled with a huge bale of second-hand clothes, for Sophia's clothing business. The remaining space was taken up by a chair next to a small table, with a few of Joy's books.

The room was served by one light bulb, dangling from the exposed mabati galvanized roofing. No luxury of ceiling boards in this abode.

Joy, the immediate follower of Sophia was a first-year interior design student at the national university. Emulating her sister, Joy had studied hard, though under financial hardship, to qualify for the much sought-after design program. Joy continued to work hard, though her completion of the study program depended on Sophia finding a job, to pay her university fees.

When Sophia entered the house, Joy stood beside the bale of second-hand clothes, humming one of the latest hip hop songs while busy sorting, folding, and bagging clothes, in readiness for sale the next day.

"Hi Sis, tell me how the interview went," Joy chirped, welcoming her older sister into the house.

Placing her handbag on the table, Sophia said. "The first part of my day pray you don't get to hear. The second part, my interview at Akoth Towers, went well. I answered all the questions." Completing her response, she walked a few paces back and sat on the sofa.

Joy, holding a mauve trouser, looked at her sister expectantly, waiting to hear more.

Sophia looked up, saw Joy's quizzical expression, and added, "But you know the unwritten policy in the job market, no personal reference, no job. Networks." Sophia uttered the words with resignation written all over her face, which made Joy drop the next question, about the first part of Sophia's day.

Joy lifted her head from the bale of clothes and turned to say something but stopped. Sophia looked more tired than when she arrived a few minutes ago.

Immediately Sophia had sat down on the sofa, her mind had raced to the early morning accident. She felt very tired, as aches from her fall flat on the concrete returned to her bruised body.

Joy returned her attention to the clothes.

Sophia stood up and pulled down a red basin from a nail on the wall, saying. "The thing I need most is to bathe. Better do it now, before everyone is back and ready to wash away their day's sweat."

She picked up some soap and removed a towel from another nail on the wall and walked outside.

At the only communal tap for the thirty rooms, Sophia filled the basin and hauled it into one of the two-bathroom stalls marked 'women only'.

Joy wondered how Sophia could say the interview was okay yet look so tired and con-fused. She decided that Sophia could be hungry, or as usual, worried about their two brothers in secondary school, but were home now due to lack of school fees.

She abandoned arranging clothes and moved to the kitchen side of the room. She touched the twenty-liter plastic container they used for fetching water from the communal tap. Satisfied that she did not need to fetch more water, she lit the kerosene stove and hummed a song as she prepared an early supper. By the fourth song, Sophia entered the house as Joy covered the steaming ugali, a cake-like meal cooked out of corn flour and water

"You are too much..."

Sophia's words startled Joy into an upright position. Her eyes followed Sophia as she re-placed the basin and towel on their hooks as she completed the sentence, "You read my mind like an open map. How did you know food is what I wanted most?"

Joy smiled, more out of relief, than her wise decision to prepare supper early.

Sophia said a prayer of thanks for the food, including a thank you to God for protection on her travel back to the house. She then served ugali and *sukuma wiki*, Kale, sat down on the sofa and ate without talking.

Joy joined her in the meal. She ate slowly while stealing frequent glances at Sophia, hoping her sister would talk, say something about the interview, to break the silence.

Halfway through the meal, Sophia forced a cough, to which Joy responded by looking up, as Sophia spoke. "Guess why I have enjoyed the meal?"

"Hunger of course," was Joy's response, before she heard Sophia say, "No. Were it not for God, you would be an exhausted girl right now, from mourning."

Joy, holding a piece of ugali midway to her mouth, held it there while looking at Sophia, confusion written all over her face. Sophia must have read Joy's questioning expression and continued, "I almost died from a car accident, this morning."

Joy pushed her chin upwards to reveal a sunken line between her eyebrows. She put her plate of food on the floor as Sophia pleaded. "Please, never try to cross a road if a matatu waits for you and there are cars of rich people behind. I tried that this morning, and still regret my decision."

"What happened?" Joy asked, and Sophia continued, "My favourite purple and lime green matatu stopped on the opposite side of the road, so did the shiny black Mercedes right behind the matatu. I checked the opposite side to be sure the road was clear to cross. Midway across, I saw the Mercedes swerve onto the road, right into me—"

"Uuuuuuui!" Joy screamed, then held her mouth with her left hand, to quell her noise, before she said, "Oh no, how could they?"

Sophia continued with her narration. "When I came to, I was lying on the other side of the road, right in front of the matatu."

With tears flowing down her cheeks, Joy looked at Sophia, picked up an empty plate and covered her half-eaten food as Sophia spoke.

"What woke me up from the shock was the crowd of people who had gathered around me and were chatting. I could hear some people asking what happened, whose daughter I was, and if I was still alive."

Throwing both arms up into the air, Sophia added, "Anyway, I am alive. Please do not tell Mum. She'll tell Dad, and that will be the end of our stay in the city." She chuckled. "Dad will come and take us back to the village, costs less to transport us while we are alive."

Joy's wet cheeks rose with a smile, which faded when she heard what Sophia said next. "But returning to the village will be the end of your university education, and my job-search, and the education of our four brothers."

Joy stood up. "I better go bathe. More residents just walked into the compound. The queue will grow, and I do not like the late hour, when very few people are outside." She stretched and unhooked the basin as Sophia said, "I thought I was seriously injured, until a good Samaritan helped me to my feet. That is when I realized that, apart from a few pains and a soiled skirt, I was okay."

Sophia urged her sister to go bathe. "When you finish your bath, I will tell you how I arrived at Akoth Towers in a clean skirt."

Joy smiled and walked out, closing the creaky door behind her.

~ ~ ~ ~ ~ ~

The time was long past seven o'clock, and a cold March breeze had set in, though no rains yet. Joy did not stay in the bathroom for long, partly because the tap water was very cold at that time of the evening.

Sophia unbolted the door when she heard Joy sing a popular pop song, announcing her return.

As Joy entered the house and latched the door behind her, Sophia, who was busy sorting and folding more clothes from the bale, looked up and said, "From what I saw at the open market today, tomorrow should be our day. Very few of the clothes on display can compete with ours, and their prices were a little higher."

"Really?" Joy said while looking at her sister who continued to talk. "I plan to take a risk tomorrow. Instead of you carrying your usual bag of clothes to sell at university, leave it at our market for me to sell. Double load."

Joy would have wanted to argue, let Sophia know that they had enough clothes in the bale, so she could sell at the market while Joy carried her usual load. Joy did not utter a word for she was busy juggling words in her head, trying to find the best way to ask Sophia to narrate her arrival at Akoth Towers for the interview, in a clean skirt.

When Joy looked up at Sophia, she saw her sister's mouth open, ready to say something, and she heard it. "I will tell you something, this city is full of good people, and a few bad ones."

Joy thinned her lips as her oval eyes widened, showing confusion, urging Sophia to continue. "The first good people are the matatu owners, for covering the seats with plastic. Other-wise, I would have ruined a seat for the day, with my soiled skirt."

Joy, though not wanting to interrupt, found herself asking, "I thought you said you arrived at work in a clean skirt?"

"After a long internal debate to go or not go for the job interview, I decided to go, and if they turned me back, at least I would have tried."

Joy nodded, as Sophia said. "Always open your eyes, wherever you are." The words prompted Joy to turn and look at the door to their house, as Sophia continued. "The minute I alighted from the matatu at the city center, I spotted a hair salon across the street, which gave me an idea."

Sophia paused from talking, holding a maroon trouser to her waist, gauging if it would fit her.

Joy looked up from washing the dinner dishes, to establish why Sophia had gone quiet. Seeing the trousers, she said, "Nice, put that one aside, looks like it will fit you well."

Satisfied with her find, Sophia threw the trousers into the used clothes bucket, and continued to sort out more clothes while talking. "The hair salon must be one of those that open before sunrise, to cater for some office workers, especially women who find it hard to style their hair from home, and easier to part with money. I followed my first instinct, walked in and tried—"

"Ooh yes, it's always good to try." Joy interrupted, before she let Sophia continue with her narration.

"Considering that it was past eight o'clock and my interview was at nine, I walked in, and asked a salon attendant if I could borrow a little soap and their hair blow dryer. Her response drained the remaining energy out of my body."

Joy once again looked at Sophia who then explained that the lady was not willing to help her, for fear of losing her job if the boss discovered that she had given out the items.

The words had reduced Sophia into tears, though she did not tell that part to Joy. Instead, she continued her narration. "I was surprised when an older salon worker, who was busy sweeping the floor when I entered, stopped and gave me the two items without uttering a word. I accepted them and marched into a washroom within the premises.

Twenty-five minutes later, thank God it was early morning, when not many clients use the washroom. I walked out in a clean and dry skirt."

Joy put down the water-dripping cup, then clapped her hands. "I see you going far in life, far. You never run out of clever ideas. God bless the lady who helped you, and the people who interviewed you for the job."

Chapter 4

A week later, or more specifically, seven whole days of continuous angst, marked by juggling more job applications with sorting and selling second-hand clothes, Sophia slowed down to check her email.

She noticed a message from three days before, which she read four times, before shouting to her sister. "Joy come read this message. Two sets of eyes are better than one," she said, meaning to whisper but ended up speaking loudly.

Joy read the email message once, turned and hugged her sister. "I'm supposed to go eat chips with Suzy, but we must get you ready for this job. If you cook chapatti for us tonight, I'll come up with two weeks' worth of high-class good looks for you."

Sophia, still tongue-tied from the good news of a job offer, said, "Whatever you ask for will be yours, except my first pay cheque."

Happiness overcame her. She embraced Joy before sitting down on the sofa and covered her face with both hands, in disbelief of the good news.

Joy smiled nervously, seeing her sister overcome with joy, tears streaming down her cheeks, and spoke. "Good to start on the right footing. You never know, one day when you get promoted to manager, you should not have a reason to look back and regret about your attire on your first day at work."

Sophia uncovered her face, no longer hiding her tears. Joy smiled and said, "You will be my styling experiment."

Sophia stood up from the sofa and moved to help sort more clothes from a new bale they had received earlier in the day. Holding onto a dress she had picked to fold, she looked at Joy, about to say something, but she was met with a beaming smile and a stretched-out pinkie. "Promise me, you will be strong, and take no shit from anyone," Joy said.

Sophia, holding three of her fingers under her thumb, stretched her pinkie and sealed the deal, as Joy spoke, "One more thing sister, remember we are in business. These clothes are not for free." She winked at Sophia. "You will pay back every penny, not tomorrow, but some day."

Sophia burst out laughing, loud enough to drown out the words from Joy.

Joy feigned annoyance as she held one hand akimbo. "Congratulations sister, go out there and continue to make Dad proud." She paused, as she elbowed her sister with a smile and added, "Dad's girl from the village."

~ ~ ~ ~ ~ ~

Joy's words rang in Sophia's ears as she walked into the lobby of Akoth Towers.

Dressed in a navy-blue shirt dress - three-quarter sleeve, mid-length and supremely starched, along with high sheen black loafers that matched her trusty black leather bag. The outfit gave her the appearance of somber efficiency.

Sophia cleared with security on the first floor and walked into the elevator. She was now a proud wearer of a badge. Her work ID, with the Mwasimba Group of Companies logo on the top left corner, had her photo in the middle, and her name below - Sophia Mariko.

Sophia could not be more proud, as she rode in the elevator to the 52nd floor of Akoth Towers. During the long ride, she wished her mother and father were nearby to witness this momentous day, her first day at work.

Being early in the morning, she imagined that Mariko, her father, must be busy, four hundred and seventy-five kilometers away, at one of the local markets where he was a live-stock trader. Mariko worked hard, but if working hard pays, as they say, then it should have paid her father by now, ten-times or a hundredfold with riches.

Sophia quickly chastised herself for the thought. Was her father not blessed with a wife and hard-working children? With a daughter, who had not only proven herself worthy of education but was now in an elevator to the top floor of a tower, a tall building that she had known only from the outside, until last week?

On her ride to the top, Sophia tried to recall a time she took an elevator to the 52nd floor of a building. Nothing came into mind.

The elevator stopped on the 25th, 37th and 43rd floors, and then Sophia got into a panic, on realizing she was now the only passenger in the elevator, still going up, so high.

The bell chimed as the elevator stopped and the two doors separated, to let Sophia out. She walked out and turned to her right-hand side, as earlier instructed. She scanned her newly gotten staff ID and the glass door opened. She walked into a large reception area, prompting Liz, who was talking on the phone, to direct Sophia with a hand, to wait.

Sophia took note of Liz's nails. They were long enough to suggest style, but short enough not to seem too impractical or tacky. Her clothing, although interchangeable in colour and tailoring, pulled enough quirky details from Nairobi, Paris, and London, giving the effect of a familiar and crisp foreignness.

After about two minutes, Liz replaced the phone receiver and stood. "Good morning. How may I help you?"

Before Sophia could return the greeting and explain that she was the new PA, Liz reached out her hand, asked for Sophia's staff ID card. She scanned it on a small machine by the reception desk. In an almost inaudible monologue, Sophia heard the few words uttered by Liz. "Registered. Passed. Okay. Good to go."

With a smile and one hand akimbo, Liz handed the card back to Sophia.

Liz, with hair that was a little past her neck, but not below her shoulders, her style spoke of moderated pushiness.

She checked Sophia from head to waist, smiled and walked away, beckoning her to come along. "Follow me and I will show you where to start."

Sophia was offended by the terse welcome from Liz, but there was not much she could do. She had no idea who Liz was, and most importantly; she had been unemployed for six months, she needed the job, to be able to help her family.

She followed Liz until both were in a large office space, a breathtaking room, where Sophia's induction into the Mwasimba Group of Companies began.

Liz looked around the large room, then walked out, saying, "Human Resources will arrive soon, to rescue you from your loneliness."

~ ~ ~ ~ ~ ~

Sophia found it hard to digest this woman who matched the opulence of the room, a room that was to be her office. She stood in the middle of the room, wondering what to do with all the space, No doubt, a spacious area three times the size of her one-roomed house.

Busy admiring the room, Sophia was startled when a middle-aged woman opened the door with a broad smile, uplifting her spirit that had been dampened by Liz. Sophia felt at ease and returned the smile.

Offering her hand, the woman said, "I am Cecilia, head of Human Resources. Welcome to Mwasimba Group of Companies, glad you accepted to join us."

Sophia said, "Me too, I am very happy to be here."

"As you already know, you will be working directly with the Director of Marketing, next door." Cecilia walked to the front door, opened, and held it for Sophia to walk out.

Cecilia closed the door behind her, turned to her right and walked side by side with Sophia, down a corridor. They made a stop at the next door. Cecilia knocked, and while holding onto the handle, looked up at the embossed golden nameplate, prompting Sophia to lift her eyes to the sign, *Mr. Michael Mwasimba, Director, Marketing.*

Cecilia opened the door and stepped inside. Sophia followed, and for a moment thought she recognized the assured looking man settled at the far end of the office, behind a huge desk.

He rose as Cecilia approached the desk, shook hands, and accepted greetings. The medium built man stood six-foot two-inches tall, with broad shoulders and a matching smile.

Cecilia turned to Sophia. "Meet Mr. Michael Mwasimba," as he extended his hand to Sophia. "Nice to meet you Ms. Mariko, glad you made it. You impressed most of the panel members during the interview."

"Thank you, Mr. Mwasimba, I look forward to working with you." Sophia responded, remembering now where she had seen the man before.

Mr. Mwasimba next comment threw her off balance. "That is the last time you will call me Mr., and Mwasimba. Those, we have reserved for the real Mwasimba."

Cecilia laughed, saying, "Ooh, I like the way you are scaring your PA, on day one."

Looking at Sophia he said, "I have two names, Mr. Michael when I am in boardrooms and other meetings. Otherwise, all staff call me Mike."

Sophia grinned, taking her boss' comment as a joke. No way would she refer to him as Mike. At worst she would try 'Mr. Michael.' But she looked forward to working with him, he was welcoming.

Cecilia glanced at Sophia, then back to a conversation with Michael. Their chat centered on how far the Human Resources Department had implemented the training sessions recommended from the last company board meeting.

Sophia, not wanting to appear to be listening in, studied the walls of the expansive office. The large mahogany desk dwarfed a bookcase by the left side of the room, on which Sophia noted many books and print journals on marketing, finance, and management.

The mention of her name brought Sophia back to the conversation between Cecilia and Michael. Sophia caught the last part of Mr. Michael's sentence on how he would join some of the training sessions, now that Sophia had reported to work as his PA.

With a smile, Sophia waited to be told something. Instead, the two went on with their conversation, allowing her to continue admiring the office and beyond.

At one point, Sophia looked out the four-panel window right behind Michael, surprised that most of what she saw outside the building, was trees. She wondered how a building in the middle of a concrete built-up city could have a view of trees.

Not wanting to be caught staring at her boss, Sophia turned her head and her eyes rested on a mahogany door, near the bookshelf, as she heard her name again.

Michael asked if she had been shown around the reception and her office. Before she could respond, Cecilia stretched a hand to Michael. "Thanks for welcoming us into your office, I will introduce Ms. Mariko to Human Resources, and the staff who will be with her during orientation week."

Sophia understood the message. She stretched a hand to Michael. "Nice to meet you Mr. Michael, I look forward to working with you." She saw him smile, and knew it was all about the 'Mr.'

Cecilia led the way to the door. On their way out, Sophia noticed that there were only two doors along that side of the corridor, her door and that of Mr. Michael.

~ ~ ~ ~ ~ ~

Mesmerized by the expansive corridors, Sophia was determined to learn her way around the offices.

She noted down in her writing pad the location of her office along the zigzag corridors, and the many tasks of a PA. She also absorbed a ton of information from presentations about the Mwasimba Group of Companies.

At four o'clock, Sophia finally sat down at her office desk, on the plush, black Portuguese leather that made her office chair too comfortable. She marveled at the fact that she was positioned behind the mahogany desk, reading a booklet marked Human Resources. She read instructions and filled in forms, then read the company rules, ranging from company confidentiality, acceptable office clothes, to office romance.

Sophia smiled. She found the rules and guidelines easy to follow. Joy had promised to dress her as a PA, and she had no plans of ever wasting time on romance. She had not done that before, even at university. She would not let romance interfere with her office work. Her goal was to work hard, give her best to the company that had just given her a chance to lift her family out of poverty.

It was past six o'clock when Sophia walked out of Akoth Towers headed for the house she had left twelve hours ago.

Chapter 5

The queue at the bus stop was not what Sophia expected to find. One look and she wondered if everyone had been working late like she did.

She stood behind the last person in line, assuming she would be the last one in the queue. No. As soon as she stepped in, more people joined the line behind her. The only consolation was that there were many matatus on route 46, the reason she boarded one within minutes.

Surprised at how stuffy and noisy the matatu was, before she remembered it was the first effect of going from the serene air-conditioned Akoth Towers, into a packed vehicle. She added the need for a mild perfume as part of her office attire. She could not afford to enter the Towers smelling like the interior of a matatu. However, she had no immediate solution for the noise.

Vendors squeezed themselves into the matatu passageway, looking each passenger in the eye, like people owed them a purchase. "*Kumi, kumi, bei ya jioni ni tano. Kumi, kumi, Auntie, toa tano.*" Ten shillings, ten shillings. The evening price is five. Ten, ten, but ladies can pay five.

There seemed to be some unknown arrangement between the matatu attendant and the vendors. As one vendor jumped out, another one boarded, making the journey a non-stop dis-play of items for sale.

Sophia was more than relieved when the matatu made a stop for her to alight. Jumping out, she watched the vehicle speed off, finally free to take in some fresh air.

She was glad to be away from the preacher who talked non-stop, putting passengers on the ready, to duck spits escaping from his mouth.

Gone was the loud hip hop and Christian music, that many passengers loved and hated at the same time. Anyone who sat right below the large speakers hated the loud boom, boom noise. Yet some passengers loved their first encounter with a just released song.

Like a released prisoner, Sophia escaped from the sweaty smells of the cramped vehicle, though she felt de-pressed with her destination. Such a contrast between the office she walked out of an hour ago, the overcrowded matatu, and the room she walked into in only ten minutes.

~ ~ ~ ~ ~ ~

Sophia arrived home, exchanged greetings with Joy, then went to take a bath.

The moment she hung up the bathing basin and towel on their hooks, Joy made an announcement. "Im-agine, today the Professor cancelled our class. I was a little ticked off, because all my preparations and travel time were wasted."

Looking at Joy, Sophia said, "I am sorry to hear that, hope they will find an agreeable time for a make-up class."

Making herself comfortable on the sofa, she heard Joy defend her Professor. "No problem if the Prof. does not make it a habit. I made effective use of the time. Studied with Liz and Alex, took a matatu during the low fare hour, sorted more clothes to sell, and now supper is ready." Joy explained before inviting Sophia to eat.

Sophia took a long breath, then exhaled. "I like the aroma from the vegetables. What's up today?"

"I increased our debt at the food kiosk."

Joy had added two eggs to the *sukuma wiki*, a technique learned from Stella, their mother, on how to stretch a balanced diet.

Joy had taken the liberty to get four eggs on credit and cooked a healthy meal to celebrate Sophia's first day of work. Joy knew that when Sophia received her first pay at the end of the month, they would clear their ever-growing food debt at the kiosk.

After dinner, Sophia began sharing details of her first day at work, but Joy cut her short with a whispered reprimand. "You are a fool, to bring office information to the house. Sister, our walls have ears, especially the thin mabati wall separating us from our next-door neighbour, and from the outside world."

Sophia, eyes, and mouth wide open, lifted her left hand and covered her mouth, to prevent more words from spilling out.

She led Joy in a prayer before they retreated to their shared bed for the night.

While in bed, Sophia uttered her last words for the night. "Kick me out of bed tomorrow morning. I need to be in the office by seven."

The sisters drifted into a deserved sleep, more out of tiredness than any comfort offered by their worn-out mattress.

Chapter 6

On her second week at Akoth Towers, Sophia was introduced to more offices and employees. A walk-through the various offices within the Tower revealed more twelve-foot-high ceilings, floor-to-ceiling windows, with remote control operated curtains.

Sophia had never imagined that work desks could get to be the sizes she saw in most of the single-occupant offices. The irony was that most of the work was done on a computer, located on a mini desk beside the main desk.

Orientation continued through several departments, meeting and greeting many people, too many to ever recognize if she came across them out in the streets.

Sophia wondered if the company had guidelines on the type of men and women to employ. Mere coincidence could not bring together so many well-built, flat-chested, broad-shouldered men, with large hands, all clad in designer suits. The few ladies on the upper floors were equally fit and attractive. They dressed in designer dresses or skirt suits, five-inch heels, always walking in quick short steps, their heads held high, and waists kept thin.

Though Sophia could compete on waist size, her slim waist related more to hunger and not self-denial of food, the case for many other women in the city.

Sophia knew one thing for sure, that Joy would spend a day admiring and talking about the attire worn at Akoth Towers, like the clothes were individual people with a heart and soul.

Sophia was introduced to the transport department, with its fleet of cars and drivers at her disposal whenever she needed to travel on company business.

By the end of her orientation, she had concluded that politeness was second nature at the Mwasimba Group of Companies. Though her conclusion conflicted with stories out in the streets on how mean bosses in huge offices could be.

She noted that the people she met at Akoth Towers were nice, appeared to love and respect other people, making it easy for her to fit in.

Though Sophia was aware that she was born into a poor family, she also knew that her family overflowed with strong values, respect, kindness, and love. She was brought up to respect all people, young and old.

Growing up in a village in Dhala District, Sophia learnt from an early age to be obedient, and respect those around her. These values were held dear by her family, including members of her church, school, and the larger community.

By her third week at work, Sophia was knowledgeable on the objectives of the Mwasimba Group of

Companies and their activities and locations around the world.

She had also undergone an intensive week of training on communication, leadership, and team-building skills, among many other topics.

~ ~ ~ ~ ~ ~

Orientation within the Marketing Director's office demanded that Michael opened and closed many files from Sophia's computer. That way, his PA could get a complete picture of folders where company operational and marketing 'details' were saved, a softer term for the company's top business secrets. "PA confidentiality" popped up in Sophia's mind.

Seated right beside Sophia, Michael was focused on showing her documents she would need in her daily tasks. At other times, Sophia sat on her leather chair while Michael stood close by, holding one side of her chair, leaning over to touch folders on the computer screen with his index finger, while he explained.

"This one contains sub-folders with individual client files. Okay, close that and open this one, it has minutes from all the company directors' annual meetings. This other folder has multiple files, mainly copies of letters from the Chairman and heads of our other departments."

The tour of computer folders and files lasted more than two days. Little did Michael know that his proximity frightened the life out of Sophia. Knowing very well that she needed the job, or rather, the salary it paid, she had no choice but to endure.

Being keen on details, Sophia quickly found a way to overcome her proximity-related fear. Keeping an eye on the circle of gold on Michael's finger helped calm her racing heart, so she could focus on the important task of learning her PA duties.

Each time Michael got close to her, Sophia's body would break into a sweat, introducing a new concern, body odor, as each day progressed. By lunch time, Sophia would have changed her blouse, if only she had carried an extra one in her bag.

Sophia spent a lot of energy divided between learning and fighting with the fears in her mind. "What should I do if Liz, or another staff member, or visitor walks into my office?"

Her first thought was that would be her last day at the office. She quickly rejected the thought, remembering how many people were waiting for her monthly pay cheque - university fees for her sister, school fees for two brothers in secondary school, and some necessities for her parents, before food and rent for Joy and herself.

The urgent need for a salary forced her to consider a new idea, the need to tell Michael how uncomfortable his proximity made her. But then she worried in what way she could communicate the message without offending him.

Sophia focused on learning her PA duties. She made a mental note, that later in the day, or even while in a matatu going home, she would come up with a strategy on how to handle the situation, without jeopardizing her employment, her only reliable source of income

Orientation continued for the next three months, with greater focus on Sophia's duties. The orientation officially ended when she received a letter on the company letterhead, signed by Mr. O. F. Mwasimba, Chairman, Mwasimba Group of Companies. The letter confirmed her as an employee of his company, a member of their large family of employees.

Chapter 7

Patty knocked at Sophia's door and invited her to lunch.

"Is it okay if we go at lunch time?" Sophia asked, casting her eyes to a clock on the wall.

"No need to worry about the early break. Mike is aware of that. The lunch is part of your orientation." Patty closed the door and walked towards Sophia's desk. "Best to go early, ahead of the hungry crowds that fill the place at one o'clock."

Sophia typed a message to let Michael know where she would be. She locked her computer screen, picked up her bag and walked side by side with Patty, to the elevator and out into the restaurant on the second floor of Akoth Towers.

Though she could not explain it, Sophia felt a sudden connection with Patty, and considered the talkative girl as her first office friend.

During orientation, Sophia had learned that Patty was a manager in the Finance Department. She had joined the company after graduation from university in Malaysia. Sophia wondered how some people became managers when still in their twenties.

Patty introduced Sophia to some of the restaurant workers. She also introduced her to a punch-in machine, for a monthly credit system, used by any staff who might need it.

Patty guided her through the buffet lunch where they filled their plates with food from a three-course set up. They sat at a table for two, at one corner of the large restaurant.

Though hungry, Sophia chose to be slow with her eating, taking time to watch and learn from Patty, on the etiquette of eating at the Akoth Towers restaurant.

"So, are you enjoying your work this far, or planning on how to dash out?"

Patty's question startled Sophia. She looked up with a smile while thinking she could never abandon her job, whose benefits she had started to enjoy. She responded. "So far so good. In the beginning, I wondered how I would ever learn all the tasks, but I did. Mr. Michael is patient, ready to teach me, whenever I ask."

Patty laughed aloud, confusing Sophia. She looked around the restaurant, trying to find out what could have amused Patty, as she heard her say, "Sorry for my outburst. Surely, you haven't called Mike Mr. Michael?" Patty laughed again, "Please do it and let me know his response. He has a funny answer to whoever calls him Mr."

Sophia ate another spoonful of her broccoli soup, not telling Patty that she had heard the response on her first day at work. Instead, Sophia changed topic. "How long have you been with the company?"

Patty, waving to an employee from her department, said, "Not long and too long. I have been here for two years, though I did a lot of internship work before, on every university holiday."

Sophia, impressed that Patty could afford to travel home for holidays, knew she needed to say something. "Interning must be good, gives one prior orientation to a company. I guess once you reported as an employee, you did not require much orientation."

By the time the two finished eating dessert, Sophia had eaten enough to last her until the next day and learned how to enjoy a decent meal at that restaurant. She knew that two more trips to the restaurant would make her a veteran, just like the many people she had seen moving through the serving line with ease and enjoying their lunch.

Walking out of the elevator, Patty stopped and turned to Sophia. "Thank you for coming with me for lunch."

Sophia did the same, thanking Patty for the invitation and good company.

"Let me know when we can go for tea, I am always available," Patty said while walking to the left side of the elevators.

Sophia turned right and walked past the reception desk, into her office. She was happy that a company manager had been so kind as to take her out for lunch.

Back in the office, Sophia sat in her leather chair and drifted into reflections on some of the details on staff relationships that Patty shared. Who was who at the company, whom to fear, who to smile at, who barks a lot but never bites, which men were jokers, and the women who breathe fire?

The information contradicted the impression Sophia had formed during her first week of orientation, when all she met were polite and welcoming people.

Fear gripped her, and she wondered how long she would last at the Towers, before being entangled into one of the groups. Sophia wondered with whom she would make friends in the office, and from which of the many hidden groups?

The thought motivated her to focus on her PA duties, the reason she would receive a pay cheque at the end of the month.

~ ~ ~ ~ ~ ~

Sophia punched in a password to unlock her computer screen, and the first message she saw was an email from Michael. "Type the hand-written minutes on your desk, read files five and seven in the Mapera folder. I will need a three-page summary, outlining factors the marketing staff could consider for the success of that project."

She picked a pen from the pen holder on her mahogany desk and scribbled on her sketchbook, "three pages of facts to consider."

She read the message again and noted that Michael completed the email with the line, "Hope you will be available to accompany me to the meeting, as will be the norm in future."

Her first thought was to ask why she should go with him to meetings of bosses? Then, she held her tongue between her teeth, to be sure no word escaped involuntarily from her mouth. "That would be the end of my job and my pay cheques." Sophia scolded herself. "Who am I to disobey my boss?"

She completed the assigned task in record time. She would have won a trophy, were it a competition.

With a paper folder in hand, she hesitated at the door connecting her office to that of Michael. She pushed her shoulders back, licked her lower lip, and bent her knuckles for a soft knock.

"Yes. Come in," was the response, in a very authoritative voice from the other side of the door.

She opened the door, almost peeping before walking into the office. "I have the minutes and three-page report ready for you."

Michael stretched out his left hand and took the file while pointing to a chair with his right, an invitation for her to sit.

There was silence in the room while Michael read the printouts.

Sophia turned her concentration to the outstanding items in the office. On the far end wall was a framed work of art. Before she could jog her mind for the name of the artist and potential cost of the painting, she heard Michael clearing his throat to recapture her attention.

She turned, only to meet a scrutinizing stare. She felt her face heat up as her heart pounded beneath her blouse. She wondered how long Michael had been staring at her.

Michael chuckled, getting Sophia's eyes to involuntarily widen, as she tried to find the reason. Had he found a mistake with her work even after she had read her report several times and run the spelling and grammar checker twice?

His next words quieted her pounding heart. "I see you are an amazingly fast learner. Excellent job, keep it up."

"Thank you," were the only words that escaped from Sophia's mouth, as she stood to leave.

Michael said nothing, only stared at Sophia. His gaze made her more uncomfortable. She turned to her right, hoping to see another person in the office, that Michael could be looking at. With disappointment written all over her face, she confirmed the room had only the two of them.

Sophia's heart was pounding hard, prompting her to involuntarily glance at her chest. Her first thought was of stories she had heard about what some bosses do to young women, right in their offices, after work hours. She prayed he was not such a boss.

Her silent prayer was at answered when he said, "Let us meet here tomorrow morning at seven, to leave for the meeting before the crazy traffic builds up." Before Sophia could say yes, he added, "I will ask one of the drivers to pick you up."

"Thank you. I will make it here on time," Sophia mumbled as she quickened her stride towards the connecting door. Afraid, that if she delayed, Michael would ask where her residence was, and insist on her being picked up. Sophia had no intention of letting anyone at the office know where she lived. Not now.

Sophia imagined one of those sleek company cars, meandering along the narrow dusty road to the entrance of her estate. Due to the narrow space between the two rows of houses, only people and bicycles could go beyond the entrance.

She had another larger fear. If the landlord, who lived within the larger first room in the compound, saw the company car and tracked it down to her, rent for her room would skyrocket, without the mandatory notice.

Then she thought of the loitering boys who demanded money or stole from pedestrians, especially if they knew where one worked. Sophia was sure the thieves would wait for her and demand money, which she did not have.

Back in her office, she completed a few more tasks, before she walked the long corridor to the elevator. On her walk, she realized the total silence in the building was a sign that company staff had long left for home. Fear gripped her as she walked out of the elevator, past the ever-manned main reception desk and entrance, out into the dark streets.

Chapter 8

Sophia arrived in the office at six-forty the next morning. As she settled down at her desk, the connecting door opened, and Richie entered her office.

On seeing Richie, she put to rest her fear of being in the office alone with Michael that early. She returned his morning greeting, while reminding herself that she was at work, not available for an early morning chat about the stock exchange and global money markets.

In the past, as early as two weeks into her employment, Richie had made it a habit to stop by her office and engage her on current issues in global financial markets. So, when Richie appeared, Sophia knew he would, as always, get into extended discussions.

Sometimes Sophia felt conflicted about the use of her office work time to discuss global finance and markets with Richie. Whenever she alluded to that, Richie's explanation was that the topic was very much what the company did. As an employee, it was more than okay to take part in discussions for the benefit of the company.

Each time that happened, Sophia made a mental note to raise the issue with Michael, a promise that she had not implemented to that day.

While waiting for her computer to finish booting, Sophia acknowledged how hard these rich people worked for their money, by arriving at the office so early.

She wondered how most men at the Akoth Towers found extra time to work out at the gym, maintain their broad shoulders and flat chests, with Michael and Richie at the top of the list.

Sophia retreated into her office posture, and from the corner of her eye, she noticed that Richie was staring at her. Without caution, she heard words escape from her mouth. "Is staring at people common for men?"

Richie reacted with a loud laugh.

Instantly she wished there was a delete button, for everything, including spoken words. Since there was nothing she could do, she wished it was time to leave for the meeting. She found solace on the computer screen.

Meanwhile, Richie had invited himself to a seat by the small round table at one corner of her office, staring at his phone.

She read her email messages and arranged and re-arranged the few items on her desk. She stopped her fumbling when she heard the connecting door open.

Michael walked into her office. "Hello Sophia." He looked at Richie and back to Sophia and chuckled. "Why is the office dead quiet, yet there are two people here?"

While still focused on the screen of his phone, Richie answered, "Because we are two busy people, getting morning work done."

Laughing, Michael asked Sophia if she was ready to leave. `Prayer answered,' Sophia thought while shutting down the computer. She picked her second-hand designer bag and leather office bag which contained a laptop, office diary and documents for Michael's two meetings that day. She walked out of her office, Richie and Michael followed her out.

Sophia stopped at the reception desk to greet Liz before she walked to the elevator. As she approached, she saw Richie, leaning against the wall with crossed arms, waiting, staring at her as she approached. Michael had said he would stop by the Finance Department to consult with one of the managers, then proceed to the meeting using a different vehicle.

When Sophia arrived at the elevator, Richie pressed the down button, checked her from head to waist before he said, "Enjoy your day out at meetings. See you soon," and walked off the direction of his office in the South wing.

Sophia felt overpowered, before reminding herself that Richie's action just balanced out with her words to him in the office, when she asked why he was staring at her, no more guilty feeling.

She chuckled, as the elevator chimed and opened. She stepped inside and pressed ground floor, where a company driver was waiting, to chauffeur her to the meetings.

Life is full of surprises, Sophia thought as the car sped out to the streets and onto Uhuru Highway, towards Hills Two, the venue of the first meeting.

On the way she thought of how she was liking her PA duties as days went by. Between reading many documents and preparing comprehensive summaries for Michael, answering his office phone whenever he was away, and participating in frequent in-house learning sessions, Sophia continued to appear refreshed and ready for more PA tasks. To her, more work tasks meant assured employment, and a pay cheque at the end of each month.

One of the important tasks of a PA was to go with their boss. Therefore, Sophia was the bearer of Michael's official diary and meeting briefs. And she put in extra time to learn the re-quired skills, including how to walk into official meeting venues and rooms.

By now, the more energy and time Sophia put into her PA duties, the more the tight knot in her chest loosened, an opposite reaction for most people.

Her PA tasks were demanding, with long hours of work, but that did not bother her at all. During her six months of unemployment, she never stopped praying to find a job. Better still, she was now PA to Michael, a boss who always arrived in the office long before 8:00am, the official reporting time.

However early Sophia arrived at the office, the latest being 7:30am, to beat the morning traffic, she found Michael already in the office, except on the days when he traveled out of town.

The other striking part was that Michael had made it his duty to open the connecting door for morning greetings. His friendly manners left Sophia confused; trying hard to balance his good gesture with what she had learned while growing up, that the young or junior were expected to greet their seniors.

~ ~ ~ ~ ~ ~

Sophia's mind drifted back to the evening before, to a telephone conversation with her mother. Stella was incredibly grateful that her two sons were back to school.

The conversation had reminded Sophia that almost her entire pay cheque went into paying owed fees at the school. What kept her strong was the acknowledgement that, with each passing month, she got a chance to ease life for her family, especially her parents.

The chat Sophia had with Stella had brought back memories. Sophia recalled how earnings from her second month allowed one of her brothers, Silas, in his final year of school, to return to class.

Silas had been home for more than three weeks, waiting for their father to save enough money for school fees. After receiving fees for Silas, the school authorities allowed Kevin, Silas' younger brother, back into school, on Sophia's word that she would remit some money for his fees, the next month.

Soon after, Sophia's two youngest siblings were proud owners of new school uniforms. Sophia was happy when everyone in the family was happy, giving her more motivation to per-form her duties as a PA.

Despite the heavy financial burden on her shoulders, Sophia had learnt to walk with her head held up. For her, the way to progress at her place of work was by blending in, not standing out. Time spent worrying about the poverty in her home would mean less time working hard to end the poverty.

On a few occasions she had heard Michael wonder aloud, about what he would do with-out her. Such comments made her uncomfortable, partly because he was her boss, and because he sometimes acted too friendly, something she did not want.

All she wanted was to work hard, and in return, receive money, not friendship. For now, money meant a lot to her, not as an individual, but to her family back in the village.

Sophia was very much aware that her parents were barely getting by, especially with the Cooperative loan her father had taken to pay for Joy's education through secondary school. Thank goodness, that part of the tuition fee for Sophia's university education was covered by grants reserved for students from poor families. Her high academic achievements placed her at the top of her class in the first year of university, qualifying her to receive grants reserved for academically outstanding female students.

Now Sophia felt obligated to help her parents. Her reasoning was that, by paying school fees for her two brothers in secondary school, she would give her father an opportunity to re-pay his loan using interest earned from his livestock business, with its ever-increasing interest rates. That would leave Stella to till the small family farm and feed the family.

Through quick calculations, Sophia realized that in the next eight to twelve months, she would have stabilized everyone at home, then she would contribute more towards Joy's university tuition.

Joy was a happy soul that circumstances had forced to put in double effort each day. She had to focus on her demanding design courses, and in between classes, sell second-hand clothes to fellow students.

The forty-five-minute drive to Hills Two was quick, surprising Sophia when Elvin stopped at the guest drop-off point. He hopped out and opened the back door for Sophia, as the guard at the main entrance lifted his right hand into a salute.

Getting out of the company car, she picked up her bags, thanked Elvin, acknowledged the guard, as she marched into the building, leaving behind the click, click sounds of her three-inch-heeled shoes.

One thing that Sophia had learned as PA, was the need to wear heeled shoes with the right click sound, especially when attending official meetings. A properly heeled shoe, with the right short-quick steps, and her official badge dangling from the left side of her waist, opened doors for her.

At the reception desk, Sophia paused just long enough to exchange greetings and receive information on the meeting room. With one turn, she marched into the elevator and up to the fourth floor to get acquainted with the room set up and greet early arrivals, long before Michael and other superiors arrived.

A thirty-minute drive to One Point for the second meeting, and the same click, click walk into the building got Sophia into the meeting room.

That controlled sound of high-heeled shoes was like the right knock, knock on doors. Doors opened for Sophia. Those nearby lifted their heads to check on the new arrival and acknowledged her with a smile and greeting. What more could Michael's PA ask for?

The two back-to-back meetings passed very quickly and with good outcomes, at least as communicated by the pleased look on Michael's face.

After depositing the official documents back in the office, Sophia vehemently turned down an offer of a ride home, even after being told that the drive was necessary whenever company staff worked late.

Sophia found it embarrassing to explain the absence of a road to her doorstep. But her greatest worry was that the company car would attract unwanted attention at her residential area. Though it soon turned out that there was attention drawn anyway, even without her dis-embarking from the backseat of one of the company lustrous vehicles.

Chapter 9

Six months into Sophia's employment at the Mwasimba Group of Companies, and seven-teen long months since she was last in the village, due to lack of money for transport, Sophia took Friday afternoon off to visit her family in Kabogege village, four hundred and seventy-five kilometers from the city.

Sophia knew that all her brothers would also be home, since August was a school holiday month.

Armed with a few clothing items from Joy's business, Sophia boarded a bus and counted the many hours of travel to her local town. She then took a matatu and alighted at the main road, from where she trekked the two kilometers to her home.

After forty minutes of walking, stopping here and there to exchange greetings with familiar people, she arrived home, the place she knew so well. A homestead dotted with three structures, surrounded by a live shrub fence.

After a second look at her parent's main house, Sophia added `plaster the house,' to a growing mental list of ways to support her family.

She also noted that the one-roomed house, the sleeping quarters for her brothers, needed expansion. Though the room was still practical, since Kevin and Silas were in boarding school, only sharing the space with the younger boys during school holidays.

Sophia smiled as she approached the front yard of the main house. The grounds were well swept, the live-fence well-trimmed, the grass well cut. Nor was there any litter on the grounds, in stark contrast to the rubbish covered walkways at her residence in the city.

Screams of excitement from Babu and Charlie startled her. "Mama, Mama! We have a special visitor," her two youngest brothers exclaimed, with the kind of genuine laughter that she had missed for so long.

Sophia embraced the boys, letting her bag drop. She then lifted Babu, the youngest in the family, to her waist, and looked at his smiling face. "You have grown. The last time I saw you, you were just a baby."

With tears burning her eyes, she put the boy down before giving Charlie a soft pat on the back. Just then her mother appeared from the smoky one-roomed kitchen, located between the main house and the boys' sleeping quarters.

Sophia increased her stride, meeting her mother halfway, into a tight hug.

"My daughter, welcome back. I have been praying that you find time to visit us, and here you are" Stella said as Kevin and Silas emerged from the goat shed.

The boys ran towards their sister.

Looking beyond the double embrace from her brothers, Sophia noticed that her aunt, the wife of a cousin to her father, had walked out of her house, looking over the fence, to see what all the laughter was about. They exchanged greetings, and Sophia turned back to her happy family.

Since darkness closely followed the setting sun, the family assembled in the kitchen, to prepare the evening meal, and share information.

The two older boys, Silas and Kevin, helped with the cooking of vegetables and ugali.

Charlie sat on his banana fiber football, while little Babu sat on the mud floor, smiling, and listening to on-going conversations, and responding when Sophia asked him a question. "Boy, you are no longer a baby, how are you doing at school?"

Babu responded without looking at his sister. "I like school, when it does not rain on me and my books."

Charlie chipped in while pointing to Babu. "He has a plastic paper to protect his books." He turned the direction of his mother. "Sometimes I ask him to walk closer to me, take shelter under my banana leaf."

He stopped talking when Babu elbowed him on the side. "I want an umbrella like my friends, not banana leave umbrella."

"Okay, one day Mama will get you a small umbrella, if you promise to take care of it," Sophia said before she turned to Kevin and Silas. "Big boys, how's school and life in general?"

Before any of them could respond, Stella asked if Sophia had a cold when she coughed.

Sophia was quick to respond, "No, no. I was fine before the trip, could be the effect of long hours in the crowded bus." In truth, she knew her cough was a reaction to the smoke in the one-room kitchen.

Sophia was humbled, seeing how happy her mother and siblings were, despite the poverty surrounding them.

Mariko arrived later in the evening, to an exchange of enchanted greetings with Sophia, although she was puzzled by her father's uncharacteristic happiness. Either she had been away in the city for too long, or her father had made a huge profit at the livestock market where he spent his day. It did not take long for the answer to come.

After dinner, eaten by everyone huddled around a small table on one side of the living room, Sophia opened her bag and gave out the clothing gifts she had brought for each family member. She was amazed at how the second-hand clothing items brought such joy to her family.

Without minding privacy, Babu removed his clothes and pulled on the long-sleeved white shirt and grey trousers. He walked and stood beside Sophia. "Do I look smart enough to come with you to the city?"

There was laughter in the room before Silas turned to Babu. "People travel to the city only if they are going to university, which means you must work hard at school."

Kevin laughed, stopped, and turned to Silas. "Work as hard as brother here. Did he tell you he received a prize at school for most improved student?" Kevin chuckled. "One of the teachers said Silas is now university material, for working hard and improving his marks."

Sophia extended a hand towards Silas, "Receive my high-five for setting the right example for these boys," she turned and waved her hand from left to right, where her other brothers sat.

Mariko interjected. "You set the hardworking example, not Silas."

"Papa, I set the example for Joy, now Silas is setting an example for the boys," Sophia said as she yawned.

Stella reminded the children that it was time for bed. The four boys obeyed. Kevin picked a flashlight from under the table and his siblings filed behind him, out of their parents' house, into the boy's sleeping quarters.

Sophia and her parents stayed on and continued chatting.

They talked at length about her brothers' performance at school, the health of relatives in the village, the crops just harvested and those planted on the family land. They also talked of students from the village who had qualified for university.

Then Stella mentioned that visitors were coming to their home tomorrow, Saturday after-noon.

Seeing confusion on Sophia's face, Stella clarified. "Remember the teacher in the village secondary school, the one who has always admired you? Now that you are here, his family will visit, to formally introduce the parents."

Afraid of falling off her seat, Sophia gripped the dining table, her heart pounding in her chest. She turned to her father for support, but he only nodded his head, up and down in approval.

"But Mother, I am not ready for marriage. I just started at a new job, to pay school fees…and to…"

Stella turned to Mariko as he interrupted with his hand raised. "My daughter, never let a good man go by. Mwalimu Cleophas has been waiting all these years, for you to complete your degree program."

Jerking her head sideways, Sophia immediately regretted the pain it caused in her neck.

She looked at her mother as her father continued to talk. "My daughter, with your degree from the national university, you will get a teaching job at the school, or as a government officer in our town."

Sophia opened her mouth to talk, though all she managed to say was, "But," on realizing her father had not completed his talk.

"You are at the right age, and I am not ready to be known as the man who gives empty promises."

Sophia moved her toes on the hard clay-finished floor, to reassure herself that this was not a dream, though she was aware of that from the tears streaming down her face.

After a long silence, Mariko excused himself, saying he had a long day ahead tomorrow.

When Sophia heard the bedroom door close, she looked at her mother with begging eyes. "Mother, do you seriously think I should abandon my new job in the city?"

Stella did not answer.

After another long silence between mother and daughter, Sophia stood and walked to the girls' bedroom, located within the house of her parents.

Chapter 10

It was Saturday morning, just after five o'clock. Sophia would have given anything to sleep longer, a luxury she rarely took due to her busy work life in the city.

The thought of sleep brought back the suppressed anger she felt the night before, that had kept her awake most of the night. She was alert to the sound of her father as he left the compound at his usual time, 6:00am.

She lost hope, thinking he might not go to the livestock market, since the family was to receive visitors.

Her heart sank into her stomach, then rose, on hearing Mariko's words. "I will focus on selling a few goats, and return by ten or eleven, with meat for the visitors."

She smiled to herself, knowing that her brothers would have enough meat for weeks to come. Although that would depend on whether the visitors would agree to eat or walk away once they arrived and found that the woman they were to propose a marriage to had left for the city.

Sophia waited for thirty minutes, long enough for her father to walk to the main road and turn right onto the road to the market, not left, the route to town.

Sophia was heartbroken, knowing that her brothers would find her gone when they woke up. With her mind made up, there was little else she could do.

As tired as she was, she lifted her small travel bag and walked out of the bedroom, to say goodbye to her mother. "Good morning Mama. Just… I... am leaving for the city." Sophia struggled to utter the words.

Stella stopped, stood upright as the broom dropped out of her hand. She looked at Sophia who said, "I have decided to go back to my job in the city."

"You arrived only last night, why must you leave so fast?"

Sophia, looking down at her shoes. "Mama, my boss and other people in the office have spent many months teaching me how to perform my duties. It will not be proper if I fail to re-port to work on Monday."

Sophia wished she could stay one more day, for the sake of the expression on her mother's face. Yet, she knew she must leave, before the visitors arrived and construed her presence as consent to marry.

Stella broke into silent sobs. Sophia hugged her, and whispered "I am sorry," picked up her bag and walked out of the house and compound.

On hearing an approaching matatu, Sophia ran the last stretch to the main road and boarded the vehicle. In town, she was lucky and got a seat on the early morning bus to Nairobi.

Six hours later, Sophia was still dazed when she arrived at her residence in the city, to the total surprise of Joy, who was not expecting her until the next day.

Sophia chatted briefly with Joy, saying everyone at home was fine, before asking for a favour. "Please call home and let Mama know I arrived safely."

Joy walked out of the house as the phone on the other side rang and rang. An hour later, she returned to the house after an hour. She put the cell phone on the table, walked to Sophia and gave her a hug, saying, "I wish I could understand what it is with our father and marriage. I know marriage is not a bad idea, after all, that's how we are sisters." She chuckled. "But I do not understand father and his unwillingness to change with the times, in some areas of life."

Sophia said nothing, her tears streaming while a visibly agitated Joy cooked food.

By the time the sisters finished eating, Sophia had shared the main details of her short stay in the village. She stared at Joy and said, "Joy, sometimes I want to laugh, and then cry, though the crying comes faster. What do our parents think? That we are still in the 1900s, when some people did not have choices?"

Though Sophia tried to make fun of her experience in the village, she ended up very agitated, completing her sentence on a high pitch.

Joy stepped on some clothes on the floor to reach the bale that she had been sorting when Sophia arrived.

Joy had earlier decided that on a Sunday, it would be better to carry clothing that people would relate to after attending the Sunday service, the style of clothes they normally wear to church.

Holding onto a white silk blouse, Joy looked at Sophia and cleared her throat. "Do you have any office events soon? This blouse is screaming out, party."

Sophia's face brightened up with a smile. She stood and took the blouse from Joy and held it across her chest to gauge how it would fit. Satisfied, she flung it into a nearby plastic bucket, containing their dirty clothes.

Sophia turned and looked at Joy, like she was expecting more clothes. Instead, she heard Joy say. "Dad is furious that you let him spend his money to purchase meat and other goodies he cannot return to the sellers. Remember to add that when you next send money home, at the end of the month."

Focusing her gaze on the pair of shorts in Joy's hand, Sophia said, "Good. At least I gave him something to think about."

Sophia was glad that Joy had thought of refunding money to appease their father. What her father needed most was money.

Sunday went well, with better sales than Sophia had expected in mid-month. She realized that with schools closed for holidays, many youngsters were in search of new clothing.

The sisters returned home at sunset, with Sophia acknowledging that the ups and downs of life come and go.

Her Saturday was the down, Sunday had been the up. Her prayer was that the next day and the rest of the week would be ups. Though, respecting the graph of ups and downs, Monday would be a down.

Chapter 11

One late morning, Richie appeared from Michael's office, exchanged greetings with Sophia, before explaining his presence. "Time for lunch girl, all on my tab, or the company, that's if there is a difference."

Sophia glanced towards Michael's office and back to her computer. "I am busy right now, completing documents for a meeting. Can we enjoy the lunch another day?"

She was focused on editing an eight-page fact sheet, which she had condensed from a 90-page report. She needed to discuss contents of the new document with Michael before she could print a final version. Given thirty more minutes, she would be done. She also knew that if she gave Richie any attention, they could get into a long discussion, delaying her completion of the fact sheet.

Richie persisted. "Michael is aware, and if the company is paying, it means you will be on official duty, eating lunch with me." He rested a hand on his chest.

Sophia did not look up. She bit her tongue, to prevent the words in her mind from escaping through her mouth. She wanted to say that next time, he should at least have the courtesy to call and give her notice. Better still, consult her first so she could inform Michael of her whereabouts. Sophia knew that voicing the words would lead to a time-consuming debate with Richie. Instead, she chose her words carefully and said them slowly.

"Hope you will be okay to spend an extra ten minutes in my office. I need to complete this, for Michael to read while I am gone, to enjoy lunch with you."

Her choice of words worked. Richie smiled, pulled out his phone and sat on the chair right in front of her mahogany desk.

She took one look at him and wished he had not chosen that seat, directly opposite her. Now she would be distracted and need more than the ten minutes to complete the task.

~ ~ ~ ~ ~ ~

Richie guided Sophia to a building located about a kilometer east of Akoth Towers, an-other tower called Truphena Towers.

As the guard by the revolving door exchanged friendly greetings with Richie, Sophia was busy wondering why the people who afford such huge buildings, liked to call them towers. She realized that most were known by female names, a fact she liked. With that thought, she gave a silent appreciation, to whoever owned or named the buildings.

Sophia believed that anyone who recognized women, whether in a matatu, office building, meeting room, or home, deserved credit. For example, her father, though poor in money, he respected his wife and daughters. He showed this by the struggles he went through to educate his daughters, something that some of his age mates shy away from.

Growing up, whenever her father returned from his livestock business, he would call Stella his wife, and give her a portion of the day's profits. Sophia recalled her father's familiar words. "Mama Joy," her father having taken the title of Baba Sophia when she was born. "Here are some shillings to purchase meat for the children." He would hand her sixty or ninety shillings, not a lot, but very meaningful.

Mariko's gesture did not mean that the family ate meat that often. It would take three to four times that much to buy enough meat for the family. Of course, occasionally, especially when the money had accumulated, the family would eat beef or goat meat, stewed to last several meals.

Sophia's thought process was interrupted, as they were promptly directed to a corner table, where she noticed a reserved sign. Before she could digest the idea that she was on a well-planned lunch, Richie pulled a chair for her to sit, then pushed her closer to the table before he took a seat opposite from her.

To show her gratitude, she said, "Thank you," while wondering if Richie had booked the table days in advance. Thinking to herself, "that must be how the rich operate," Sophia settled herself well, on the already comfortable dining chair.

She became reflective, searched her memory for an occasion when someone pulled and held a chair for her to sit. No such occasion came to mind.

None of her fellow students at university, the few she occasionally ate out with, ever got that close. "This is a first," came to her mind as a waiter appeared next to her and asked if they were ready to order. Sophia asked for orange juice, no ice. Richie asked for mango juice.

Staring at Sophia instead of the menu, Richie asked, "Afraid of some chili pepper?"

"I only do mild," Sophia responded.

Richie suggested she try the Lancashire hotpot, a dish the restaurant was renowned for.

Sophia agreed without asking what the dish comprised of. She sipped her juice, with di-vided attention; wondering what to do if the food turned out to be one of those dishes served as rare, or raw. Should she turn it down or just struggle with the meal?

She sipped more juice, while playing with words in her mind. She was planning to ask Richie if he would survive the lunch without doing what he had done since they arrived, staring at her the entire time. Before she could coin the right words, he asked.

"How are you finding your PA position so far?"

She used the question as an opportunity to stare back at him. "Good, though I have no prior experience to compare with. I can say I have learned a lot about the company and how to get Mr. Michael ready for business meetings."

Richie, holding his glass of juice on the table with both hands, said, "Sounds good. And you are right about the learning. The one you call Mr. has already praised your excellent performance."

Richie kept smiling and staring at Sophia.

Secretly, Richie was attracted to Sophia since they first met at university. Each time he set eyes on her, it was either his way of marveling at the smart academic responses she provided, or, at how her oval-shaped eyes fit well into her oval face, complimented by her well-kept short hair.

Little did Richie know that Sophia chose the short hair style because of limited finances. Otherwise, she would have preferred to grow her hair long, add hair extensions for daily variations in hair length, as most women in the city did.

Sophia was amused at his use of the word Mr. She turned her eyes to his hands and registered that he had not sipped from his glass of juice. She stared while guessing if the company paid lunch meant that she had to politely answer all questions about work. Otherwise, she would have liked to ask, to know the occasion when Michael commented on her competency as his PA.

Richie was still staring.

Lifting her glass of juice, she added, "I have learned so much from Mr. Michael, and am enjoying my duties."

"Be careful you don't annoy your boss with that Mr. and Michael. He sure detests titles."

Sophia responded. "Tried but failed. I need a day-off, to say 'Mike' a million times, for my brain to listen, and my tongue to adopt."

Richie changed the topic. "Sometimes I miss being at school. How do you find life out of university?"

Sophia looked up from her half-empty glass. "Ooh, those were good days..."

He smiled, ready to hear what she could have found as good as the expression on her face. She explained, focusing more on her experience at university. "Good days in their own way, though I cannot take any amount of pay to repeat my years at university."

Richie's eyes widened as he listened to her next words. "I am now making effective use of my days as an employee and liking it at the Mwasimba company," she said, putting emphasis on the name Mwasimba.

Sophia was relieved when the waiter brought a large white flat plate holding a steaming bowl filled with meat stew, carrots, potatoes, and onions.

Richie appeared amused, one side of his mouth lifted towards his cheek as Sophia inhaled the aroma, announcing, "That smells delicious, I am happy with your choice."

"My pleasure, I hope you will allow me many more chances," Richie said. Though his main thought was different, he was thinking about how natural she was, seemed to have nothing to hide. He wished she had seen the reaction of some of the ladies he sometimes ate lunch with, picking at their food like it bites.

Halfway through their meal, Sophia looked at her watch, then at Richie, who returned her gaze. "I know we have enjoyed our lunch for close to an hour, don't let that worry you."

Sophia, surprised by his perceptive reply, said. "I see it is time to get back to work. I have enjoyed lunch. I must go help your brother to get ready for tomorrow's meeting."

Richie laughed, a little too loud, causing some nearby patrons to look at them.

With both hands on the table, Richie leaned towards Sophia. In a whisper, he said. "Allow me to repeat myself, we are on a working lunch."

She looked at him, with a full smile, revealing her deep dimples. She then frowned on hearing his next point. "Your turn now to ask me any question. You have burdened me with the task this far."

Before Sophia could censor her reply, she heard herself say. "Questions? I have many. For example, what joy do you find in staring at me for hours?"

Richie was quick to respond. "I find my heart liking you more by the day. I hope yours gets the infection soon and does likewise."

Realizing that her question was fodder for Richie's response, Sophia found no reason to protest to what he had just uttered. Instead, she chose her next words carefully. "Why don't we limit our good discussions to more interesting topics like global money markets?"

Richie smiled at Sophia while returning a wave from a customer at one end of the restaurant, as Sophia continued. "If I have not mentioned to you before, the words love, like and such, do not exist in my vocabulary, especially at my work environment. Please replace those words with work, and I am in."

She stopped talking on detecting the changed expression on Richie's face, from smiley to serious, as he said. "A challenging task to ask of me, and I guess of you. Time will tell."

For dessert Richie drank tea. Sophia enjoyed a banana-chocolate cake. She was reflective. Here she was, seated with a former classmate, now a company manager. Not just any company, but the prestigious Mwasimba Group of Companies, a company with operations in real estate, banking and finance, manufacturing, and agriculture, beyond the national borders, to many other parts of the world.

She further wondered how things happen amazingly fast for some people, while for others, like her, it took a great deal of sweat to get a job.

Little did Sophia know that she would still be walking the streets of the city, in search of a job, had it not been for the morning accident on the day of her interview. Though she had per-formed well during the oral and written interview, she was not to get the PA post, already earmarked for another interviewee with an internal recommendation.

It was long past 2:00pm when Sophia returned from lunch. She sat at her leather chair, reflecting on how lucky she was to have her stomach full of delicious food and a job as PA to the Director of Marketing.

She lifted her feet off the floor and swiveled the leather chair for a three hundred and sixty view of her office. And then she saw the hand-written note on her desk, which made her dive back into work-mode.

Chapter 12

Exactly one week after the end of October, Sophia and Joy returned home in the evening, to find there had been a break-in at their one-roomed house.

Though the house was scantily furnished due to lack of money, whoever forcefully entered, took most of what the girls owned: a quarter of a bale of their second-hand clothes, three aluminum cooking pots, cups, and spoons.

Thanks to the bed cover overflowing to the floor, the thief did not find their shoes, two boxes of clothes and books stored under the bed.

Sophia sensed more trouble. Someone within or outside the estate must have been keen on her daily early exit and late returns. Someone must have noticed her smart office attire, and mild make-up, and even followed her until she disappeared into Akoth Towers.

With a heavy heart, Sophia knew they must vacate. Find a house to rent at a different residential area in the city, though relocation meant digging deeper into her meagre savings.

A weekend spent walking in and out of high-rise building estates, yielded a two-bedroom apartment. Though the rent asked would leave Sophia with no savings, she accepted the unit, being the only one readily available.

The sisters agreed that Joy would find two university students to share and pay for the second bedroom. Sophia and Joy would continue to share a bedroom, in an apartment that now included a separate kitchen, bathroom, toilet and living room.

The sisters vacated their one-room, though they had paid rent to the end of the month.

Once they were settled in their new residence, Sophia was happy. The residential apartment was worth their money in terms of security. And she had already used up all cards from her excuse box, on why she did not need to use company transport, even when she worked late.

Two weeks into their new residence, Stella called to inform Joy of her planned travel to the city. Joy now had no choice but to tell Sophia of earlier phone calls from the village.

Since Sophia had constant access to a telephone at the office, she had given Joy their shared cell phone. Joy thus answered most of the phone calls from their parents.

Not wanting to upset Sophia at her new job, Joy had decided not to inform her, that the many phone calls from home had changed from the need for money, to a call for

Sophia to travel home, and take part in planning her looming marriage.

In her search for answers, Sophia chastised herself for lacking courage. Courage to make it known to her parents that marriage was not part of her plans.

On arrival in the city, Stella was happy with the progress made by her daughters, now residents of the third floor of a high-rise apartment building.

Except for their books, clothes and shoes, every other item in their apartment was new from a hire purchase shop in town. The shop was a high interest rate credit store where customers signed out furniture on credit and made monthly payments. The understanding was that the shop owners would repossess the furniture if a customer defaulted on the monthly payment.

Sophia and Joy happened to be terribly busy during the week of Stella's visit, leaving at sunrise, only to return at sunset.

Stella spent three days in their apartment, having nowhere to go as her knowledge of the city was close to zero.

Stella made effective use of the time, self-learning the intricacies of operating household items, many of which were new to her - a gas-cooker, a television, indoor toilet and more. She also helped to sort and iron the second-hand clothes in readiness for sale.

On Friday night, Stella knew she had to deliver the message that brought her four hundred and seventy-five kilometers to the city. The message was Sophia's marriage.

Stella started the discussion by asking, "I do not know where to start or how to say it, but have you thought about marriage since you were last in the village?"

"I have been very busy at work Mama, it will be good if you give me more time to think about marriage, let alone a boyfriend."

Stella smiled at the confession made by Sophia that she had no boyfriend, which could also mean the extra time she asked for was to think about Cleophas, the teacher.

"Most ladies marry immediately on completion of their studies from school or university, do you plan to go beyond that stage?" Stella asked while looking down at the cream cement floor of the living room.

"I asked for more time, to think on how to abandon my job and apartment in the city, to be married in the village."

Sophia wondered how to explain to her mother that some of the men, her former university classmates that she would consider for marriage, were yet to find jobs. And the few who had jobs, earned too little to support a wife and pay school fees for in-laws.

Joy said, "Mama, what is your wish, you and Dad? Do you want to see me homeless? By now you should know there is no way I can afford to pay rent for this apartment." She waved her hand from left to right. "Do you wish me back to the room we were forced out of?"

Stella, choosing to look at the television, gave herself enough time to think about Joy's questions. She wondered what life would be like for Joy, without the television set and the many modern household items in the apartment.

"I would not wish you to return to the sad one-room house. My motherly instinct tells me the person who stole your items would come back, next time to defile your bodies. And that would break my heart."

Both turned to their mother, Sophia, with a frown, and Joy with a smile.

Sophia had never thought of the burglary that way. That, with one push of the door to the one-roomed house, a man would have gained entry and imprisoned them for a whole night. There had been such break-ins in the compound, and not once did any neighbour open their door to help a victim. Everyone feared being assaulted also. Sophia added the fear she felt, to her list of reasons to stay. She would never have a peaceful night, if she left for the village, leaving Joy alone in the mysterious city.

Joy's smile was to acknowledge that, their mother had an ideal excuse to convince Mariko not to marry off his daughter, the only guaranteed bread winner in the home.

Stella left the city for the village on Saturday morning. She was pleased with the improvements her daughters had made to their lives that far. She admired their dedication to work and studies. Leaving their apartment at dawn and come back in time to eat and sleep.

Chapter 13

The Mwasimba Group of Companies was renowned for its office parties, though limited to two or three per year

The December party was the one to remember, because invitations went beyond company staff, to include business associates.

To an outsider, the end-of-year party was more of a show, of who was who in and out of town. And many turned up with friends and family members.

To novices like Sophia, there were many things going wrong at this end-of-year party, from the outfits worn by some of the younger attendees, to unreserved words thrown amongst some attendees.

Sophia was oblivious to the cause of the instant hatred towards her by some socialites at the party. She would soon learn that many who sacrificed time and money on attire for the par-ty came with romantic objectives.

Some women and girls turned up to witness who got the latest clothing fashion right. There would be whispers and scorn on those who failed. The young, the bold, and even some of the older and restless, flashed the latest styles in clothing, hair design, nail colour, accessories and – of course – heels.

Many in the older generation watched and registered whose daughter walked in with whose son. Some parents liked the game. For them, intermarriage meant business conglomerates. Not a bad idea.

A fast and keen learner, Sophia was known in the office for her attention to detail, but she missed one detail at the party; Richie had a tough time turning his eyes away from her to the other ladies. At some point, Richie joined a group whenever he noticed Sophia chatting with his age-mates, aka, competitors.

Sophia was angered by two affronts. Richie, who made himself her guardian without consulting, and the scornful ladies, envious that Richie was not giving them hoped-for attention.

The evening game turned into a sort of cat and mouse game. The more Sophia tried to run away from Richie, the more other men at the party sought to be by her side. And, the more Richie tried to shield her from other young men, the more scorn she received from the socialites.

After four hours, spent on sampling the uncountable food displays, chatting with guests, and avoiding eye contact with the socialites, Sophia decided there was not much more left to enjoy. She announced she wanted to leave the party, to Richie's dismay.

Unknown to Sophia was that Richie and his friends had made plans for an after-party destination. A place with a dance floor, away from all the old people. Sophia refused his invite, intent on exiting the party. So, the least Richie offered was to drive her home, an offer she also turned down.

After Richie recited the company regulations, reminding her that eleven at night was late, and office policy demanded that employees must be seen home safely, Sophia gave in to a ride home by a company driver.

She arrived at her apartment just before midnight, her very first company ride home. She was almost grateful for the robbery that had catapulted her and Joy from their one-room house, into a decent residential area. At least the company car was able to drive all the way to the front of the building.

As she opened the door to her apartment, she was glad that the office would be closed during the December holiday, to reopen January third, two weeks of holiday. The holiday would be enough time for her to dump the party fiasco into the back of her mind, before resuming work in January.

As she retired to bed, where Joy was already fast asleep, a better idea came to her mind. She would spend the free days helping Joy with the clothing business.

Being a few days before Christmas, clothes were sought after, especially by urbanites looking to buy gifts to deliver to relatives back in their rural villages.

Sophia pulled a bed sheet over her head, on remembering that she would not join her family, for yet another Christmas holiday.

She woke up the next morning, a Saturday, oblivious to events at the party she had left unceremoniously.

Minutes after Sophia was driven out of the Rundika exclusive club, there was near chaos from the many well-dressed ladies at the party. Richie caused the chaos, when he opted to chat more with a group of women, colleagues of his mother, to the annoyance of his mother and the socialites. Patience, his mother, expected him to mingle with the socialites, daughters of her colleagues.

An inebriated lady had latched onto Richie. Not just any lady, but Wendy, the tightly and well-dressed daughter of Salome, his mother's best friend.

Before Richie could untangle himself from Wendy, another more-than-tipsy lady spilled a glassful of wine, all over Wendy's red gown.

In the blink of an eyelash, all hell broke loose at Rundika Club. Though Richie escaped unscathed, the same could not be said for some of the ladies who managed to end up on the floor, along with broken wine glasses, lost earrings, and even some torn articles of expensive women's clothing. Indeed, an end-of-year party to end all parties.

Chapter 14

Two weeks later, it was time to return to work. After a lengthy morning prayer with Joy where Sophia asked for a better new year ahead, she left for Akoth Towers. Part of the prayer asked for a busier year, to help Sophia forget some of the troubling events of the year before.

She arrived on the 52nd floor, exchanged New Year greetings with Liz before proceeding to her office.

On her way, she wondered why Liz did not look as happy as many people do in the New Year, especially that she had no school fees payments to worry about.

"Who is out to make me lose my job?" Sophia mumbled after she opened the door into her office. It was not possible to mix work and romance, one would suffer.

A second look and she confirmed that she was not dreaming, there were red roses, waiting to welcome her to her mahogany desk.

Though very confused, she liked the scent of the flowers. She walked closer to the flowers, while mumbling, to calm down her racing heart. "Someone must have made a mistake. The flowers probably belong at the reception desk."

Her mind drifted back, to her arrival on the 52nd floor. She tried to connect the flowers to the strange look she received from Liz, a look of envy and loathing.

Another glance at the flowers, another breath taken in of the captivating scent, brought sweat to Sophia's brow. She could feel her make-up melting on her face.

With trembling fingers, she opened the second drawer of her desk and deposited her handbag, in readiness to leave the room, to find out the source of the flowers. She pushed the drawer closed as she unwillingly dropped onto her leather chair.

Sophia almost jumped up out of fear. She had not heard a door open, but she saw Michael standing inside her office. She held onto the top of the desk, to hide drops of sweat she believed were escaping from her face. Though she did not see any mark on the shiny desktop.

A new thought flashed through her mind, that good manners require one to always greet people, especially in the morning. And to greet someone, one needed to look at the other. Was that not what she grew up learning and doing?

She pulled herself together and greeted Michael. "Good morning and how was your Christmas and New Year holiday?"

Her misty eyes were met with a smile. The smile made her tense. She wished the floor beneath her would open, so she could disappear. Instead, she forced a smile.

Sophia's brain was now on overdrive with questions. Who brought the flowers? Could the flowers be a result of the company's New Year policy, to deliver flowers to individual offices? Were the flowers brought to her desk by Michael, otherwise why would he have such a broad smile? Or, were the flowers from a secret admirer?

Sophia's glimpse of consolation came from the thought, that the flowers were a mistake, and the company florist would soon open her door, apologize, and walk out with the roses. The last thought led to the idea that she should go to the reception desk and check if Liz had her usual flowers.

Lost in thought, she missed most of what Michael said before he left her office. All she remembered was, "Come for a meeting at nine."

In her mind, the day would be her last day at work. She wondered if she had been too busy, absorbed in giving her best as PA, to ever consider that her employment with the company would one day end.

She was grateful to have until nine o'clock, enough time to go cry, stop by Patty's office to share the sad news, before going for her last meeting with Michael. Flowers, roses on her office desk, meant that she had broken company rule c251 on romance in the office.

As Sophia pulled the office door behind her, and turned left, on her way to the washroom, out of the corner of her eye she saw a person approaching from her right. In confusion, she took long strides past the reception desk and out into the washroom. On entry, she was thankful, that being so early in the morning, few people were visiting the washroom.

She entered one of the six toilet stalls. Then a thought hit her. "What am I crying about, I forgot to check the reception desk for the usual flowers."

More time in the washroom could mean that Liz was busy making phone calls to the florist, to inquire about the day's delivery.

She left the toilet stall, washed hands, and had a quick check of her face in the mirror, and was surprised to see that her make-up was intact.

On the way back to her office, she paused at Liz's desk and her heart broke, the reception flowers were there, fragrant, and fresh, like the New Year.

She now had a new problem. She could not go back to the washroom to cry as earlier planned. Anyone who had seen her appear from the washroom, walk to the reception area, and turn back to the washroom would for sure be tempted to ask if she was unwell. Though she would confidently answer such a question; because right then, on that morning, her first day back to work in the New Year, it was a yes, she was unwell. So, Sophia thought, until she opened her office door, and froze at the threshold.

She did not turn to look back. Anyone could tell that not all was well with her, since she arrived in the office, less than an hour ago.

Aware that Liz must be watching her from afar, Sophia paused by the entry to her office for a long moment. Feeling awkward, she gathered courage and walked past Michael and Richie, who were in her office, engrossed in a lively conversation.

She walked to her chair as she mumbled a New Year greeting to Richie and was outraged by the response she heard.

"Is that your new year greeting? I assumed I would receive a hug," Richie said as Michael laughed aloud and patted Richie on the shoulder. "You see, another reason to visit my house more often, to learn that men give hugs, not ladies."

Sophia chose not to look up, though she felt four manly eyes digging into her skin. She switched on the computer, to busy herself, and catch one or two words, of the issue making the two men jovial, while she suffered.

Michael and Richie continued with their discussion on some company expansion project.

Sophia looked up on hearing her name, and saw Richie look at the flowers on her desk and then at her.

This time, Sophia was certain that sweat dripped from her face onto the desk, though she saw none.

Michael lifted his left arm, took one look at his Rolex, and walked towards the connecting door. "I need to make some phone calls before our meeting at nine."

The words troubled Sophia. She wondered if Michael, from the way he had looked at her, was planning to ask her about the flowers on her desk. She turned back to the computer screen, read email messages before the meeting.

Richie went and sat on one of the two visitor chairs next to her desk, and the office went quiet.

Sophia perused through her email messages, pausing to read twice, no, three times, the message from Michael, letting her know of the nine o'clock meeting, to discuss an important matter that had arisen. On the fourth read of the same message, she noticed that email came in at 7:00am, and she was reading it at 8:35am.

What type of PA reads an important message two hours late? Was what she thought of as she typed an acknowledgement, clicked send and glanced at Richie. He lifted his head from the iPad on his palm and looked at her as she turned back to the computer.

All she saw was a blank screen, as she wondered. "Why is he torturing me?" She wished Richie could say something about the flowers, before her nine o'clock meeting with Michael.

For a moment, she thought of going to ask Liz if she knew anything about the flowers. An idea she at once abandoned, because she had no plan of what to say, if Liz mentioned Michael or Richie, or another man within the company as the source of the flowers.

She decided that she would wait to establish the source of the flowers at, or after the meeting. For now, she needed to prepare for the meeting.

Instead of focusing on work, her mind wandered away on why she felt that everything was wrong about her first day back to work, the work that paid her a salary, so needed by her family.

Sophia hit the computer keyboard hard, to distract herself from the scary thought of losing her job. Instead, she drew Richie's attention.

He pushed his chair back and stood. Sophia reacted by looking at the computer screen, then turned and touched the sketchbook on her desk before she turned back to the computer. She saw that in less than a minute of distraction, she had received a new email message, without her hearing the notification which was still turned on.

Richie stretched his arms upwards, beyond his head, without making a sound. He turned and looked at Sophia, at the flowers, and back to her with a smile.

He took short strides to the connecting door, held the door handle without turning it downwards to open the door, and looked back at her. "The flowers are nice. Is there a vase we can arrange them in? That way you can enjoy their full beauty."

Sophia looked up, just in time to see Richie pull the connecting door behind him.

Another look at the flowers, she saw something new, eyes on the petals, looking up at her, begging for something from her.

"Ooh, this Monday morning," the words jumped out of her mouth. She immediately held her mouth, on seeing that Richie did not fully close the connecting door, it was ajar.

A quick look at the clock on the wall, Sophia saw that the minute arm was at :55, five minutes to the meeting time. She took a quick glance at the computer screen just in case another new message had dropped in from Michael.

As a PA, she knew it would be awkward to turn up for a meeting and be asked about an item in an email message she did not read. Such a situation would bring her reputation for de-tail a notch lower. Being meticulous was a talent she was now known for within the Company, to the extent that once she checked official documents, Michael would usually append his signature with confidence.

~ ~ ~ ~ ~ ~

Armed with a writing pad and laptop, Sophia walked towards the connecting door, paused, then turned and walked the opposite direction. She walked out of her office, into the corridor.

She stopped at the reception desk, her brows pulled in, on seeing that Liz was not at her desk.

She bent over the desk, pulled out a stick-it pad, wrote three words, threw the pad back into place and walked away.

She entered Michael's office using the front door and met with laughter from the two brothers.

"Are they laughing at me?" was her first thought, as she lowered herself onto the empty chair, right opposite Richie.

Michael, on his high leather chair, had his hands busy, unearthing something from the bottom of his in-tray. He fished out a bound document, before turning to face forward.

"The deal we have been chasing went through. Chairman has requested that we travel to China and sign some important papers with the partner company and government officials in Beijing."

Sophia lifted her head and squared her shoulders, an involuntary response to the news, as Michael continued.

"Our travel office is already aware. Be ready to leave tomorrow morning."

Sophia wondered what Michael meant by saying we, for there were three of them in the room. Was he referring to Richie and Michael, Michael, and Sophia, or the three of them? She quickly reminded herself that she was at the meeting as the PA, she must wait for instructions.

There was a brief silence, which Sophia took advantage of to enrich her role of PA. "May I have a list of documents to prepare for the trip?"

Michael opened to a page in the bound document. "Read from that section forward, to establish what we shall need," he spoke as he handed it to her.

Sophia took the document, noted the page on her sketchbook, closed the document then looked back at Michael.

At the end of the twenty-minute meeting, Sophia stood to leave when she heard Michael say. "Once you have all the documents ready, you may go home."

Surprised, she turned and looked at Richie, then Michael, just to be sure the words were meant for her, and not Richie.

When her eyes met Michael's, he added. "A driver will be available to take you home via the shopping mall, in case you need to pick up items for the trip or for Joy, while you are away in China."

The mention of Joy touched Sophia's heart, that her boss had recognized the short travel notice, even though that was part of her terms of service as PA.

"Thanks. I will decide about the transport after I put all the required documents together."

"Remember to keep the receipts for reimbursement as part of your travel," Michael added.

Sophia opened the connecting door, while she wondered what receipts for her house expenses had to do with travel expenditures. She dismissed Michael's remark as one aimed at easing the pain of a less than twenty-four-hour travel notice.

She entered her office and was surprised to see the roses beautifully arranged in a vase, before it occurred to her, she had asked for a vase, and Liz did a fantastic job of arranging the flowers.

Sophia moved closer and inhaled the scent from the roses, as the connecting door opened.

Richie entered her office and closed the door behind him. He walked over and stood next to her and uttered words which confused and informed her, all at once. "They are attractive. I hope you will carry them home when you leave for the day."

He must have noticed the confusion on her face. He lifted his right hand and touched her left shoulder. The touch sent sparks down Sophia's spine, and froze her on the spot.

Another look at the flowers, and again she saw many eyes on the petals, begging eyes, looking back at her for a choice, between romance and her job.

After a long stare at Sophia, Richie walked towards the door while talking more about the flowers. "I knew the short travel notice would upset you. The least I could do was bring you flowers, to cheer you up. See you to-morrow at the airport."

He pulled the door closed behind him, giving her no chance to respond.

~ ~ ~ ~ ~ ~

Sophia sat down with a heavy sigh. Then, one look at the document in her hand remind-ed her she was a PA, not employed to look at flowers, however nice the scent emitted.

Next, she remembered the promise she had made to herself on getting the job, that she would put in her best effort.

The same effort she had put in through school, from primary to secondary, and to university. A qualification which earned her the title of smart village girl, though full of insinuations. The only reason Sophia did not fight against the title was because of the admiration she had earned from her father, and from the village people.

She could not ask for more, except to keep her reputation as a hard worker.

She wished there was a way to inform her father, that even at her place of employment, she had achieved a trophy for being keen on details, though it was only an imaginary one.

Would her parents understand, or would they hear the achievement in terms of more money? Would her parents ever understand that the reason she always looked forward to traveling, was because each trip out of the office was an impromptu salary raise, though temporary?

For Sophia, six days away in China, ten days plus travel days, meant that she would re-turn with enough savings to keep one sibling in secondary school for at least two terms.

Sophia had a self-made money saving policy in place. When on travel, she made sure to eat a fully balanced breakfast, that way she did not need to spend much of her meal allowance on lunch and dinner. She achieved that by waking up earlier than her colleagues, to eat break-fast long before the others. Her excuse was that as a PA, she needed to be at the meeting room in time, to have everything ready before her boss arrived.

Her thoughts on efficiency as a PA yielded a new idea which helped relax her facial muscles. She thought of how one day she would write a book for Personal Assistants, a manual on how to keep one's job.

She guessed that the book would be popular, to one day make it to one of those *Best* in categories. Sales would be high considering the many stories in town, how PAs were failing at their jobs, mixing work with romance. Not her.

With the last thought, she looked at the flowers on her desk, then wondered if she had joined the interminable list of PAs failing at their jobs. She whispered, "No," pulled the computer keyboard closer to her hands and put her whole mind and heart to the PA task before her.

To keep her trophy of *keen on details*, she read the document from cover to the last page. There was no need to read the selected pages, just to miss a critical issue, and discover that on arrival in Beijing, which happened to be far, over fifteen hours of flying. 'Unimaginable' Sophia thought.

~ ~ ~ ~ ~ ~

Sophia locked all the official documents for their travel in the office safe. She was ready to walk out of her office, to the car waiting for her outside when she heard a knock on the door.

The doorknob turned, and the door opened as Patty marched in with a broad smile, not waiting for a response to welcome her.

Sophia looked at Patty and assumed Patty had received information about their travel and had come to ask her to buy some items from one of the expensive duty-free shops. Sophia had never understood why Patty had a soft spot for items from expensively priced shops.

Small regular items she could buy from shops in town. Then she remembered that Patty always gave her enough dollars for whatever item she needed. Sophia was always willing to buy items for colleagues in the office, the ones who gave cash, especially those whose job duties did not include travel, even out of Akoth Towers.

Sophia never reached her luggage limit since she rarely shopped. She preferred to save her dollar allowance, which as per her interpretation, had small watermark prints with the words school fees, school fees, written all over.

Patty sat on the visitor`s chair, and immediately stood up, like there were needles on the chair.

To Sophia's surprise, Patty stretched and touched the flowers. "Aaah! These are the flowers. They are befitting of him." Without even batting an eyelid, Patty continued, "And I hear you guys travel together tomorrow. Make sure you have fun, that boy has an eye for you. And the earlier you acknowledge that, the better."

Sophia, visibly agitated, turned to Patty and forced a smile. "Please, I am not looking for a man." She chuckled. "I will let you know if I ever do."

Patty smiled and then quickly changed to a frown as Sophia added, "I am already having fun doing my job."

Patty stretched her pointer finger and poked Sophia on the arm, in a friendly manner. "You should be grateful that Richie brought you flowers today, as an announcement to the world. He just saved you from Beauta, Michael's wife." She chuckled as she made eye contact with Sophia. "Are you aware she is traveling to China as well? Her plan is to come, embarrass you and make sure you come back to no job."

Sophia restrained her tongue, she extended her hand, touched her chair and sat down, to prevent herself from falling. She asked for more information, and got it, Patty style.

After a thirty-minute chat, Sophia took note of the time on the clock, 1:00pm, time for Patty to be at her office desk.

Sophia stood up and gave Patty an unusually long hug, then said, "Thanks. I will remember that."

One of the things Sophia learned from their chat was that Liz was a niece to Beauta.

Sophia reversed her earlier resolve to leave the flowers in the office. She would carry them home, and on arrival, go down on her knees in prayer.

Though she liked her current PA job, she resolved that she would not like to be accused, of having a love affair with her boss.

She walked out of the office, to the elevator and down to the car waiting for her. She re-minded herself that after the trip to China, or even while on the visit, she would start searching and put in job applications to other companies.

Chapter 15

On arrival at the airport, Sophia was welcomed by Janet, one of the staff from the company travel office.

Janet helped Sophia through check-in and walked with her upstairs, an act which Sophia registered as different from previous travels. In the past, the last time she saw staff from the company travel office was at Akoth Towers, or at check-in, helping Michael when they traveled on the same flight.

Sophia followed obediently, walking into the executive lounge. She hesitated at the entrance, then called on her courage and walked inside, her very first time in an airport executive lounge. Soon after, Sophia's feet felt like heavy stones, a reaction to the people she saw.

Richie watched her from afar. He stood and walked to her side, taking the carry-on office bag as he guided her to the leather sofa, where he had been sitting. Sophia exchanged morning greetings with Michael and Beauta, then sat down next to Richie.

As soon as Sophia's body hit the chair, she heard Richie talk about breakfast. "We have already ordered breakfast, and since you had not arrived, I made a guess of what you would like."

Sophia mumbled, "I am okay," though what she would have liked to say was how dare he assume that she would eat breakfast, worse still, what she would enjoy.

She ate all her food, partly because all she had earlier for breakfast was a glass of juice. She involuntarily moved closer to Richie, a reaction to the constant stare from Beauta, seated on the opposite sofa.

After breakfast, Richie stood, picked the office bag, and extended out a hand to Sophia without saying a word. She obeyed, picked her handbag, and rose to her feet, while wondering if Patty had briefed Richie on the rumours, the trouble she could face from Beauta.

Sophia hoped that the rumour was not an office whisper that only she was not privy to. Had Patty not alerted her, she would not have offered her hand to meet Richie's.

Richie, standing close to Sophia, turned to Michael. "We want to stretch a bit, see you at the gate when the flight is ready to board."

Just like that, they walked away, Richie's hand on the small of Sophia's back.

Sophia could feel her pulse pounding in her forehead. Sweat dripped down her back, and she hoped that Richie's hand had not felt it.

At one point, she had a mind to pull away and walk ahead, away from Richie. But she still felt the stare of Beauta on her back, as she recalled Patty's admonition.

"You should be grateful Richie brought you flowers today as an announcement to the world. He just saved you from Michael's wife."

~ ~ ~ ~ ~ ~

When the four arrived at the boarding counter, Janet handed out passports and boarding passes.

Michael and Beauta walked in first, with Beauta supporting her head on Michael's shoulder.

Sophia and Richie were next, walking side by side.

Richie and Sophia arrived at the entrance to the plane. Within a short moment, a quick walking middle aged hostess guided them into the left row. She stopped at the third set of seats, for Richie to take his seat, before she led Sophia to her window-seat in business class.

After buckling her seatbelt, Sophia closed her eyes as her mind drifted back two weeks ago, to the Christmas party, and then yesterday at the office.

Her thoughts were interrupted by a strong arm weighing down her shoulder. She turned to see Richie, inviting himself to the seat beside hers. He started a conversation which did not get far.

A male passenger appeared in the aisle, looked at his boarding pass and back at Richie.

Richie eyed the man who appeared to be in his thirties. He turned, kissed Sophia on the cheek before vacating the seat with a complaint. "I wish this was my seat, and not the one a mile away from you."

With a frown, he touched Sophia's hand before walking back to his seat in first class.

Sophia, angered by Richie's behaviour, busied herself by looking out the window.

She heard the passenger next to her mumble something as he buckled up. She turned, greeted the man then refocused her attention back to the window, thought. "It would be rude not to greet a person seat-ed right next to me. If something goes wrong at 38,000 feet above sea level, he could be the only person to save me, not the one in first class."

Sophia was tired and sleepy, having slept for less than four hours the night before. After preparing supper, chatting with Joy, and packing for the trip, it was well after midnight when she went to bed.

After eating the meal served in the plane, she drifted off into a deserved sleep.

Sophia was awakened by a strong hand that cuddled her left shoulder. She woke up, squeezed her eyes for a clearer view, and remembered where she was. She saw Richie's hand stretched out towards her, with a red rose.

"Good morning Sunshine. I brought you a morning wake-up call, the scent you love."

He placed the flower in her hand and walked away, as she shouted after him. "Is there a flower garden in first class?" She turned and looked out the window, on realizing that nearby passengers were looking at her.

After a moment, Sophia decided that it could be early in the morning whenever the plane was, not a proper time to be annoyed. Worse still, she remembered that they were too far up in the sky, a place where no one should even think of having a verbal fight.

She held the rose to her nose and breathed in, then exhaled, stood up, excused herself to the passenger beside her to pass, and walked to the washroom.

Upon her return, she ate her snack in silence, while taking frequent sniffs of the rose, enjoying its per-fume. After the meal, she was busy reading a book when Michael cleared his throat to draw her attention.

From her seated position, Michael appeared unusually tall, helping Sophia to understand the reason the Mwasimba sons always travelled in first class. They needed more leg room.

He appeared tired, without his usual pleasant expression, his office face, the one that made him likable to most of the company staff. Standing there, he appeared subdued, though still tall, and muscular, as always.

Michael asked Sophia about her travel comfort, and then informed her of an email, just in from their Beijing office, with more good news on the business side.

Sophia thanked Michael for the update. As he walked away, she wondered how a company director, traveling in first class, on his way to sign a big business deal, his wife by his side, could not appear happy.

In the past, when Michael and Sophia had traveled with other company managers, he would take frequent walks from his first-class seat to business and economy classes to chat with staff members. Today he did not appear as energetic or happy.

Sophia put on headphones and searched for a cartoon channel to keep her entertained, on the remaining part of the long flight.

Landing at Beijing International Airport was as smooth as the earlier stopover and take-off. As Sophia walked out of the plane, she was surprised to find Richie standing by his seat. He let her walk ahead until they reached the exit of the plane where he took a long stride and joined her side, his hand on her back.

Richie's actions since Sophia arrived at the airport executive lounge had raised questions in her mind. She wondered if he was traveling to co-sign documents with Michael, or was he on a joyride, on a first-class ticket?

Sophia hoped that Richie was on a business trip. She dreaded her next thought, wondering how the trip would be with only Michael, Beauta and her. She sighed, trying to imagine which of the two was a better choice, with or without Richie on the trip? What if Richie had not traveled, then Michael forgot and made one of his many jokes, or held her shoulder, in the presence of Beauta?

~ ~ ~ ~ ~ ~

Sophia waved bye to the trio as she walked outside and boarded a taxi to the hotel, where she checked into her room. She remembered to turn the deadbolt on the door, always preferring the double security it offered.

She tossed her handbag on a coffee table and dropped down on a nearby two-seater sofa, for some rest.

As soon as she landed on the sofa, the hotel phone by the reading desk rang. She jumped and picked it up without checking the caller ID and heard Michael's voice.

"We have our first meeting with our liaison office people in seventy minutes. Read the package in your room and be in the boardroom at least five minutes to start time. Okay?"

He hung up before Sophia responded, though she still did, saying, "Yes, I will be there," into the dead phone line.

Sophia was now fully awake, at least to the objective of her very first trip to Beijing, PA duties.

She made a quick tour of the room, taking note of the splendor in the tastefully furnished sit-ting area, a nearby kitchenette to her right and a door to her left, opening into a spacious bedroom, half of it taken up by a king-size bed.

On seeing the bathroom, with its Jacuzzi bathtub, she thought of having a bath, but then remembered the folder that Michael mentioned. She walked back to the sitting area.

The folder was easy to pick out because of the familiar Mwasimba company logo. It did not have many documents. A welcome note from Chaoxiang, Manager, China office, and a de-tailed schedule for each of the days they would be in Beijing.

Sophia noticed that the official program was interrupted by group tea breaks, lunch breaks and dinners.

She wondered if it meant she would not have a chance to spend some of the wad of dollar notes she was given from the Nairobi office, for her meals and incidentals.

She had always asked for a flat rate allowance instead of the other choice, where employees received an amount of dollars from the office, spent and kept receipts to later account for the money spent.

Without wasting time, she did a quick mental calculation, and an involuntary smile lightened up her face. The dollars she had, once converted into Kenya shillings would do wonders to her family, in the form of school fees. She had almost a year's worth of fees for secondary school.

She whispered to herself, "What more could a girl ask for, except a quick shower, dress like a PA, and be in the meeting room, to work for the company that just solved my main challenge, money."

~ ~ ~ ~ ~ ~

Sophia walked to the elevator and rode up to the top floor, she walked along a corridor and into a magnificent meeting room.

She got busy admiring the room set-up. A smile engulfed her face while she thought of how the place would have looked out of place, the many red decorations, if outside of China. Then she looked out through the windows and saw trees and many buildings.

She continued to stare outside, beyond the tall buildings, until the opening of the door attracted her attention. Richie entered with a large group of people. Some she recognized from their previous visits to Akoth Towers. Two were managers from the Nairobi office, while the rest were not familiar.

Many handshakes were shared, and self-introductions made, before individuals occupied chairs around the large oval table.

Another swing of the door, and in walked a man in a black suit, white shirt, black tie, and dark glasses, with Michael on his left side. Sophia watched, expecting to see Beauta, as the door swung to close.

Michael walked to a vacant chair at one end of the table, taking a folder that Sophia handed him, as he made himself comfortable.

Sophia sat nearby, not directly opposite, but from where she had an unobstructed view of Michaels' eyes and hands in case he missed to find a document in his folder.

Over time, Sophia had extended her PA skills to include an understanding of the non-verbal signals from Michael, and it had so far worked. She could correctly guess when to hand over a document or say a date he could not recall fast enough.

A quick glance around the room, Sophia saw Richie, in focused discussions with the man earlier introduced as Chaoxiang. Standing tall, though not as confident as Michael, Richie dressed for the official meeting in a grey pin-striped Armani suit. He had on a complementing shirt and necktie, and black leather shoes.

The room went quiet when Michael greeted those present. Richie and Chaoxiang swiftly walked over and took seats on different sides of the table.

Sophia was glad thus far, for Richie had not bothered her. He was as business-like as could be. She made a mental note to say a prayer later; at break time or when the first meeting was over, before they transitioned into the second, a dinner meeting.

Sophia reflected on the many people in the room and concluded that human beings were marvelous creatures. How they made such quick transitions, remained a puzzle to be solved.

A short time ago, on the flight, Richie and Michael acted different. Michael was reserved and appeared edgy, while Richie was all romantic, with roses and casual words on the plane.

Now in the boardroom, Michael was as jovial as in the Nairobi office. Richie was very official, from his attire to keeping his distance from her. She told herself that she might accept Richie as a friend, only if he continued to act that way—official when he should be, that included not dropping anonymous flowers on her desk in the office.

The next day's afternoon meeting included more Chinese people compared to the morning meeting. The session was filled by one PowerPoint presentation after another.

Though Sophia enjoyed her PA work, the jet lag and presentations were taking a toll on her. But she regained her alertness when Richie walked to the podium and took charge of the meeting, starting with a PowerPoint presentation.

Discussions from the meeting continued during a catered dinner, followed by a short briefing from Michael. After the meal, everyone was free until the next morning.

Always keen on events nearby, Sophia noticed when a man dressed in a black suit entered the room and walked out with Richie and Michael.

~ ~ ~ ~ ~ ~

"Did I enter someone's room?" was Sophia's first thought as she stepped into her hotel room. It was transformed by a bouquet of beautiful flowers, their heavenly scent filling the air.

A small note on the side of the vase caught her eye. "Hope you enjoy smelling the flowers as you wake up in the morning."

Wake up? But this was evening, before bedtime. Sophia wondered if the person who brought the flowers, confused time, imagined that she was already in bed. Or, she would enter the room, and miss to see or smell the flowers, until morning.

"Whatever." she said aloud, decided there was no need to spend time agonizing over flowers. What she needed was to sleep, in readiness for another long and important day.

After a long hot lavender scented bath in the expansive Jacuzzi, Sophia retired to bed from where her thoughts reverted to Beauta. She wondered where Beauta could have been, while the trio were busy in meetings. Maybe Beauta stayed in the hotel room to watch movies or catch up on sleep.

Sophia woke up to the familiar melody of her alarm clock. She was happy with the way she felt, relaxed, and she could smell the flowers.

Within forty-five minutes, she had gone through her morning ritual of getting ready for a workday. Her regular activities included a shower and applying make-up after choosing clothes for the day. She then realized that she had ten extra minutes before breakfast time as shown in the brochure in her room.

The scent from the flowers was soothing, so she gave them her attention. Once again, she saw many eyes appear on the petals, as she inhaled their calming scent.

She walked to the window and pressed the remote to open one side of the curtains. She was attracted by the beauty outside of her room, a beauty she had overlooked since her arrival.

"Is that a park and playground for the hotel or public?" Though it was early in the morning, there were already several people outside, enjoying a walk or a slow run on the neatly cut grass. Amazing to be in such an expansive city, home to more than twenty-one million people and see such open spaces with so much green.

After breakfast, she went back to her room, retrieved the official documents from the safe and added them into the office bag. She picked her handbag holding personal items, including an extra blouse. It was a blouse she called 'just in case,' she soiled her blouse while at an important meeting and needed a quick change. Off she went to the hotel lobby, to wait for Michael and Richie.

Richie was already at the lobby, dressed in a black suit, white shirt, and necktie. Seeing his shoes, Sophia wondered if he had them shined daily or if he brought along many polished pairs, one for each day.

Michael arrived, and they walked outside and into waiting cars, and were driven off to their first meeting of the day.

The two morning meetings were document-signing sessions. The bosses, mainly men, and a few women, sat on large, comfortable chairs, at the front of the hall. Document after document was brought to each representative, and shown the exact place to sign, indicated by a coloured sticker.

Sophia was keen on how the signing was conducted, with people moving along the tables, removing a sticker after each signature. She looked forward to a day when she would have the task of showing people where to append their signature.

She would apply the knowledge she had just learned on use of coloured stickers to indicate places where a signature was needed. That way she would not confuse where to point each person to sign.

After four days of signatures, meetings, and more signatures with interludes of group teas and lunches, each ending with official dinners. The dinner on day four, a banquet to celebrate the signing of business contracts had very many people in attendance.

Beauta resurfaced, with elegant heels clicking on the marble tiles. Her Ellery dress ended right above the knee with the glossy leather tailored to give her a party-ready look. She must have had some transformation to her looks, most probably at a beauty salon. She had been MIA for four days, while her husband was busy signing contracts and agreements.

The meeting with Michael at the end of the banquet was brief. It was a reminder that the next day's meetings would be visits to government officials, to thank them for the good business relations that the Mwasimba Group of Companies enjoyed.

Chapter 16

Everyone retired to their rooms for the night. Sophia looked forward to the next day, after which she would have time to rest, or even sleep in.

A ringing phone startled her as she locked the official documents in the safe. She answered the room phone on the fourth ring, and almost dropped the receiver on hearing the voice on the other end of the line.

"Did I catch you at the wrong time? This is Beauta. I am on my way to your room, see you soon."

The line disconnected as the receiver dropped out of Sophia's hand. She felt her body warm up as her face broke into a sweat. She involuntarily wiped her palms on her skirt to stop the sweat from building up.

Sophia wished Richie was by her side.

Questions flashed through her mind and out of her mouth. "Why would anyone want to spoil my night, my name? Worse still, get me out of a job, the job that has brought happiness to my family?"

She paced the bedroom while muttering to herself. "Has this woman not had enough evidence that the only interaction between me and her husband is office work, me the PA and he the Director?"

Sophia screamed, "No way," as more sweat drenched her back in response to her pounding heart.

She then heard a soft knock on her door, and immediately contemplated to run all taps in the Jacuzzi, pretending to be busy in the bathroom. Or she should have switched on the tele-vision to high volume. That way, Beauta would hopefully hear the noise and assume that, either Sophia had a visitor or could not hear her soft knock.

She decided that she would gather her courage and explain to Beauta that whatever she had heard, were all rumours.

Sophia knew that if there were rumours, they must be based on Michael's easy-going be-haviour with staff in the office. And she shared an office wall with him, and there was a door connecting her office to Michael's corner office.

She should explain to Beauta, that the few times Michael had held her shoulder, meant nothing between them. It was his way of introducing her as his PA to his business colleagues.

Michael's hand always seemed to land on her shoulder whenever he called her over for introductions, even at company meetings.

She would further explain, that on a few occasions, she had seen Michael hold shoulders of other company staff as well. She would ask Beauta, about the person who was spoiling her good name, through rumours.

Another soft knock on the door startled Sophia from her thoughts. She mumbled, "Whatever," opened the door to find a smiling Beauta.

Beauta entered Sophia's room and handed her a large paper bag. "I brought these for you. I thought you might like them," as she looked at a nearby seat and back at Sophia.

Sophia realized her poor manners, quickly ushered Beauta to a nearby over-stuffed chair. She then offered her a bottle of water from the fridge in the nearby kitchenette.

Beauta declined, politely. "I flew out to visit some friends. They insisted on giving me a tour of their new shopping mall. I had to show some politeness by purchasing items from their designer store." She shifted on the chair, like she was trying to find a more comfortable position. "I bought the clothes for you. All my clothes come from my personal shopper and the head seamstress of a design house in Paris."

Sophia's lips parted, though no words came out, as Beauta continued. "Try on the items, and hopefully they fit, though you cannot wear them to the office."

Sophia smiled. More out of relief from her earlier fear, than the gifts in the bag which she was yet to open and see.

"Thank you very much for thinking of me. So nice of you." Sophia said with a brightened face.

Beauta announced her departure. "Good to see you happy. I should let you sleep. I know how busy you are."

She readied to leave the room, and Sophia saw her off at the door, thanking her again for the gifts. Beauta walked away, followed by a security man.

After securing the latch on the door, Sophia picked the clothing bag and walked to the bedroom where she saw a lovely bouquet of flowers on her bed.

"Okay, flowers can wait," she muttered as she opened the bag to reveal the clothes that Beauta gave her. One look at the items and Sophia found herself almost falling over from too much excitement. She took two steps and sat at the edge of the bed. Three pieces, dream pieces, as only seen in movies and fashion shows. No likeness would ever be found in their many bales of second-hand clothes.

She tried on each dress, and gave a congratulatory message to Beauta in absentia, for getting her size ten, right. Checking herself several times in the full-length mirror, she wished Joy was nearby, to rejoice with her.

After one hour of soaking in hotel bathing salts, Sophia went to the bedroom, picked a rose from her bed with both hands, inhaled and put it back. "Lucky girl."

An idea popped up in her mind, to call Richie and say something about the flowers. She picked the phone, then put it back, deciding it was a bad idea. She needed to first decide on what to say to him.

She climbed into bed and switched off the lights. Her mind went back in time, to the line of events since the week began, up to that night. She was reflective as she drifted off to sleep.

Chapter 17

Sunday passed amazingly fast for Sophia, with quick visits to five offices, all courtesy calls. The last meeting was a group dinner.

Apart from Richie's eyes focused on her, all went well. She was happy, satisfied with the success of the official business that brought her thousands of kilometers from home.

The evening ended with an exchange of country-specific gifts, and semi-emotional goodbyes.

On the drive to the hotel, Sophia's mind was on the next day. Since there were no scheduled official activities for the morning, she planned to sleep in.

Sophia decided that going to bed right away with a stomach full of food would not be good for proper digestion.

Though it was past ten in the night, she made a mental list of activities to do before retiring to bed. Check email, watch a movie on TV, and take a hot bath. She added, step out on the balcony to admire the night skies.

A soft knock on her door scattered the plans in her head.

She walked to the door, checked on the peephole, swung the door open and stared at Richie as he slurred. "May I come in for a meeting?" As he invited himself into the room, not waiting for a response to his request.

Richie entered and pushed the door to close behind him. He paused, and then sauntered towards the balcony door where he checked the outside.

Sophia's eyes followed Richie. She liked how elegant he was in casual wear. Black trousers, a mauve pull neck with a gold neck chain breaking its flow, and sports shoes that gave him a springy step.

He walked back, picked the TV remote, switched on the TV, then threw himself on the two-seater sofa. "Exactly like my room. Did they think we are twins?" he mumbled, beckoned her with his left hand before he patted sitting space beside him.

She responded as directed. To her, Richie said he had come for a meeting, and he brought along his laptop.

She sat with hands folded across her chest, partly hoping to quiet her pounding heart.

Richie stretched his left hand to her shoulder and continued to watch news on TV.

After about five minutes, Richie stood up and pulled Sophia along. "Have you had time to enjoy the beautiful night view from your balcony?"

Sophia pulled away. "My week was full of important matters, I have not had time to do that, though it was on my evening line-up."

He opened the balcony door, held Sophia's right hand, and guided her outside while saying, "Not one night have I retired to bed without enjoying some fresh air and nightly views from my balcony."

"So, when do you go to bed and wake up for the official meetings?" She found herself asking.

Richie made eye contact. "I can show you tonight."

Sophia did not respond, wanting to avoid the discussion on sleep and wake up times. She held onto the rail of the balcony and looked at the far end of the field. She stared at couples with intertwined hands, walking slowly, while others sat on the long benches at the park.

She stared until Richie disrupted her focus. "Have you had time to use the hotel gym?"

Sophia bit her tongue, not wanting to tell Richie how foreign that question was to her. The last time she visited a gym was while at university. She'd followed her friends, more out of curiosity. She needed to see the various exercise machines while her friends used them.

Her silence gave Richie an opportunity to continue. "There is one exercising machine I identified for our Nairobi gym. I can show it to you tomorrow. What time do you normally visit the gym?"

She chose to stay mum, contemplating on how best to answer his question, without get-ting into a long debate.

On further reflection, she decided that since she had had a long week, which demanded that she be alert at every instance of the many official meetings, what she needed then, was less argument, and more peace of mind.

She waggled her head up and down and smiled as he did the talking. The only thing that bothered her was the large hand on her back. The feeling was good, but she had no courage to accept it.

As the night progressed, Richie and Sophia retreated into the living room where he selected a movie that they watched together.

When the movie was over, Richie changed the channel to sports. Sophia looked at him and announced. "Tomorrow is Monday."

"Sure, today being Sunday, tomorrow must be Monday," He replied.

Sophia chuckled. "I would like to retire to my bed, after you leave for your room."

"What if I join you in bed tonight, won't that be the best for both of us?"

Fear gripped her. "I would prefer you slept in your room, not spend the night here."

There was silence between them. Richie continued to watch TV while Sophia sat with crossed arms. At one o'clock, she turned and made eye contact with Richie. "Good night," stood and left the room.

~ ~ ~ ~ ~ ~

Immediately her alarm went *kring, kring, kring*, Sophia switched it off and went back to sleep until nine o'clock, when she got out of bed.

Confused by the noise from the next room, she tiptoed out of the bedroom and noticed that the television was still on, Richie on the sofa, fast asleep.

She went back to the bedroom and re-emerged with a duvet and covered him. She switched off the television, and looked at him while thinking, "So peaceful, so harmless. He is not a bad man."

Sophia walked away. She reached her bedside table, picked up the rose and inhaled the scent. She put it down and went ahead to the bathroom where she enjoyed a hot bath. She appeared from the bathroom dressed in a three-quarter sleeve cream blouse, and navy-blue jeans.

Ready for Monday, Sophia walked to the door to go for breakfast, but changed her mind before she could open the door.

She went and sat by the edge of the bed and thought of waking Richie up, so he could go sleep comfortably on the bed. After a moment, she decided that was a bad idea, for he might interpret the act, made purely out of compassion, to mean an invitation to her bed, something she had never considered doing.

Sophia picked up the book on her bedside table and continued from where she had put a bookmark. She read until someone standing next to her interrupted.

"Good morning Sunshine. You look great, did you sleep well?"

She tilted her head upwards, to look at Richie and wondered how to respond to such a greeting, from a man who owed her an explanation, why he did not leave for his room last night.

Then, she recalled what her mother had taught the family about the start of a good day. Stella always reminded her children of the need to empty their mind of sadness before retiring to bed and fill the mind in the morning with positive thoughts. And that meant starting the day with a pleasant greeting to whoever one met with.

"Good morning. I hope you had a good rest. How was your night?" She enquired.

Richie's face brightened with the rays of the morning sun shining through one end of the window curtains. She interpreted that to mean they would have a good day together.

Her eyes followed as he and walked into the bathroom and emptied his bladder without closing the door behind him. Next, he washed hands and face, while calling out, "Any of those hotel toothbrushes around here?"

"Not my type of toothbrush."

"Sunshine, remember this room is just like mine." He chuckled. "I found them."

After about five minutes, Richie walked into the bedroom, bare feet, in his black trousers, a white vest that clung to his muscular chest.

Sophia ogled as he walked into the sitting area while talking to himself. "I will call room service. Anything special for you, or the usual?"

She chose not to respond, deciding to wait and see what the usual included.

After about ten minutes, there was a knock at the door. Sophia ran to get it, not wanting anyone to see Richie in her room. She checked through the peephole before she opened the door and received a trolley filled with an assortment of breakfast food items. "Thank you," she said before the hotel staff wished her to a good breakfast and left.

She pulled the trolley into the room and as she turned to close the door, Richie wheeled the food away.

He was busy setting up breakfast on the coffee table when she joined him in the living room.

She stood akimbo and wanted to ask him what people would think, now that breakfast had been wheeled into her room. She changed her mind, deciding to hold the question for later, it was too early in the morning to pick a quarrel.

As they ate breakfast, Richie asked, "Have you ever thought of relocating?"

"Ooh yes. I have often entertained the idea of moving back to the village. Whenever I visit, the place is quiet, peaceful, so welcoming." She let it at that, for him to decide if she misunderstood his question, or she decided to interpret it her way.

Richie remained quiet. She guessed he was confused by her response. She stared as he refilled their cups with tea.

While he served tea, she reflected on her response, which she knew contradicted her plans. In no way would she abandon her PA job. A job that she liked, a job that had made an enormous difference to her life, lifted her family out of poverty, to better circumstances. The job that enabled her to fly to faraway lands where she attended VIP meetings. She knew it would be hard for her to move to the village, especially with her father waiting to marry her off to Cleophas the teacher.

For a moment, Sophia wondered whether the other women she knew were fortunate and unlucky at the same time, like her. With a respectable job, and parents wanting to marry them off.

Richie stood up and pushed the food trolley aside. "While you are deep in thought, I will dash to my room and get ready for the afternoon outing, unless you want me to bring my clothes and get dressed here?"

Sophia waved him away without uttering a word.

He extended a hand which she held onto for support and stood, telling herself she needed to go bolt the door.

They walked to the door and Sophia was surprised when Richie turned abruptly and faced her. Before she could react, he held her face between his hands and planted a kiss on her lips.

The more she struggled to break away, the tighter he pulled her to him. She gave in, encircled her hands round his neck and returned his passionate kiss. When he released her to catch his breath, she stepped back. He looked at her and beamed. "Thank you very much for everything, I hope you've enjoyed our morning." He opened the door and walked out, pulling it behind him.

Sophia bolted the door with trembling hands. She walked to the sofa, picked up the duvet and went to the bedroom where she let the duvet fall on the bed, followed by her body. Her heart throbbing out of her chest.

Once she felt that her pounding heart had slowed down to near normal, she turned and lay on her back, staring up at the white ceiling of her hotel room.

She lifted both hands and covered her face, like she was shy. She lowered her eyelids and felt like she was somewhere, a good place, suspended in happiness.

Lowering her right hand to her chest, she whispered, "This must be the feeling that makes girls to follow men to their houses."

Feeling shy, she lifted her hand to join the other hand in covering her eyes. She stayed still, reminiscing on events of that morning, and only stood up when she started to fall asleep.

She checked email, just in case Joy had any updates for her, but found she had no new email. She checked her Facebook page, though she rarely posted anything herself. She noticed her sister's update with a happy face on completion of a class project. With that, she guessed all was well at home, signed out and continued to read the book from where she had stopped.

~ ~ ~ ~ ~ ~

Sophia heard people talking and laughing out in the corridor, before she heard a soft knock on her door.

She checked through the peephole and saw Michael. She opened the door and exchanged morning greetings before he asked if she was ready for the day. Sophia picked up her sweater and handbag, and off they went.

The drive in two four-wheeler vehicles to the countryside was relaxing. Sophia welcomed the fresh air, away from the city of Beijing, with its multitudes of people and back-to-back meetings.

The afternoon leisure tour ended at a shopping mall for those who needed to shop. Sophia joined the group of three other women present and they walked in and out of clothing and beauty product stores. Having converted her travel allowance for her siblings, she did not buy much, except items for people who had given her money. After, the group, including the security men and drivers proceeded to eat dinner.

Sophia looked around and felt that the day was different in many ways. She was in a good mood, though she could not explain how she got that happy.

Michael and Richie were jovial, which Sophia attributed to a lack of their usual business suits. The two security men going with them had exchanged their black suits for jeans and casual shirts, though their dark sunglasses remained in place.

Seated next to Chaoxiang's wife during dinner, Sophia wondered how easy it was for men to transform, from busy bosses signing contracts and facilitating meetings, into sharing jokes and laughing aloud. To sleeping on sofas and still being jolly throughout the day. She wished she had that type of stamina.

For a moment, Sophia wondered if the men were that free and jovial with their families. She never saw such laughter in her father. She attributed his sadness to the poverty he had struggled with for so many years.

Sophia was hopeful that just like the men she was enjoying a meal with her father would one day transform himself from sadness to happiness, now that the financial burden was being lifted off his shoulders by her pay cheque.

~ ~ ~ ~ ~ ~ ~

Michael, Beauta, Richie and Sophia traveled to the airport for their long journey back to Nairobi.

On the flight, Richie spent the first leg of the journey walking up and down the aisle of business class. This time Sophia occupied a seat next to a woman traveling to Rwanda, via Nairobi.

Richie must have slept on the remaining part of the flight to Nairobi, he did not appear on the aisle.

On arrival, the foursome appeared sad as they entered cars waiting for them. The source of sadness for each was different. For Sophia, in the hour it would take to get from the airport to her apartment, she would be back to reality, to hear who else looked for her hand in marriage, while she was gone.

Chapter 18

Sophia took advantage of the long Easter holiday weekend and traveled to the village. The aim of her visit was partly to appease her father and clear the guilt that had followed her since August when she'd left without saying bye to her father. Against all hope, she convinced herself that this time things would be better at home.

Since Stella left the city in October, she had been calling, and once asked Joy if Sophia was already married, adding that she better not be, as there were good men waiting for her back home.

With little understanding of university study programs, Stella alluded that Joy should find a decent job in the city to support herself, allowing Sophia to get a job transfer to their local town.

Little did Stella know that the corporation Sophia worked for did not have offices in their local town. And chances of Sophia ever finding a well-paying job outside the capital, like her current PA post, were close to zero.

Sophia traveled to the village, much to the happiness of her parents and siblings.

Two days into her arrival, she overheard her parents discussing to invite some visitors, without naming names. They asked Sophia for money to buy food for some visitors. When Sophia enquired about who the visitors were, the answer was that they would be a surprise, and a good one.

Though it was past seven and dark outside, Sophia walked out of the house and made a phone call, whispering into the phone. "Joy, our parents plan to have surprise visitors while I am here. The information has made me uncomfortable"

"Could you return to the city tomorrow morning? Your objective was to visit, which you have done and…"

Sophia heard her name called, disconnected the phone call, and retreated into the kitchen where she heard her mother complain. "In the village, people do not walk outside in the dark, especially unmarried women."

On seeing Sophia, Stella changed the topic. "I hope my good daughters have not become friends of the dark..."

Babu, the last born in the family laughed until he fell off the stool he had sat on, as Stella added, "How else does your sister walk outside in the night, without asking one of you to escort her. Whom is she talking with on the phone, that she does not want others to hear?"

To indirectly answer the question raised by her mother, Sophia looked at Babu and Kevin seated nearby. "Joy sends her greetings to each one of you."

The two boys tilted their heads towards Sophia in unison, excited as Charlie voiced his need. "Please call so we can talk with Joy. She has been away for too long. I wonder what she looks like now?"

Sophia, in tears from Charlie's plea, about missing Joy, and knowing that Joy also missed her brothers, wished she could help. "I do not have enough credit on my phone right now, I will buy credit tomorrow, then we shall call her."

Stella voiced another complaint. "Why people want to waste money on phone calls, I do not understand," she said as she absentmindedly lifted a wooden cooking stick from the ugali she was stirring on the three-stone fire, into a nearby pot of ready vegetables.

Stella then turned the direction of her sons. "Why ask to speak on phone? Are the greetings passed to you by Sophia not enough?"

The boys did not respond. Sophia could tell where her mother's random scolding was pointing, the money her parents had asked for earlier, earlier in the day.

Sophia consoled herself that Stella had little knowledge of cell phones. Otherwise, she would have complained about the prohibitive cost of Sophia's phone, a newly released smartphone.

Text messages from Joy started to drop into Sophia's phone, prompting her to mute her phone, before reading the messages. Sophia was right on silencing the incoming messages, otherwise, Stella would have complained about the many pings made by the stream of SMS messages.

Sophia scrolled and read all the messages, while keeping a straight face. But her anger brought some warmth into her body, in the cold April evening. Using a lot of *rs, ws,* and *4s* to save on the number of SMS messages, therefore phone credit, Joy suggested to Sophia that the visitors could be her potential in-laws. With a suitor for her.

Sophia put her cell phone away and tried ridiculously hard to keep a neutral facial expression. She engaged in family discussions while they ate dinner from the main house.

Once Sophia was in the girls' sleeping quarters, she sent an SMS to Joy. "I had a similar idea but was giving them the benefit of doubt. These guys are serious."

Sophia saw the blue light flashing on her muted phone, signifying the arrival of a new message. "Give me a few minutes. I will come up with a suggestion."

Sophia was angry that her parents could have plans about her marriage without involving her or getting her consent. She argued that at the age of twenty-four, she was certainly old enough to be involved in such an important matter.

She felt sad, that her parents had entrusted her with heavy responsibilities of educating her siblings but could not consult with her on issues affecting her life.

With tears streaming down her cheeks, a new idea came to her mind. Before she retired to bed, she set her alarm to wake up early.

~ ~ ~ ~ ~ ~

Sophia woke up early and cooked breakfast of milk tea which she served with bread for the family.

From the kitchen, she could tell that her father was awake and ready to leave for the live-stock market. How she wished to inform him that breakfast was almost ready but did not. She guessed that such an invitation would get him to ask why she was up so early. And Sophia had not gathered courage to make her announcement known to him. She decided it would be easier if she told her mother first.

Once Sophia finished eating breakfast with her mother and brothers, she entered her sleeping quarters and read an SMS from Joy. Joy's suggestion was in total contradiction to her decision.

Sophia planned to travel to their local town for the day, hopefully meet with old friends and laugh away the anger in her heart.

When she re-emerged from the bedroom, smartly dressed, and carrying her handbag, Babu stood still with a broad smile on his face. His posture told her the young boy must have thought Sophia had brought out more gifts for them.

On arrival, three days ago, she had given a designer clothing item to each of her family members. Clothes carefully picked from the bales of secondhand clothes that Joy had become an expert trading in.

They loved the gifts. With Mariko talking often on how he could not wait for God to bring important visitors to his home, so he could wear his first ever suit, a gift from his educated daughter.

One look from Stella and Sophia began explaining. "I am leaving for town. I will be back before the end of the day."

She walked out of the house as she heard a warning from Stella about town. "Be careful. There are many bad people, and strange vehicles in town, now that many families are home for Easter."

Sophia only said, "See you later," as she walked out of the compound, to the bus stop.

On arriving in town, Sophia decided to visit some of the older shops she was more familiar with, before she would venture into the large new stores.

By one o'clock, she had walked the better part of town, stopping often to exchange greetings with familiar people. She also tried on clothes and shoes, in several stores.

Feeling tired and hungry from her long walk, she entered one of the big new restaurants in town, to treat herself to a lunch. She walked in with her office step of confidence, to a corner table. The table was strategically placed, she could watch people as they walked in and out of the restaurant.

A waiter arrived. While holding onto a menu, Sophia asked him to suggest their favourite dish for the day, and that would be her choice.

She vacated her chair, her handbag on her shoulder and went to the hand-washing sink. The sink was at one end of the sitting area, near an exit marked staff only. Little did she know what lay beyond.

Sophia squeezed liquid soap and got busy washing her hands, observant, to clean out the many handshakes she had made with people along the streets.

Suddenly, she felt a large hand grab her shoulder, another hand over her mouth, and she was whisked away, out the staff exit to the backyard, into a waiting car.

Before she could catch her breath, find her voice to scream, or energy to struggle with her abductor, the car drove off, at high speed.

After what felt like a long drive, which she could only guess, because her head was face down onto a large thigh, wearing faded jeans. She felt the hand which had pressed her head to the thigh, loosen.

Still very scared, she lifted her head, wanting to see her captors. Her eyes peered outside through the windscreen, where she saw a two-vehicle accident, right in front of them. And then she read a nearby yellow beacon, *road closed*.

In more panic, she turned her head, and was surprised to see the face of Turuki, the eldest son of Onono, a well-known businessman in town.

In the driver's seat was Mechando, his younger brother. Immediately, Sophia broke into a fresh sweat. She was confused, wondering if she should be relieved that she knew her abductors or even more scared, especially with the words she heard next, from Turuki. "This is my lucky day, an Easter wife, until some son-of-a-bitch decided to cause the accident and block the road."

Sophia involuntarily clicked her tongue, annoyed by the curse words uttered by Turuki.

Too scared to talk, she looked straight ahead at the accident. Then a shiny sweat on the neck of Mechando caught her attention.

Without uttering a word, Mechando reversed the car, to Sophia's horror. Fear suppressed her impulse to scream and attract attention from the crowd that had gathered at the scene of the accident.

Mechando made a U-turn and drove back, towards the town center.

A kilometer into town, the vehicle stopped, and Sophia heard words that calmed her pounding heart. "Get out and go home. The ride was my gift to you, not to be mentioned to anyone." Turuki told her with a wry smile.

Before Sophia could doubt the words she just heard, there was a click from the driver's side of the door, releasing all the door locks.

She jumped out of the car, uttering a breathless "Thank you," fearing that if she did not show some gratitude, the men might change their minds on setting her free.

Out of the car, she hurried off, in the opposite direction. She only realized her mistake when she saw a matatu driving the opposite direction, with a sign showing town center. She waved it down and jumped in, taking the first available seat, and holding her head in both hands, feeling the sweat on her face.

On arrival in town, she alighted near the police station and walked in without looking back in case someone recognized her.

At the station, it took her more than an hour to convince the officer on duty to allow her to record a statement. His argument was that being a holiday season, many ladies were known to enjoy meals paid for by boyfriends, then scampered away, feigning abuse. An argument the officer completed with words that infuriated Sophia. "Those Onono boys are good kids. They cannot be involved in such a demeaning act."

On hearing the words, Sophia knew that if she expressed what was in her mind, she would be accused of verbal abuse. With tears streaming down her cheeks, she recorded a statement, left the police station, and boarded the next available matatu home. On arrival, she met with Babu and Charlie whom she told she was tired and needed some alone time.

When her father arrived home in the evening, Sophia, having cried all her tears out, reported the horrifying incident caused by Turuki and Mechando.

She hoped her father would make it his next day's morning assignment, to visit the shop of Onono, and talk with the elderly man, about his sons.

Sophia was very shocked by what her father said. "Now, more than ever, it is time to speed up your marriage to Cleophas the teacher, to avoid such incidents in future."

Sophia turned to her right side, in case her mother was nearby and heard the response from her father.

Instead, she heard more words from her father. "There is protection in marriage. No one in their right mind will kidnap another man's wife."

The words momentarily touched Sophia. Growing up, she had never heard of someone's wife kidnapped. But, many times, single girls were, and their parents never seemed bothered by the disappearance of their daughters. Then, months later, the lost girls would be found at another village, as someone's wife.

More anger crept into Sophia's heart, as words poured out of her mouth. "But Papa, have you not heard of individual rights in our new Constitution? Freedom of individuals, whatever their age or gender, to be treated with respect, and make their own choices?"

Mariko looked at his daughter, like she was speaking in a foreign language. Seeing his cousin approach the compound, he waved Sophia away and went outside.

Sophia spent the rest of the evening reflecting on her new challenge. What would her life be like now, if, like most ladies at university, she had left with her degree and a boyfriend or a husband. If she had done that, she would be having someone in her life, to counter her father's preference for Cleophas, the teacher, for whom she had no feelings.

Two days later, Sophia boarded a bus to the city, acknowledging that she would need, either a well-paid lawyer, or several trips back to the village, to attend court sessions for her kidnapping case.

Chapter 19

One Thursday evening, Richie entered Sophia's office carrying a single red rose. She accepted the flower having missed Richie who had been away since Mon-day, facilitating a workshop at a venue in the outskirts of the city.

She pushed her chair back from the desk and brought the rose closer to her nose as her eyelids closed in contentment. She opened her eyes on hearing Richie speak, in a whisper. "I stole a moment to scan some ladies at the workshop."

The rose dropped out of her hand to the floor. She bent to pick up the flower as Richie added, "And all that I saw was you with me. Tomorrow is the workshop closing ceremony and participant send-off party. Please…"

Sophia turned from the computer screen and looked at Richie, as he completed the sentence. "Please, promise not to say no—"

"I cannot say no to something I have not heard," She interjected.

Richie's face brightened up with a smile. "That is even better, getting a yes before my re-quest."

He pushed his hands into his trouser pockets and closed the space between him and Sophia. "Tomorrow, please accompany me to the ceremony at 4:30pm."

"Why, when the official work time ends at five o'clock?"

"Ask your boss. He will tell you that, since it is a company function, you are free to at-tend. Everyone from our department and some people from Truphena Towers will be there."

Her dimples sank deeper into her cheeks. The smile was her response to his mention of the tower. His mention of Truphena Tower reminded her of her first ever meal with Richie, long before she knew the Tower was another property of the Mwasimba Group of Companies.

"I will consider your request."

Richie lifted Sophia's left hand, inspected her fingers before he kissed her hand and spoke. "It will not hurt if you dress for a Friday evening out. Call a company car if you need to go home for a change of clothes." He left.

Sophia picked and sniffed it before refocusing on the half-completed task on her computer screen.

~ ~ ~ ~ ~ ~

On Friday morning, Sophia arrived in the office with her handbag and a dry cleaner bag, containing evening dress.

The day dragged on, and she never stopped checking the clock on the wall. She was waiting for the time she would go to change into her evening dress. She needed to see the ladies at the workshop, the ones Richie confessed he had tried to admire.

Sophia hoped that none of the women at the party would be in attires to compete with her. She had chosen a light purple Recho Omondi dress, complete with subtle darting and long sleeves that offset the length of her hemline. Her nude brown strappy stilettos, a splurge from a few weeks ago, made her chandelier style cowrie shell earrings, and equally loud, intricately beaded Bea Valdes clutch, come together in a restrained expression of the ostentation

She arrived in shared transport with Patty and two other company staff.

Patty, still in her office suit, looked sternly at Sophia. "I am annoyed with you, but envious of Richie. Why you did not alert me to also dress up, I cannot guess."

Sophia looked at Patty and wished she could explain that her change of clothes was Richie's idea. She could not share that information as she did not want the other company staff present to overhear.

They joined the workshop participants at a cocktail party and for closing remarks. Sophia followed Patty around. Having been one of the trainers, Patty already knew most of the participants drawn from business enterprises in the Eastern and Southern Africa Region.

Richie, as the organizer of the workshop, gave his speech of thanks to the participants, then walked away from the podium in the direction of Sophia and Patty.

He touched Patty on the shoulder and kissed her on the cheek. He then held Sophia by the small of her back and gave her a quick kiss on the mouth before he continued to chat with some participants nearby.

Sophia, still confused by Richie's action, did not notice when Patty sneaked away.

After eating *a la carte dinner*, as participants enjoyed desserts and drinks, Richie elbowed Sophia's arm. "Please acknowledge your friend who has been eyeing you the entire evening."

Sophia's eyes followed Richie's to three tables away, and there was Patty, almost unrecognizable. She'd changed into a bareback evening dress, and there was a man next to her with his hand on her back. Sophia smiled and waved.

The last activity of the evening was a dance in a hall near the dining area. During the dancing, in the middle of a song, the music suddenly stopped, to the annoyance of the revelers.

Richie, who had walked with Sophia near the DJ, took a microphone, and apologized. "Sorry for holding your steps in limbo, you will proceed momentarily," as the dancers responded in unison, "Aaah," from the floor.

Richie, with a hand encircling Sophia's waist, gently pulled her closer to his side. He put a hand into his inner breast pocket and pulled out a small black velvet case.

Confused, Sophia's eyes darted from Richie to the crowd and back to Richie as she saw him go down on one bended knee, right in front of her. She cast her eyes back to the crowd as their cheering increased. "Do it, do it."

Her lips parted but no words came out as she saw him open the velvet casing. He retrieved a ring, and she was touched by the begging eyes that looked up at her.

When the clapping finally stopped, and the music was back, a tear dropped from Sophia's left eye, as she looked at the one Carat diamond ring on her finger. She wondered how she said yes, to what she now considered an ambush, in a crowded public space.

She would let the evening party go ahead without her causing a scene. She would revoke the engagement at the office on Monday. She needed the weekend to strategize on the best way to do that without starting a rumour at the office.

Next, she pondered on how long it would take her to find another job, a job like her current PA post.

Sophia considered taking leave from work, pack, and retreat to the village to contemplate the engagement. But her parents might construe her return as agreement to marry the teacher. Should she take leave and stay in the city? That would depress her, for her PA work was, not only her source of income, but how she loved to spend her weekdays.

Then Sophia thought about the cost of disappointing her parents, the very people who sacrificed so she could complete her education in secondary school and university in the city.

Chapter 20

On Monday morning, Sophia came face to face with a large bouquet of flowers.

Seeing the eyes from the flower petals, looking back at her, only added salt to her Friday injury, the engagement ring. Though still on her finger, she planned to remove it when she went to Richie's office, after she filled an application form for leave of absence.

Sophia encountered more surprises when she logged into the computer to read email and complete the online leave application form.

With elbows resting on her work desk, she supported her head between her hands, wondering. "Another trip on short notice? Why is everyone making my life a whirlwind? Is this really my life?"

She shifted her eyes back to the computer and read the details of the trip. "The company is being expanded, in the form of a new building. The land deal just went through, and company representatives from head office have to be present, to break the ground for the new building."

She saw an attachment to the email message, an extensive list of items she was to have ready, for the trip in two days' time.

On Wednesday, Sophia was on a flight to India, and she still had the engagement ring on her finger. She had been too busy the last two days to implement her plan of returning the ring. Between getting all the required paperwork ready for the trip, and responding to frequent phone calls from her mother, Sophia had no time to spare.

Sophia had not forgotten how things went yesterday, on Tuesday. Stella called her eight times. On the ninth count, Sophia accepted the call, just to hear her mother on the other side. "Your kidnap case was thrown out due to lack of evidence. The argument put forward by Turuki was that you are his girlfriend and were on a friendly date."

In between wanting to hang up the phone, and wanting to cry in the office, Sophia had resolved to remain strong, give her mother time to finish speaking, just to stop her phone from ringing.

Stella did not pause even to catch her breath, as Sophia listened. "The judge also noted that none of the parties involved were married, and they are over eighteen years. There was no case."

By the time Stella paused, Sophia was furious, beyond madness. A type of anger she had never felt before. Sophia wondered how Turuki and Mechando could win a case on false hood, telling herself that if she had time away from work, she would have traveled home to appeal the ruling. Though she was still afraid that her parents might take her arrival as a chance to convince her to marry the teacher.

As they checked in and boarded the plane, Sophia could tell that Richie was excited, by his confident stride. She guessed the happiness was from seeing that she still had his ring on her finger.

On arrival at Mumbai International Airport, the trio were whisked away in two cars, closely followed by two security men in black suits and dark glasses. Sophia recognized the men as from the Nairobi office.

On the drive to the hotel, Sophia, seated next to Richie, wondered if she was slowly being made a family member without her consent. Otherwise, why had she been included in the transport detail with Michael and Richie, unlike in previous travels.

The trio arrived at a different check-in process. Unlike in past travels, when Sophia's settling into a hotel started with filling and signing forms at the hotel reception desk. Now she ac-companied Richie and Michael as they were escorted into an elevator to their hotel rooms, bypassing the form signing process.

While in the elevator, Sophia feared the three of them would be allocated rooms on the same floor and corridor.

The elevator stopped on the 18th floor where one of the two hotel staff in the elevator announced, "Madam and Sir," his eyes shifting from Sophia to Richie. "Your floor please."

Sophia walked out without looking back, lest she read any telling expression on Michael's face. Richie followed, and placed his hand on her shoulder as they walked on.

She was aware that her breathing was not normal, for she could hear her heart beating hard, as they followed the hotel staff along a corridor. She pulled her jacket together, to pre-vent the people near her from seeing the rise and fall of her blouse, in rhythm with her pounding heart.

By now, Sophia was convinced that she knew what people meant when they said some-one suffered a heart attack, which she believed would be her fate soon.

She felt sweat roll down her back, as the hotel staff leading the way stopped in front of a door, inserted a card, and pushed the door open. He stepped aside. "Madam," and signaled with his right hand, for Sophia to enter.

Sophia stepped in and received the key card as she heard, "Enjoy your stay with us."

She smiled back. "Thank you very much."

Based on the events since Friday when the ring was placed on her unwilling finger. Then the flowers in the office on Monday morning, the one rose in the plane, and the many times Richie's hand had been on her back, Sophia feared for the worst, being booked to share a room with Richie.

Sophia was more surprised to see her luggage, well placed on a stand next to the wardrobe. No more struggles, she thought.

Thursday afternoon and Friday were filled with long meetings at the Mwasimba Group of Companies Mumbai office. There were also discussions with some businesspeople and government officials followed by the signing of documents.

Saturday was jammed with dancing, music, and a ground-breaking ceremony.

The Mumbai office had printed thousands of T-shirts with the company logo and colours. Subsequently, the people attending all wore the company uniform.

Sophia made a quick note, to look out for the next day's newspaper, the photos would make great news back in Nairobi.

Just before Michael held a spade and dug out a large mound of soil, the women entertainment group invited women from the VIP tent to join them. Sophia and three other women responded and were swiftly helped to dress in new silk *Saris* as part of the ceremony.

At one point, while busy enjoying the song and dance, Sophia saw one of the men in black suits move closer to the dancing group.

She got very worried, for in no way would she want to live like a prisoner, under constant watch, being guarded by security men. She made a mental note to have a meeting with Richie, or Michael.

On further thought, she wondered, what her complaint would be about. What if she asked and received no answer? What if she asked and was informed that her role as PA de-manded that type of security while away from the home office. Would asking make others perceive her as an uncommitted PA?

The ground-breaking ceremony ended with Michael and Richie planting tree seedlings at one corner of the property. The ceremony concluded with a lavish public lunch, which extend-ed into a dinner for select dignitaries. By the end of the evening, Sophia was very tired, partly from her extensive dancing.

She was happy that she had learned so much from her first participation at a ground-breaking ceremony. She now had detailed information on what transpired during discussions and arguments in meeting rooms, before everyone appeared, in a happy mood at document signing ceremonies.

Reflecting on events she's watched on TV and read in newspapers back home, she now understood why the media was never allowed into closed door meetings. The media was then invited to witness the last stage where officials appended signatures and shook hands.

Chapter 21

Though she was getting used to flowers appearing in her room, things had not remained constant. Parts of her body were awakened, each time she spotted a flower. Not the flowers she saw along the streets and in other people's offices, but the flowers meant for her.

On her way to the bathroom to bathe, she saw a red rose on the bathroom countertop. The more she stared at the flower, the more the eyes on the petals appeared to return her stare.

After brushing her teeth, she immersed herself in a hot bath, filled with lavender-scented bathing salts, picked from a basket of scents in the bathroom.

Lately, Sophia had discovered that lavender helped calm her mind, to a nice resting place, a place with good memories, or a place with no memories, just peace.

After a long soak in the huge bathtub, she decided it was time to read a book, and then sleep.

The moment her left foot touched the bathmat, the ringing phone startled her, almost throwing her back into the bathtub.

Clinging onto the towel wrapped round her body, she ran into the bedroom, lifting the receiver as the ringing stopped. The ringing was back immediately she put the receiver down. She accepted the call, wanting to hear what Richie had to say at that time of the night.

"You sound out of breath; did I startle you?"

"No. I just got out of the tub, been enjoying a relaxing bath."

Immediately the last word left her mouth, she regretted what she said, asking herself why she felt the need to explain that she hurried from the bathroom to pick up the phone. Her thought was interrupted.

"I miss that, hope we can have one together soon."

She burst out. "You are going to wait a long, long time for that to come. Maybe after I turn fifty-five, when I retire from your firm."

"My girl, I am ready to wait a thousand years, knowing that one day our love will become our life." He chuckled. "Just take one look at my ring on your finger, it will tell you how long I am willing to wait. Happy?"

Sophia pressed the reject button on the phone and put it back on the nightstand. She walked to the wardrobe for a nightie as the phone started to ring.

She walked back and accepted the call. "Did you not just say you will wait a thousand years, that wasn't even a minute."

Richie laughed aloud.

Sophia, taking advantage of that, disconnected the call and proceeded to get a nightie, as the phone started to ring, again. She walked back, pressed reject and got dressed, though she suddenly missed the ringing of the phone.

Sophia looked at her cell phone and saw it flash a blue light, sign of a new message, which she read. "Do you have plans for tomorrow, after the meeting? If not, I have a grand one for us:)"

She typed :/," and pressed send.

Immediately her phone lit up again. "I read your response as no plans on your side. Thanks, I will organize for all the minutes until when we leave for the airport in two days' time."

Sophia read the message with a smile on her face. She decided there was no need to argue with Richie about his wishful thinking.

She logged into her email and saw two messages from Joy. She clicked the messages with urgency, starting with the latest and read. "I thought by now you would have responded, the weekend is here, and Dad is furious with the visit."

"What visit?" Sophia murmured as she read the first message with lightning speed.

She closed her phone, sat on the edge of the bed, and felt tears stream down her face. When she finally stopped crying, she picked up her phone to call Richie, then changed her mind. She needed to compose herself first. Not good to sound agitated, a thing she had heard pleased some men.

Sophia went back to her phone and read the messages again. She typed one sentence to Joy. "Please call our parents and tell them something, then we can discuss when I get home."

Sophia broke into a monologue, asking what she did to the gods, so that no one seemed to consult her, even on personal matters. First, it had been her father, wanting her to marry the local schoolteacher. Now, she just read a message from Joy that there was an emissary sent by her ultimate boss, not Michael, but Mr. Mwasimba himself. The objective was to ask Sophia's parents to set a date when the two families could meet to discuss her marriage to his son.

The challenging part, as briefly mentioned by Joy, was that Mariko, their father, was furious, that Sophia had fallen for one of the city boys, whom he referred to as "no good as husband material."

A line of questions ran through Sophia's mind. Who was her father to say that? What did he know about the city and its people? The city that had helped make his life in the village bearable, the city that gave her the highest level of education. The city that gave her a job she loved, the city that she had come to like, the city…"

Sophia woke up to her alarm and was surprised how fast the morning had come, before she could enjoy a restful night, which followed her the rest of the day.

Chapter 22

Sophia went to the morning meeting, though all the speakers sounded more like far away voices. She was easily irritated, especially on noticing the constant stares from Richie, while he made a presentation to the group.

She waited for midday, when the meeting was scheduled to close, so that she could retire to her room and catch up on sleep.

She was more than grateful when the meeting was over. As she marched out of the meeting hall, a strong hand grabbed her by the shoulder. "Is everything okay with you today?"

Before she could even reflect on the question, she heard words from her mouth. "Ask your brother."

Michael's hold on her shoulder tightened as he said, in a lowered voice, "Ooh, you guys had a long night? No problem, you will soon get used to that."

Sophia's body literally froze as Michael walked with her to one of the two vehicles waiting outside.

As they approached the cars, one of the men in black suits opened a back door. Sophia noticed that the man did not look at her face, an act she silently appreciated, while thinking, "Good, these men are trained not to stare at the face of their bosses, they would read stories. But I am not one of their bosses, just an employee."

Michael went back to the meeting room where Sandeep, the local office manager, and other staff members were waiting to have an informal meeting with him.

After what seemed like an eternity, though it had been only twenty minutes, Michael, Richie, and Sandeep emerged from the building and walked to the waiting vehicles. Michael sat with Sophia, while Richie and Sandeep got into the other vehicle.

They were driven out into the countryside with scenic hills and valleys covered with food crops.

The breathtaking views must have been what Sophia needed, to loosen the knot in her chest.

Michael went out of his way to chat with her for most of the tour, pointing out historic sites and provided detailed information on each.

In the elevator to her hotel room, with one security man in tow, Sophia did not notice as Michael and Richie walked off to the hotel bar.

She entered her room and latched the door. As she threw her handbag on the coffee table, she noticed a new vase of roses staring back at her.

She sank into the two-seater sofa, switched on the television, then switched it off. Telling herself that what she needed was a quiet room, and maybe to check her email, in case Joy had additional information.

Sophia checked her email and there was no new message. She closed her phone and put it on the table as it began to ring. Without hesitation, she answered the phone as the voice on the other side asked. "May I come over to talk?"

To Sophia, Richie wanting to talk was her prayer answered, "Yes," she said.

Minutes later, she responded to a soft knock on her door by swinging the door open, without using the peep-hole. She was face-to-face with Richie and Michael. She slammed the door shut and went back to the sofa. On sitting down, she regretted her action.

She heard another soft knock, which she termed as her second chance, walked to the door, opened it and walked back to the sofa, without checking to see whom she had opened for.

Richie walked in, closed the door behind him, slowly, then took long strides towards Sophia, an action that got her heart racing. She stood up, out of fear. Before she could react, he was holding her face between his large palms.

Sophia, very confused by his action, stood still. Before she could react, he lowered his face to hers and kissed her lips until she gave in. He then sat on the sofa with her before he said, "I am sorry."

Sophia turned and faced him, wondering if he was sorry for the long kiss, or, for the sad-ness that his father had brought on her?

There was an extended silence before Richie spoke. "My initial plan was that we would check into one room, so that by now I would have told you of the planned visit to your parents. I had wanted to tell you about the room on our flight here, but then changed my mind. I decided it would be better to let you be in your own room, that way you could perform your PA duties to your usual high standard."

When Richie paused, Sophia feigned ignorance and asked. "What was it that you needed a shared room to tell me? You may as well say it right now since we are in the same room."

Richie lifted Sophia's left hand, turned the engagement ring around on her finger, then kissed the ring. "I talked with my father about you and me, that I love you and want to spend my life with you, and we, my father had no objections. He likes everything he has heard about you. That is why I proposed to you at that function. That is what I planned to tell you."

Sophia pulled her hand away and folded her arms across her chest, as Richie continued. "I also agreed with my parents that they could initiate discussions with your parents about our marriage."

The words knocked into Sophia's heart like boulders. To protect her throbbing head from further harm, she bent her head to her knees, with both hands shielding the back of her neck, as she sobbed.

Richie switched on the television, though he did not look to see what channel was on. He put the remote down and brought his left arm around Sophia's waist, cuddled her to his side and waited.

After a short while, the sobs lessened, before she said, "No one respects me. No one sees that I too should be consulted, no one wants to hear if I have an opinion on their plans."

She yanked out a tissue from a nearby box, blew her nose before she continued. "No one notices that I am a grown woman, with grand ideas, and big plans, for that matter. All that you are doing is to get me out of a job."

After another cry, she stood up, walked to the bathroom, and ran the tap, occasionally lifting water and splashing her face. The feeling was soothing. Sophia smiled at herself while thinking, "Did the tears just clear my mind, give me the confidence I have so yearned for?"

She walked back to the sitting area and sat on the over-stuffed chair. When Richie looked at her, she addressed him. "Tell me, why do men find it easier to make decisions for other people, instead of consulting with them?"

He continued to stare at her while scratching his chin. "Which men?"

"You, your father, my father, and I guess most other men out there."

"I can only speak for myself, which I have just done. Please come and sit beside me while I explain. I do not bite, I promise."

She went and sat beside him, needing to hear what else he'd planned.

He put his hand on her shoulder and cuddled her. "Your job with the company is secure if that is what you are worried about. I have made that decision for you, and it is not a bad one." The rest should be okay, you and I are adults.

Had Sophia been raised by parents different from Stella and Mariko, she would have slapped Richie. How dare he repeat the same mistake she just asked him about, the habit of making decisions about her and for her, obviously without even considering, consulting her.

She realized her mistake. That smile sunk her dimples in a way that usually tantalized Richie. Before she could react, he held and turned her face to his and kissed her lips. When she pulled away, he lifted the television remote, did a quick flip through channels, and settled on a comedy.

In silence, Sophia wondered if that was how the world of men and women operated, out-side of the work environment. That men made decisions they considered good for women to follow.

To her, if that was the case, there was no way she would ever be married, to live with such a man. She would rather devote her life to advocate for programs that would help change the current decision-making situation. That way, men could start to involve and consult women, before they made decisions.

With her thoughts on the future, a smile appeared on her face. Richie turned and looked at her, then back to the TV screen.

Sophia retreated to her inner thoughts, comforting herself, that one day, after her siblings completed their university education, or when the school fees responsibility shifted to Joy, she would start a movement. The objective would be to create awareness, educate women, especially young girls, on their rights, insist to be involved in decision-making, at all levels."

From the look of things, it appeared to Sophia that all men; rich, like Richie and his family, or poor, like her father, were used to making decisions for women. With that thought, she felt sorry for Stella her mother, knowing that Mariko must be the only one involved in discussions on her marriage to the teacher. Stella was only brought in to communicate Mariko's decisions to Sophia. Without warning, Sophia said aloud, "Poor mother."

Richie made eye contact, like he expected her to say more. Instead, she left her seat and walked away.

Chapter 23

Sophia and the driver were silent on the drive from the airport to her apartment. On arrival, the driver carried her luggage up to her doorstep. He turned to descend the stairs, paused, and asked her to check her email for details on her travel procedures, henceforth.

She smiled, bid him bye, and entered the house. They had recently moved into a three-bedroomed apartment, to accommodate Silas, her brother, who had started his engineering study program at the national university.

Silas was home to welcome Sophia back. After a brief exchange of greetings, he gave a quick update. "The family is fine. Mum called and left a message for you to call her."

Sophia scratched her head as she asked Silas for a favour. "Please call Mum, let her know I traveled safely back to the city. I will call her in the evening, as usual." She left for her bedroom, kicking the door closed with her foot.

She changed into a T-shirt, and sweatpants, then sat on her bed, wondering why she faced so many challenges. She thought of her father, waiting to marry her off to some schoolteacher. Her thoughts shifted to

Mwasimba, supporting Richie in his plans to marry her. And now, the driver said that her freedom had been curtailed, there would be people with cars waiting on her, whenever she wanted to leave the house or office.

For a moment, Sophia wanted to cry, but she decided otherwise. No need for tears, all she needed was courage to face each one of those men if she was to regain her freedom.

She lifted her phone to find out when Joy would be home, but instead, she dialed Michael's number. The phone rang once, twice, three times, then she disconnected.

She called Joy's number, as she saw an incoming call from Michael, which she answered. He sounded incredibly happy on the other end of the line, asking about her travel from the airport, and how the rest of her family was.

Bad idea. That was the first thought into Sophia's mind. She tried to remember why she had called him, but all she heard were words popping out of her mouth. "Mr. Mwasimba, when will you stop me from working as your PA?

There was total quietness on the other side of the line before Michael spoke. "Are you planning to resign on such a short notice? At a time when I have more work tasks that only you can help with? Remember we just broke ground for our new office in India.

May we talk first thing tomorrow morning? Please book a driver for a seven o'clock meeting. And remember to have a deserved rest today."

"Bye." With that one word, Sophia disconnected the call.

She looked at the screen of her phone as she got into a monologue. "What did I just do? Called Michael of course and without a good plan."

Another look at her phone, she noticed she had three SMS messages. She opened the one from Joy and read. "Welcome back home. We missed you so, so much. I found a part-time job with a construction firm in town. Have a good rest because I have a story for you."

Sophia clicked on the next message from Joy and read. "If possible, avoid calls from Mum until tomorrow (:"

Sophia typed back, "Ookay. I sure will do," pressed send and put her phone on the nightstand, and then remembered there was a third SMS message.

She picked the phone as an incoming call startled her and the phone dropped onto her bed. She murmured. "Mum," and buried her face in a pillow. She counted the rings until they stopped.

She stayed still and heard the phone ring again. She counted the rings until they stopped at five, then there was quietness in the room.

Sophia got up, opened her bedroom door, and called out to Silas. "Please, let Mum know that I traveled well and will call her in the evening."

Silas peeped out of the kitchen. "I already did."

Sophia retreated to the bedroom and closed the door behind her, a little harder than she would have wanted to.

One look at the phone and she noticed that she had two other new messages, which she read to establish what Richie wanted. "Hi Sunshine. Already missing you. May we go out for dinner tonight, at mine or yours will be fine?"

She tapped the phone screen and read the second message. "My Sunshine, please say something."

Her first thought was to switch off the phone, an idea that she put aside, quickly. She did not. If asked, she already missed Richie.

She checked her personal email as she heard Silas call out. "Some food for you, your favourite ugali and vegetables ready in five."

A smile spread across Sophia's face as she whispered. "Who knew this boy would grow up so fast, into a very responsible young man? The benefits of paid school fees already are flowing in."

While still smiling, Sophia opened the bedroom door and called out. "Silas. Make it ten minutes, a visitor will join us at the dinner table."

She closed the door, unlocked her phone, and typed a reply to Richie. "Our Silas is preparing a welcome-back meal for me. If you are here in ten minutes, we can devour his cooking. Promise not to overstay."

She clicked send, picked a towel from her wardrobe, and proceeded to her en-suit bathroom for a shower, to wash away everything about India, start a clean new life, maybe.

Back to the bedroom, Sophia dressed in a free flowing yellow and brown floral cotton dress. She checked her appearance in a full-length mirror on one side of her wardrobe, picked a faux gold-chain belt, and held the dress at the waist, to accentuate her figure. She pressed a cream-coloured hair band to keep her long braids away from her face to the back.

As she turned to the side of her bed, she saw the blinking blue light on her phone and guessed the message could be from Richie, asking for directions to her house.

She picked the phone to respond, then decided that it would be okay if he did not come over to her house. She wondered how she had even decided to invite him, for the very first time.

Sophia looked at the ringing phone, praying that it was not her mother. She saw Richie on the screen and decided not to answer. She had no plan to give him her residential details, fearing that he might construe that as an invitation to visit more often.

Lost in thought, Sophia put on finishing touches of eyeliner and lipstick as she heard the doorbell buzz. A minute later, she heard the front door open and her brother exchange greetings with another man. "Can't be, how did...?" she thought as she heard Silas call out. "Your visitor has arrived."

A quick check on time and she noticed it had been twenty minutes since her last message to Richie.

"I asked for it, time to deal with it." Sophia mumbled as she walked along the corridor from the bedrooms to the living room where Richie was standing.

She walked to Richie, lifted both hands round his neck, kissed him on the cheek, then withdrew her arms before Richie could react.

She called out, "Silas. You open the door for a visitor and do not seat them. That's not our house manners, bro."

Silas spoke from the kitchen, "I did sister, but he insisted, only you could seat him."

Richie looked around the living room. "Lovely place. And I like that family chat," as he grabbed Sophia's hand and guided her to the two-seater sofa.

"Thanks for inviting me over, such a pleasant surprise. And your look is killing me right now."

Sophia smiled, appreciating his compliment.

Richie picked up a remote from the coffee table and flicked the flat-screen TV on, as he heard Silas call out.

"Time to wash out all the roti and *pili pili* from your stomachs. Welcome to the table."

Richie smiled, squeezed Sophia's hand, and stood up.

They washed their hands from the sink by the dining room before lowering their heads as Silas said grace. After, they sat at the rectangular dining table, Sophia at one end, Silas on her right side and Richie on the left.

Sophia stood up, picked Richie's plate, and served food. She served in the same way she had always seen her mother serve their father; a triangle of ugali, some vegetables and beef stew.

Each time she served a food item, she looked at Richie, hoping to hear a word from him, asking for more, or saying enough. Sophia received neither, so she finished serving and placed the plate of food in front of Richie.

His eyes followed her every action, as she next served her plate and sat down to eat.

The trio ate in silence before Sophia turned to the side of Silas. "Where did you get all these cooking skills? The food is splendid, more than delicious."

"Watch me sister. One day I will open a restaurant, right here in your house."

They all laughed, before she asked. "Is that what they teach you at engineering school, to open restaurants?"

The eating session that had started off with a lot of quietness, turned into a lengthy con-versation between Silas and Richie. They discussed issues related to be a first-year student at university, his study program, and what jobs he planned to do after graduation.

When they finished eating, Silas cleared the table before he left for his bedroom.

Twenty minutes later, Silas appeared from the bedroom, walked to the main door while excusing himself. "I must leave for school, now that I have welcomed sister back from *pili pili* land."

He walked out closing the front door behind him.

Richie appeared enthralled by the impromptu invitation as he poured praise on Sophia's house, from the furniture to wall decorations.

Sophia interrupted. "How did you find this place? I thought you would wait for my response?"

He squeezed her left hand and lifted it up for a kiss. "That was a formality. What type of man would fail to discover where his Sunshine rises from?" As he kissed her on the cheek.

They sat without talking, before Sophia turned Richie's direction. "I am not being rude, but hope you will not stay long, I need to unpack and refamiliarize myself around here before work tomorrow."

He did not turn away from the television screen as Sophia spoke again. "I have a work meeting with Michael early tomorrow morning."

Richie turned towards her direction. Her eyes widened, on seeing that his face did not have an expression she could read. She wondered if she had been rude with her suggestion for him to leave. Before she could drift into more thoughts, she heard Richie say, "I already know."

Sophia felt an instant warmth, as she wondered why she had mentioned the meeting to Richie, worse still, why she had called Michael.

Lost in thought, she heard Richie say. "As I told you before, no need to worry about your job. A little worry about your father could do."

Sophia bit her tongue. She would not let any of her thoughts be known, in response to the mention of her father. How she wished Richie would leave then, for Joy would be home soon, to share the story she promised.

Like a prayer answered, Richie said. "I will be a gentleman and leave now, if that is your wish," as he stood and offered his hand to Sophia.

Sophia held onto his hand and stood. She was glad, that for once, Richie was doing exactly what she asked him to do, leave. "Thanks for coming at such a short notice."

He smiled. "You do not know what the invitation means to me. A whole new world."

Richie held Sophia closer and kissed her, she returned his kiss. When he released her, she retreated as he smiled and walked to the door. "I will walk myself out."

Sophia did not utter a word, she was busy, reflective. Did she detect some teary manly eyes?

Chapter 24

Sophia's phone rang as she walked to the kitchen to wash dishes. She took a long look at the screen and decided that touching the accept button would be breaking her promise to Joy.

For a moment, she liked her new-found courage, of getting Richie out the door, and now resisting to accept a call from Stella, her mother.

A new thought, on respecting one's parents, left Sophia wishing she had accepted the call from her mother. On further thought, she asked herself what type of message she would be communicating, if not that she accepts phone calls at any time of day, even when she was supposed to be busy at work?

Sophia loved her mother. She would have liked to talk with her at any time of day. But only if it was on different matters, other than being asked to abandon her PA job, and travel home to get married.

She reflected on how best to convince her parents that she was now an adult, old enough to be a mother, if she so wished.

Thinking of children, Sophia asked herself if she ever planned to have children of her own. She acknowledged that babies are cute, especially if parents could provide for all their needs. Children grow into young people, and one day, be inundated with constant phone calls from parents, the way her mother had been calling her.

Lost in thought on what type of mother she would make, Sophia held a cup under running water for too long. Would she turn out like her mother, calling her daughter about marriage? She poured water out of the overflowing cup and placed it on the drying rack in the ad-jacent sink.

She picked up a handful of spoons and held them under the running water, while she questioned herself how she could think about children, before she solved her current problem concerning men. Which of the families chasing after her hand for marriage would she say yes to, and on what basis?

Her stream of thoughts was in rhythm with the speed of water out of the tap into the sink, after hitting the spoons in her left hand. Sophia's mind was busy; thinking about Cleophas, the teacher, the man her father wanted her to marry, for stability, as he had called it.

What Sophia knew about teachers was from her years as a student at her primary and secondary schools. The married teachers lived together with their wives and children at the teachers' residential side within the school compound. In most cases, the wives were teachers at a nursery section of the school, or at another nearby school. For a few other teachers, the wives were nurses at the lo-cal dispensary.

The families appeared stable, though there were whispers among students, on which male teacher liked to stare at schoolgirls. And there were a few cases of a teacher caught with a girl in his house, while the wife was away at work, at the market or visiting family.

Reflecting, Sophia could not recall of any teacher who had married a wife who worked in town, at the government offices. The only place where Sophia could be employed, with her degree in Finance and Business Management.

She guessed where she would live if she were to marry Cleophas, the teacher. Would she live with him at the school compound and commute to town for her job, or would she find a house in town, so that he would be the one to commute from town to school?

Sophia thought of the sons of the businessmen in her local town. Did offices of the businesses in her local town operate like the Mwasimba Group of Companies?

What would it be like, if she was married to a son of one of the local businessmen? Would they give her a PA job at their company? She smiled at the thought, reflecting on how she would use her experience from working as a PA for Michael, to help expand the business of her new family.

Tears brimmed in her eyes, as she thought of how convenient it would be to live in her hometown, near her parents, while helping to build a business empire in her local town. An empire like that of her employer, the employer who had made an enormous difference to her life, to the life of her family.

She placed the handful of spoons in the drying rack, oblivious that some were still greasy, for she had not washed them with the soapy sponge.

Still lost in thought, Sophia picked a plate, washed it with a sponge and held it under the running tap to rinse as she reflected. Who would have ever thought that Mariko would progress from being a poor livestock trader, to his status of a happy man, operating a shop in the village, where people went to buy groceries and other household items?

Oblivious of the running tap, Sophia heard her words. "If I continue with my current job and get one or two promotions in the form of a higher salary, I can make a financial contribution to expand the shop into a wholesale store. A store that will one day expand into a chain of stores, yes, like the company of my employer, a company with businesses within the country, abroad and overseas."

She entertained the thought with a smile, as she put the plate onto the drying rack.

Sophia imagined a time when her father would expand the grocery store, into a wholesale store, a chain of stores—Mariko & Children Wholesalers. Not Mariko & Sons, as many people in her town had named their stores.

A business name like Mariko & Sons would lock Joy and her out of the pride of stores. Sophia hoped that when such a time came, her father would have stopped being the custodian of outdated traditions, like trying to marry off his children.

Surprised that she had completed washing dishes, she turned off the tap, rolled out two sections from the paper towel holder, and wiped the kitchen counter tops while in thought. She comforted herself, that in no way would her father name the business Mariko & Sons. How could he, when the first shop was financed by her money? Or rather, her exceptional work at the Mwasimba Group of Companies.

Next, Sophia's thoughts drifted to the man who walked out of her house not too long ago. The man whose brother she called boss, the man whose father owned the company that had helped change her life. The man who sneaked an engagement ring onto her finger.

She paused from wiping the counter tops, stepped on the release of the trash can, threw in the used paper towel and walked out of the kitchen. She was annoyed with herself, for keeping the ring for so long.

Sophia questioned if her keeping the engagement ring had caused Richie's annoying be-haviour of making decisions for her. She made a mental note, that the next day, she would go to his office, place the ring on his desk and walk out. Even if it meant walking out of the Akoth Towers.

On her way to the bedroom, she stopped on remembering that the next day she had an appointment with Michael, about her job. Could she afford to storm out of the Akoth Towers? What about her PA job? She could not imagine a life without the salary the job gave her.

Her thoughts drifted to the feelings she had developed for Richie, pondering, if some of her actions in the recent past could be construed as friendship feelings. Such as not fighting back whenever he held or kissed her.

Sophia bit her fingernails, like she was shy, realizing that today's first kiss was from her, a kiss to welcome Richie into her house, for the very first time. She remembered, that once or twice, she had missed Richie. Was this what other women called love? Like when Richie said he had missed her, could that be what love was all about?

Now Sophia felt the need to reflect more and reach a decision. Did she ever want to get married, to whom and for what? Would marriage bring more stability to her life, more stability than she had gained from her PA job and salary?

What would marriage add to her life, other than a new schedule. A schedule with the time to wake up and prepare breakfast, time she must be back home to cook dinner for her husband, and children.

She panicked, with a thought of what would happen to her job as PA if she got married. Would she have time to travel with Michael? How would her life be without her cur-rent flexibility? Available, and even happy to travel on short notice. Sophia was very reflective, as she closed the bedroom door behind her.

Chapter 25

Weighed down by bags of groceries, Joy opened the front door and entered the house. She kicked the door shut with her left foot as she called out. "Sophia."

She left the grocery bags on the floor in the sitting room and hurried the direction of her sister's response.

Sophia opened the bedroom door to a big embrace from Joy. "Welcome back home, we missed you. How was your trip, and how did it go with your boyfriend?"

The tight embrace between the two sisters ended with the mention of the word boyfriend. How had it taken Sophia that long to realize that now Richie qualified as her boyfriend? She turned her eyes to the engagement ring on her finger as she thought, her fiancé.

She put on a happy face. "What do you expect sister? The trip was fantastic. I am loving my job, more. I love my job. You need to fly one of these days, to comprehend what I am talking about."

"Ooh, which means I need to find a rich boyfriend, ASAP."

"No, a salaried job would do," Sophia corrected her.

Sophia reminded herself, that she needed to filter her words, the next time she opened her mouth. As of now, her responses evoked unwanted words from the listener, most of her listeners.

She made a mental note to choose her words with care. Roll them first in her mind, imagine the response from the other person, before uttering each word.

The sisters got into a lively discussion on the trip. Sophia talked about what she liked and enjoyed. Sightseeing tours and shopping. With the mention of shopping, she opened her large travel suitcase, revealing new shoes, bags, and clothes.

As they admired the items, Joy, excitement on her face, said. "One day I will go back to our clothing business. Open a boutique store at the ground floor of one of the posh hotels, or huge buildings like Akoth Towers."

Sophia, holding onto a silk scarf, looked at Joy. "Why did I think you will soon graduate into a sought-after designer, not a businesswoman selling clothes?"

Joy laughed out aloud. "Design is more in the mind than the degree awarded by universities. Yes, I have new knowledge on design, such as the classical history of design, design in distinct parts of the world, and more."

One side of Sophia's mouth twisted upwards, into a smile as Joy continued. "Yes, they teach us a lot of innovative ideas in my design study program, but clothing is where my heart is."

Sophia held out the silk *Sari* she was given during the ground-breaking ceremony. Looking at Joy, she said.

"These are the kind of gifts you get, if you worked with a company, not your own clothing store."

Joy ignored Sophia and continued to talk about business. "Looking at these designer items, the next time you travel to India I will give you a list of bags to buy for me. The price you paid is nothing compared to what people pay at those designer stores in town." She pointed to Sophia's handbag. "For this first-class leather." Joy said while smoothing her hand on one of the leather bags.

Sophia smiled. "I like it that you already know the price of items in our city."

"I can already guess which of my past clients would pay triple or five times the cost of what you paid." Joy was full of happiness as she talked about her dream business.

Sophia once again bit her tongue. She had wanted to tell Joy that she needed to aim for higher things in life. Like aspire to work with one of the better-known companies, with business activities at national and international levels.

To Sophia, Joy had studied under difficult circumstances. The best she could do for her-self was to stop thinking about a clothing business, which used to be their survival job, only source of income.

Sophia then reminded herself that Joy loved clothes, bags, shoes, and many other fashion items. Otherwise, where would she be without Joy's careful choice of items for her office attire?

Since Sophia's first day at work, Joy's choice of clothing items from their second-hand clothing business never let Sophia down. Instead, she gained respect in the office, for dressing well, as a director's PA ought to.

Sophia was aware of some ladies in the office, who, though they earned up to five times her salary, dressed in expensive clothes, but with little taste. With that thought, she resolved not to argue about Joy's idea of opening a clothing store.

With the sun setting, the room was getting dark. Joy walked to the bedroom window and pulled the two curtains together as she heard Sophia's phone ring. Both turned to the phone, as Joy warned. "Don't answer, if that is Mum."

"Yes, it is Mum. I had promised to call her in the evening. What if I accept the call, greet her and promise to call her later?" She thinned her mouth. "I have a feeling she will soon get annoyed with me for not accepting her calls," Sophia explained, in a whisper, like her mother would hear her through the ringing phone.

Joy snapped. "Better if you do not answer the call."

The phone rang a second time, a third time, and they stood there, immobile, and quiet, like the caller would see them if they made a move. They watched as the phone rang again, watched until the rings stopped, then Joy said. "Yes, you must avoid those calls for now."

Holding a pair of mauve high heeled shoes, Sophia looked at Joy who was busy talking. "Mum has never stopped calling since you left for your trip. It is about the visitors, the parents of your boyfriend. Anyway, let me start from the beginning."

Sophia positioned herself well, as Joy explained. "What I want to say is that the schoolteacher, now, more than ever, wants to marry you, and Dad is still in support of that crazy idea."

Sophia cupped her forehead like it hurt, as Joy add. "I heard from my grapevine, that the Onono boy, the bad one who tried to kidnap you, has calmed down, changed tactics, and is ready to follow the proper procedures to marry you.

Onono, their father, is said to have asked his sons to let him plan a visit to our parents."

Sophia fidgeted, like she had just sat on needles. Joy paused like she was scrutinizing her sister before continuing. "Do you remember the business competitor of the Onono family, what is his name?"

"Are you forgetting the name Ndugu, the owners of the wholesale at the new building in town where Dad purchases items for his shop in the village?"

Joy jerked out of the chair. "Yes, yes. Poor me when it comes to remembering names of now crazy people."

Sophia looked up into the light bulb, was blinded by the bright light and immediately looked back at Joy, who said, "I am told the youngest son of Ndugu is back from the USA, in search of a wife. And the only name in town is Sophia, the daughter of Mariko."

Joy sat down and looked at Sophia. "Remember how the Ndugu and Onono families have always been in competition? When one dispatched a son or daughter to study in the US, the other one did whatever it takes to send theirs to the UK. Even if it means selling part of their land or diverting a business loan."

Sophia felt the need to add. "Soo competitive. I have not forgotten how the first storied residential house popped up at Ndugu's village. It was right after the Onono family constructed a palatial home in the next village. So, the Ndugu's had to beat them, not only in size, but height wise, towards the sky. Now that village has their first red roofed storied home, all thanks to competition."

Joy looked at Sophia, like she needed to confirm she'd finished talking before she said. "I guess I do not need to say more. My guess is that immediately the Ndugu family heard that the Onono son wants you, though he used very illegal tactics, the Ndugu's must have summoned their youngest son to fly in from the USA, to compete for you."

Sophia's facial expression changed, into one of annoyance, pulled in eyebrows.

Joy touched Sophia's hand, saying, "Sophia, remember what all that comes down to? You are the best example of a strong, virtuous woman in our village and town, and now in the city. You are an exceptionally good person."

Sophia's face softened into a smile as Joy added. "Anyway, you need to call Mum. All she needs to hear from you is about your boyfriend. More so if you are the one who sent them to visit our home. Mum said there was a message to Dad, asking for a date when the family of your boyfriend could visit our parents."

Sophia's eyes opened wide, as Joy completed her advice. "If I were you, I would call and let Mum know, that such an important matter cannot be discussed on the phone. Just greet her and let her know that you will find time to travel home to discuss the is-sue."

Sophia put the shoes she had been holding on the floor, right next to the feet of Joy, a sign that the pair of shoes was for her.

Joy looked at the shoes. "Are you confused? Those shoes belong to your feet, not mine. Too good."

Sophia pointed at the shoes. "I bought them for your feet."

Joy's face brightened with a smile. "I would suggest you keep the shoes for your next date, with whoever you choose. Though I see the ring is still on your finger." She chuckled. "Any story for me about it? What happened to the removal plan we talked about last time?"

Sophia appeared reflective for a moment, before she said, "Richie was here today. We enjoyed a meal prepared by Silas."

Joy upright, from her bent position of admiring the shoes. Lifted her right hand to her heart, then said, "Please tell me more. Did he drive you home from the airport?"

Sophia ignored Joy's question, and instead, pointed a finger towards her feet. "Try on the shoes. You need them more than I do. Time for you to shine out there and get men scrambling for you." She chuckled. "As you can tell, I am already out of the market. What with...,"

Sophia paused and folded fingers on her left hand, one by one, starting with her pinkie. "One, two, three..." She stopped at four, and said, "Four men, or four families, knocking each other down, running after my hand in marriage. What would you do if you were in my situation, would you disappoint our parents?"

Joy looked up at her sister, then back to the shoes she had on, and smiled. "Look, I am taller than you now, though not as good in manners. The boys out there can follow me, or my shoes for that matter. But you know what sister, it would not be hard for me to choose."

Sophia knew that what Joy said about making a choice was true. To Sophia, Joy had courage, plus added audacity that Sophia must have forgotten in their mother's womb. Sophia knew that she needed to do something about her courage, especially in the coming days, when she must have a conversation with her parents, and with Richie.

Joy paced the bedroom floor before she danced out of the room, still in her new shoes. "I have gone to the kitchen to prepare supper. I will stay in my new shoes all evening. I like them and plan to compete with the models in town, one day."

She walked out into the corridor, reminding Sophia to call their mother.

Chapter 26

As Sophia nibbled on her breakfast, her phone rang. She saw a strange number, hesitated, then decided there was no harm to answer the call. She was still within the safe-ty of her house.

A voice on the other end spoke. "Good morning madam, Wambua here. I have arrived to drive you to the office. Come to the visitor's parking whenever you are ready."

"Thank you," Sophia said to the company driver. She ended the call and continued with her breakfast while she wondered what was going on. She'd not asked for transport, though she had received an email message to that effect.

On further reflection, Sophia decided that sitting comfortably in the back seat of a car and being driven, without worry was not a bad idea.

Riding in matatus every morning and evening, demanded that each passenger stayed on the alert. Now, no more bother of driving with the matatu driver, stepping on imaginary brakes to avoid running over pedestrians, even at well-marked zebra crossings. One had to always hold onto the rail or the seat in front, because the driver was likely to brake suddenly, to pick up passengers at none bus stop areas.

Thinking of drivers, Sophia promised herself to make time and go for driving classes. She needed to learn to drive, because owning a car, once a farfetched dream, was now closer to reality. Better still, their apartment came with two dedicated parking slots, neither of which they currently used.

When Joy found a permanent job, they would discuss family finances. The focus would be the payment of school fees for their brothers. Sophia planned to continue paying fees for Silas and Kevin, giving Joy enough time to save and pay for the education of Charlie and Babu.

By the time the two youngest boys would be ready for university, Silas would have received his degree in mechanical engineering. An engineer could not miss landing a decent job. Then he would pay university fees for his two younger brothers.

The drive to the office was faster than Sophia could ever imagine. She arrived on the 52nd floor earlier than the days when she used public transport. She now understood how the rich managed to arrive in their offices early.

During her drive to the office, she did not see any matatus compete with the company car for the road.

She smiled, those matatu drivers know what vehicles not to harass. They give way to the expensive cars on the road, like the Mercedes that she was driven in, to the office.

As she walked the corridor to her office, Sophia assumed that since she was driven in the Mercedes, then Michael would be picked up later. She smiled at the thought of arriving in the office earlier than her boss, for once.

Flowers, as fresh as ever, welcomed Sophia back to her office desk, after the trip to India.

Another look at the flowers, and she saw eyes, many eyes on the petals, looking back at her. She stopped at the front side of her desk and inhaled the fresh scent. She would not take them home, she liked them, would prefer to see them while she worked.

As she walked round the desk to store her handbag, before going to Richie's office, the connecting door opened, and Michael entered her office. "Good morning. I hope you had a good rest after the flight home."

Sophia looked up at Michael, surprised that he was already in the office. "Good morning. I did indeed have a good rest."

"Sorry to get you back to the office so fast after travel. Chairman and the company Directors are eager to receive our report about our trip to India."

"No problem. I am well rested, ready to take up work tasks.

"Since you are already here, let us meet at 7:30, to discuss the best approach to move forward."

Sophia nodded her head up and down, in agreement, as Michael walked back to his office, closing the door behind him.

She switched on her computer and saw eight days' worth of emails drop in. She used the search function to read messages from Michael. The rest could wait.

At exactly 7:28am, she picked a laptop, knocked on the connecting door and entered Michael's office. "Okay, I was not expecting this," was the first thought in her mind, the moment she saw Richie. They exchanged greetings as Sophia took the seat opposite Richie.

Always keen on details, she noticed that Michael had been looking at her. She promised herself to prove to Michael, that all she wanted was her PA job, not Richie.

She squared her shoulders throughout the duration of the meeting, guarded each word she uttered, as she made informed contributions.

At the end of the two-hour meeting, Sophia had five pages of information for their presentation to the Board of Directors. And there was a slot for her during the presentation, another first.

She clarified a few items with both Michael and Richie, before she walked out with Richie, through the main door, to the corridor.

After a short chat outside her office door, she entered and dropped into her huge leather chair, retrieved her phone, and typed a message to Joy. "Presenting to company Chairman and Directors tomorrow morning. Please do me a favour, keep Mum out of my way, today and tomorrow. I will be all hers through the weekend. Okay? I will be busy the rest of the day. Love you, sis."

Sophia switched her phone to silent mode and got to work on the presentations. She read more information emailed by Michael and Richie, before transferring them into the company template for PowerPoint presentations. She read the revised presentation again.

Satisfied, she saved the presentations on the shared drive, sent email messages to Michael and Richie, asking them to verify the documents. Once she received messages of their approval, she shut down her computer, opened the connecting door and said bye to Michael. This was not her usual practice, but just in case he had any other urgent task for her.

Eleven hours since she last entered Akoth Towers, Sophia was on her way to the basement, where a driver was waiting to drive her home. She felt accomplished, especially with her tasks as a PA.

It was only day one of being chauffeured to and from work, and Sophia was liking it. She wondered how she would have survived in a matatu, after such a long day of work.

She had been stuck at her desk all day, except for the quick lunch with Patty, who was very inquisitive about her travels. To compensate for the hurried lunch, Sophia agreed to join Patty the next day, for tea.

~ ~ ~ ~ ~ ~

Back to the house, Sophia spent time choosing and matching clothes for the next day. The clothes included an extra pair she would keep in the office, in case she one day needed a change, before an important meeting.

The idea of keeping an extra outfit in the office was easy to implement, now that she had a driver and a car, although for how long, she had no idea. She would enjoy the ride while it lasted, hoping that it would last until she went through driving school and bought her own car.

During dinner, Joy took a long look at the engagement ring still on Sophia's finger, and Sophia read into Joy's stare.

After dinner, Silas excused himself as he had a lot of drawings to do as part of his schoolwork. As he walked to his room, Joy's wisdom followed him. "Remember not to bend your head to the books too much. All the nice girls will pass you by."

He stopped and looked over his left shoulder. "Which guy, with such sweet sisters would struggle to find the right girl?" He chuckled. "Keep that in mind. I will soon ask you to bring one. Will you fail me?"

Off he went, leaving his sisters in laughter.

At 9:00pm Sophia took one look at the clock on the wall of the dining room and excused herself for the night. "Tomorrow's presentation has nerved me. I have never spoken in front of the Company Chairman." She paused when Joy interjected, "No need to be scared of your fu ture father-in-law."

Sophia rolled her eyes before she left for her bedroom.

As she walked away towards her bedroom, Joy, who was clearing the table, said, "Mum called twice, I handled her as per your request."

Sophia looked back, as Joy added. "Good night, and hey, nice car that picked you this morning."

"Thank you," Sophia said and walked on. While in the bedroom, she noticed that she had a new message on her phone, which she read. "Sunshine, my love for you grows by the day. Sweet dreams and see you tomorrow."

She typed a reply, asking Richie to stop his romantic distractions, which could inter-fere with her presentation the next day. Halfway through the typing, she changed her mind, reasoning that she was too tired to argue. Instead, she typed, "Good night and sweet dreams." Satisfied, she went ahead to the bathroom.

While in bed, Sophia wondered how married life would be if she were to try it. Would she have such leeway with her life" Go to bed when she wished, and have an undisturbed sleep?

If she married the teacher, would he sit in the bedroom, marking student assignments late into the night? If she married the son of Ndugu, would he ask her to go with him to the US, or had he come back home to join the lengthy list of returnees?

Then Sophia imagined what it would be like if she married Richie. Would he continue to arrive in the office exceedingly early, to sneak fresh flowers to her desk, long before she arrived, how-ever early she came? Would he have time to join her for dinner at home, or would he be busy in the office, working late, or out traveling…

Chapter 27

Sophia always found it hard to ignore her classic wake up buzzer. Telling herself that she had had a good night's sleep, she pulled the bedsheet and blanket off her shoulders and rolled out of bed.

It was Friday morning, the day of the presentation.

She paused and gave her thanks, again, as she disembarked from the back seat of the Mer-cedes Benz. On the elevator ride up to her office, she wondered where she would be at that time if she had used a matatu to work.

At her office, she picked a fresh red rose on her desk and sniffed the scent, before walking to the coat hanger and hanging the extra garments she brought in. Back at her desk, she responded to email messages, mostly the ones she had ignored the day before.

Sophia walked to the women's washroom, for one last check of herself before the meeting.

She arrived at the executive boardroom on the 53rd floor for the presentation. Some of the eleven Directors were already seated in large chairs at the oval boardroom table. Others stood in small groups, chatting. She spotted some familiar faces as she greeted them.

Chairman was with William, his son, and some people she had met at company functions, such as parties and meetings.

Sophia paused midway through the greeting session, on seeing Richie enter the room, with Patience by his side. Sophia cast her eyes back to the entrance to see if Patience's daughters-in-law were in tow.

Mr. Mwasimba, the Company Chairman called the meeting to order with greetings, followed by self-introductions.

Michael then took over the next session, introducing Sophia as his Personal Assistant and the connector throughout their presentations. Sophia smiled, surprised with the new addition to her PA title.

Sophia presented the introductory session before she invited Michael to talk about collaborating businesses in India and lease of office space once construction of the building was completed. She did the same, before Richie presented the second session, on the financing of the new office building and potential revenue from office space leases.

A long session of questions, answers, arguments, and clarifications followed the presentations. Sophia was impressed and amused at the same time. The Directors had transformed from their earlier friendly postures, into men and women with tough questions, needing informed answers.

The meeting ended with a group lunch and friendly chats before the Directors dispersed.

Back in her office, Sophia was relieved that the meeting and all the anxiety it brought her, was finally over.

She retrieved her phone and typed a message to Joy. "Hi, am done with the meeting." She then went to the washroom to refresh her make-up, in readiness for her planned evening outing with Patty.

Sophia walked back to her office with a lot of confidence, then hesitated by the door on seeing Richie, seated on the edge of her desk. As she closed the door behind her, he stepped down and met her halfway to her desk, embraced for long hug, before releasing her. "Let us crown the day with some drinks at the club"

"Not possible my friend…," before she could complete the sentence, the connecting door opened, and Michael entered her office. "Well done comrades. Chairman and the Directors were extremely impressed with our report."

Richie and Sophia raised their eyes, waiting to hear more, as Michael continued. "I have just received a message that we have their full support."

A full smile engulfed Sophia's face as she listened to more words from Michael. "I have an idea, why don't we fly the Directors to India, once the building is ready?"

Richie gave thumbs up.

Michael walked to the connecting door, held the handle, and turned back. "I'm off for the weekend. Bye guys and make something good out of our successful trip and presentation, at least celebrate." He took an unnecessarily long look at Sophia with a smiley face. "Our connector impressed everyone," He said and stepped back into his office as the door closed behind him.

Richie turned to Sophia. "As I was saying…," in mid-sentence, there was a soft knock on the door and Patty entered.

Immediately Sophia saw Patty, she smiled. "Okay, the sentence completes itself."

Patty looked at the two and asked. "What sentence completes itself?"

Sophia laughed. "Good you took long strides on your way here, Richie was trying to snatch me out of our tea date."

Patty turned to Sophia, both hands on her hips. "You can't allow him. Today is our day. They took you away for two weeks, including yesterday. Not today."

Without uttering a word, Richie took a step toward Sofia and put his hand on the small of her back. "You are going nowhere without me," he said, putting emphasis on each word.

~ ~ ~ ~ ~ ~

Richie, Sophia, and Patty arrived at the Gaithamu Country Club. As the trio stepped in-side, Sophia sent a message to Joy. "Hi, all is well. I have gone out for drinks with friends, will be home before midnight. Take care of calls from Mum, thanks in advance."

Sophia arrived home at 11:15pm to find Joy busy working on a self-initiated design project. She abandoned the project as soon as Sophia entered the house. "Welcome back, how was your presentation and evening out?"

"Thanks. The attendees, including Richie's parents liked the presentation. My burnt Sienna dress gave me all the confidence I needed, though it almost ruined my evening."

Sophia said as she kicked off her chocolate brown three-inch pumps, right inside the front door. She threw her brown leather handbag on the two-seater sofa, followed by herself, saying, "Do you know how large our city is?"

Joy looked at her expectantly, getting Sophia to say more. "We went to this exclusive club, Gaithamu. I had always assumed that the place is the gate and the one building visible from the road."

"Is there more? Maybe you need to remove your office dress as you educate me on the Club."

They went into Sophia's bedroom, as she continued her narration. "That place is expansive, with acres and acres of land. All the way down to some river, and up the other side. I did not get to walk outside much, but there is a children's park, two tennis courts, a leisure walking area, and a golf course, located across the river.

There are at least three restaurants, each renowned for distinctive styles of cuisine. There is a bar, and many sitting areas."

Joy, with her mouth agape, looked at Sophia. "Sounds like you had a real Friday evening out. Was it an office party?"

Sophia's face brightened up. "Nope! Just an outing with Richie and Patty, one of the managers in the finance department. Richie crashed my tea date with Patty. That is how we ended up at the club. The evening was interesting, apart from some annoying ladies at the club."

Joy jerked her head to the side, with that look of tell me more, and Sophia explained. "I now know where all those high-heeled ladies disappear to at the end of the week. To exclusive clubs. They were there in red lipstick, long eyelashes, and designer clothes. Wherever your designer imagination takes you, to all the high-end streets in Paris and London, they were there."

With one hand on her waist, Joy checked herself in the full-length mirror. She turned around like she was modeling a dress, looked at Sophia who added. "I have no problem with their clothes and lipstick, just their bad manners."

Joy smiled, urging Sophia to continue.

"Midway through our arrival, five ladies had left their boyfriends to join our table. Not just to join us but giving Richie all sorts of hugs and smooches. Imagine. One even had the guts to ask who I was, never having seen me at any of the clubs. Soo annoying, I do not think I will ever go back there."

With merciful eyes, Joy sympathized. "Ooh sorry. How did Richie take it?"

"That one is ridiculously hard to read, except for his never-ending smiles. Next time I will need one of those watches with a counter, that way, I will be able to tell the total number of kisses he gives and receives."

Joy burst out into laughter, then lifted a hand and covered her mouth.

Sophia looked at her with a smile. "When we stood to select food from the expansive buffet, his hand never left my back. You should have seen the looks I received from both the men and women at the club. At some point, Richie held my hand and kissed the ring, the only time I was glad to have had it on."

Looking upwards, with her pointer finger on one cheek, Joy interjected. "Talking about reality, Mum asked if you would travel home this weekend. I said not possible as you are busy, having just returned from an overseas trip, to the office with back-to-back important meetings. She seemed to understand, though the part of being too busy bothered her."

Joy took a long pause, like she was checking Sophia's face for reaction before she continued. "Then mother went on and on about how her age-mates are grandmothers now, that educated women never have time for marriage or babies, and more annoying words."

Joy paused and made eye contact with Sophia before she proceeded. "What if you call her tomorrow and then travel to the village next weekend? That way, you have the week to juggle the different possibilities and how to respond to potential questions."

Sophia turned to Joy, in search of some answer.

Joy said, "Better still, Mum's calls could cease with such a promise."

Sophia opened one door of the wardrobe, stood on her toes, and picked a bath towel from a top shelf. She excused herself to go for a shower.

Joy left the room as Sophia closed the bathroom door behind her. It was her way to end their conversation. The more she heard of the phone calls from her mother, now asking about grandchildren, the more agitated she became.

When Sophia retired to bed for the night, her head was heavy with possibilities. She agreed with Joy. It would be better for her to travel home and discuss with her parent their questions about her marriage.

Chapter 28

One weekend, Sophia invited Richie to what she called a proper meat eating place.

Richie arrived at her house before midday but declined an invitation to sit. "I left important things and people in the vehicle. I am afraid I can't stay."

In responding to Richie's haste, Sophia scrutinized his faded blue jeans, polo shirt, and sports shoes, before she picked her handbag, held his hand and they walked downstairs and outside to the vehicle.

On arrival, Sophia could tell that there was, not one, but many people in the green Land Rover Discovery. For a moment, she assumed that Richie had arrived with a security detail, since they were driving to Kajiado to eat nyama choma, roast meat.

A second look at the driver's seat, she locked eyes with Michael, who was quick with a response. "Today is Saturday, it will be nice if we both drop our office formalities." He chuck-led. "That way, we both get to enjoy the goat you will roast for us."

Sophia, still holding onto Richie's hand, smiled. "Deal, and that allows me to call you Mike, for the first time."

Michael broke into laughter, as Richie opened the back door and Sophia joined Patty, taking the seat right behind Michael. Richie made himself comfortable on the co-driver's seat before he turned around and addressed Sophia.

"Do not turn to the guys at the very back of the vehicle. I will introduce them on arrival."

Naturally, Sophia turned for a better view of the two men. She saw Bill with another man whose face was not new to her, though she could not place him. She waved. "Hi Bill, I know you, in a pin-stripe suit at the boardroom. Please introduce the visitor."

As Michael drove out of the estate, she heard a response from Bill. "Not now. Once we arrive, I will introduce this important boy," Bill said as he received a high five from the man.

The rest of the journey was occupied by loud chats on several topics, except work or the Mwasimba company where five of them worked.

As they drove down a gravel road, Sophia realized that they had turned off Ngong Road, no longer driving to Kajiado, her expected destination. Before she could ask, Bill shouted out from the back. "Hey Mike, drive slowly. You have boys seated at the back."

Still focused on the road ahead, Michael said, "The price you pay for refusing to drive. I will slow down, not for you, but for the sake of your dear wife."

Bill opened his mouth, but did not utter a word, as the rest broke into laughter.

"The younger Mwasimba boy here should have sat at the back," Patty quipped while looking at Richie.

Richie turned to his left, to address Patty, seated right behind him. "But I am the one with the bag of money for our feast," prompting Sophia to remind him that the trip was her initiative, so she was the one to pay.

Before Sophia could continue, she heard the man at the back say, "Richie, there comes competition. My role is to be with whoever does not win." Richie raised thumbs up as Michael parked the vehicle.

Michael and Richie walked away to the food ordering desk, as Bill called Sophia, promising to introduce her to the visitor.

The four walked to a vacant gazebo. On arrival, Bill hung his jacket on the back of a chair while saying, "Our turn, pick the best chairs, leave the worst for the driver and his co-driver."

Bill walked to the opposite side of the round table and extended a hand to Sophia. "I am William, though everyone calls me Bill, except the priest who baptized me."

Patty interjected, "Sophia, ignore him. The only person who calls him William is his dad."

Bill ignored Patty's remark, held Sophia's left hand, and turned to the other man present. "Meet Sam. Sam, meet Richie's only one, Sophia."

As Sophia and Sam's hands met in a greeting, he said. "Pleasure to meet you. Unlike most of my cousins, I have a complete name, Samson."

Sam's comment prompted Bill to give further details on the name. "Sophia, Sam is my son. I am named after Sam's father, a dear uncle, my father's younger brother."

The four took their seats and got into a conversation, Bill watched Michael and Richie walk towards the gazebo. He stood and turned to Sophia. "Sophia, my time to intro-duce you to more people, come," He said as he beckoned her to join him.

Sophia stood as Richie and Michael arrived. "Good to be introduced to people I already know," she said as she walked to Bill's side.

Bill embraced her tightly. She struggled out of his embrace as he said. "The Mwasimba boys always prefer a cuddle."

Richie ran to the side of Bill and Sophia. "Hayahayaaa. Time to wrestle my bro," raising his fists and jumping around Bill, challenging him to a mock boxing match.

Bill looked at Richie before releasing Sophia and he joined the rest of the group in laughter.

While holding onto Sophia's left hand, Bill turned to Richie. "I need a beer, for showing you how not to leave Sophia behind, next time."

Richie moved closer to Sophia and lifted her left hand, for Bill to see the engagement ring. "How long will it take you to excavate an equivalent stone?"

Sophia pulled her hand away from Richie. "No further show-offs," as she looked at a smiling Michael before she sat down, just to hear Bill say. "And she is warm," as he pulled his jacket on and sat down.

Patty, who had been talking with Samson, laughed, prompting Michael to turn her direction. "You! You still owe me an explanation, for getting engaged in private."

Patty lay her left hand on the table as Bill and Samson whistled, in unison.

Sophia looked at Patty's engagement ring, then at Richie. Her lips parted, like she wanted to say something, but did not. She would have liked to ask when Patty got engaged. It was hard for Sophia to have noticed the engagement ring as Patty always had at least two rings on her fingers, as part of her daily attire. Today, Patty wore only one ring.

Sophia's phone vibrated in her handbag. Praying that it was not her mother, she excused herself and accepted the call. Elvin informed her that a car was available if she needed to go shopping or anywhere else. "No, thank you. I am not in the house."

After a moment of silence, listening, she added. "Thank you, that was kind of you. See you on Monday, bye." Sophia said before she ended the call and went back to her chair as two waiters arrived, one carrying a glass jug filled with warm water and a slice of lemon. The other held a metallic basin and hand soap.

The group washed hands starting with the la-dies.

As the two waiters walked away, another two arrived with two trays, holding the meal—*nyama choma*, ugali, *Kachumbari* salad, side plates, glass cups filled with soup, salt, and toothpicks.

As soon as they placed the food on the table, Michael stood, picked two of the glass cups and placed them on the table near Patty and Sophia. He picked two side plates and served *Kachumbari* which he handed to Sophia and Patty as he spoke. "I watched these boys grow up." He looked around the table, from Richie to Samson and to Bill, as he continued, "I know they will consume all the food if I don't serve you first."

Laughter filled the table as Michael sat down, picked meat and *ugali* from the main tray and started to eat.

Patty looked at Michael as she pushed her plate of food to Bill. "I prefer to eat direct from the main tray, the food tastes better."

After a short while, everyone was eating the roast meat and ugali from the main platters.

When the *nyama choma* was almost finished, Samson left for the meat roasting station and returned with more meat on a plate. He emptied the plate into the tray, saying, "I asked them to go barbeque another goat."

By the time each person moved their seat away from the table, there was little evidence of the food, except for bones and some ugali crumbs.

Sophia was amazed. She found it a challenge to reconcile the thoughts rushing through her mind. She held back a smile thinking of how on many other days the people seated with her at the table wore designer suits and belonged to exclusive clubs in the city. Clubs where they were waited on at tables. Today was different, they visited meat roasting stations.

Patty held Sophia by the hand, then looked round the table, at the four men. "We are off to the restroom, to replace our lipstick." Off they went.

After a moment, Sam vacated his chair. "I better follow those two beauties and fight off whatever lions could be lying low out there." He followed Patty and Sophia.

When the three were out of sight, Michael looked at Bill, then Richie. "I love it this way, being with ladies who can eat food, not peck and complain about fatty meat and their waist-lines."

"And I like men who do not give me too much competition when eating nyama choma," Bill said before he tapped Richie on the shoulder. "Man! She is soft and warm. How do you manage?"

Richie's lips parted, about to say something as Michael laughed. "You spoiled for this boy." Pointing at Richie. "He took your advice on flowers, L.i.t.e.r.a.l.l.y. Now my office is ever filled with flowery scents, and worse, the flowers confuse the girl."

Richie rubbed his chin. "I doubt if any of you ever fought this hard for your women. She is hard to convince, though I like it that way. If Mike knew what I go through, he would give me the best recommendation thus far."

Bill slapped the table. "Hey man. Remember, Mike cannot be involved in your personal business."

Richie turned to Bill. "You missed it man. Remember, I am still on that mentorship pro-gram, under big bro. It's better if he knows the reason, I might not score my usual A rating. I am fighting harder battles but getting there. Getting there soon."

They changed the topic as Samson, Sophia and Patty walked back to the gazebo.

After twenty minutes of rest while enjoying a round of sodas, the group walked around the restaurant compound. Moving between the scattered gazebos, they stopped to greet people, many of whom Bill seemed to know.

Bill walked in between Sophia and Patty, holding each by the waist as the group went to their vehicle.

When they neared the vehicle, Michael tossed the key to Richie. "I drove you here, your turn to drive us back."

As Richie caught the key, Michael added. "After that sumptuous meal, your turn to im-press Sophia with your focused driving."

Richie drove the Land Rover while the passengers engaged in loud banter, deciding which weekend they would come back with a larger group.

The first stop was the basement parking of Akoth Towers where Bill and Michael got into one car, and Patty and Samson into another.

Sophia joined Richie at the front of the vehicle, and he drove to her residence.

On arrival, Richie walked her into the house, dropped the key on the coffee table as he sank into the three-seater sofa. "It's not safe for me to be on the road."

He stretched fully on the sofa. "The blame is on you, for taking us to the source of such delicious food," and he dozed off.

~ ~ ~ ~ ~ ~

The chauffeured vehicle arrived early Monday morning and came back late evening. security guards at the gate into Sophia's residential estate were now familiar with Sophia's transport. Unlike before when the drivers were made to sign the visitor book on arrival. They now swung the two gates open, stood at a semi-attention, holding the gates.

The drive to and from work was becoming routine for Sophia, though she sometimes missed the variety that came with traveling in a matatu where entertainment was in plenty. From the people who board and alight, to the loud rap music, especially the lead lyrics.

Then there were the hawkers who board and alight depending on how willing the passengers are to part with their hard-earned money. To the preacher trying to convert tired souls, especially on the evening ride. To pickpockets preying on unguarded passengers, and there are the masked verbal abuses from the matatu *manambas*.

The stories shared by passengers were for everyone's ears. Depending on how long one's ride was, they would hear a variety of stories. There would be stories among two or three passengers on topics such as who had married who for one week or forever. Whose house was robbed, to football and politics. No topic was left un-covered.

Now, in the chauffeured car, Sophia could enjoy only quietness, or the carefully selected classical music, usually Mozart, emanating from hidden speakers. On some days, she found the need to read a book, or the day's paper while on her ride.

Sophia had been contemplating conversation with the driver, an idea she put aside, until she could check company guidelines, or consult with Patty.

In the office, the flowers stayed a constant, though visits from Richie had suddenly be-come fewer. Richie visited only twice the whole week. This worried Sophia, wondering what she could have done to make him stay away. What if he had decided to go to the many ladies who liked him at the members' clubs? She fretted.

One day, Sophia gathered her courage and shared her worry with Patty, who laughed it off, saying, "That boy will buy me expensive red wine, when he hears that you missed him this week."

Sophia looked at Patty in confusion. In return Patty danced around in Sophia's office. "That boy has been worried that you had no feelings for him. Richie has a big heart for you, and eyes for only you. Just do the same."

The response troubled Sophia more. How much could she trust Patty, a friend that she only knew within the office? Her fears did not diminish.

Chapter 29

It had been eighteen months since Sophia received the letter that changed her life, welcoming her as the PA for Michael. Sophia recalled that it was on a Friday when she happened to read the email with the job offer. And on this day, a Friday, she sat in front of a huge office desk in an expansive office within a dark-walled glass building.

Lost in thought, a notification of a new message to her phone startled her. She read the message. "Ready for drinks tonight?"

"No." She clicked send to Richie.

Though she wished to meet with Richie and find out what had kept him away that week, she could not imagine going to one of the clubs, to risk another encounter with the bad-mannered ladies there.

While pondering the issue, her phone buzzed, which she accepted and heard, "See you at yours. I will drop in for dinner at eight."

The call disconnected before she could object. Though in her heart, she wanted to chat with Richie, before she travelled to the village the next day, for a long-awaited meeting with her parents. She typed a response.

"Not tonight. I need time to pack and go to bed early. Catching the morning bus to the village."

Two minutes later, she received a response. "See you at seven then. I will come help fix dinner, so you can have time to pack. I could even help with the packing. See you soon."

It was 6:55 when the doorbell sounded. Joy opened the door and Richie invited himself in and checked her from head to toe before he extended a hand to her. "Richie. Nice to meet you. You must be Joy."

Joy's hand met with his, accepting the greeting with a smile.

Richie spotted Sophia in the kitchen and walked there without invitation. Before Sophia could utter a welcome greeting, he embraced her with a noisy kiss on the mouth. The onions in her hand dropped to the kitchen floor.

Joy, who had gone back to the reading table, watched from the corner of her eye with a smile, pretending to concentrate on an image she was drawing.

Richie uncoupled from Sophia, while saying, "I rarely break my promise. Here I am, to as-sist as agreed."

Sophia had a mind to object to the word 'agreed,' but hesitated on seeing how attentive Joy was.

Richie washed hands and asked for his share of cooking tasks.

At 8:10pm, Silas joined the rest at the dining table. After a prayer, Sophia served Richie and they began eating and chatting. A stranger looking at them would have assumed that Richie had known the three siblings for many years.

After dinner, Joy excused herself to go pack for the trip the next day. Richie and Sophia cleared the dining table and retreated to the kitchen to clean the dishes.

"Interesting." Richie said, prompting Sophia to turn and face him, expecting to hear what could be interesting.

He added, "Had no idea you were traveling with Joy, tomorrow, I..."

Sophia, still holding a glass under a running tap, turned to the side of the dining room, though she was aware that Joy had left for her bedroom.

Richie followed her gaze while he completed his sentence. "I will be traveling to our Nakuru office and will give you a ride that far, or up to your home if you have no objections."

"We will be fine to travel in the bus."

~ ~ ~ ~ ~ ~

Sophia looked out of the car window and appreciated that the early morning departure was an excellent choice.

At nine in the morning, the Toyota Prado made a stop at the entrance of a high-rise office building in Nakuru. Richie jumped out, opened the back door, and whispered to Sophia. "Re-member to tell your mother about me. I have told mine about you." He kissed her, then Joy, and bid the trio goodbye.

Instead of Elvin turning left to the public bus terminus as expected, he turned right, into the main road and drove on, to Joy and Sophia's surprise.

Luckily for Sophia, Elvin was one of the drivers who had been driving her to and from the office. The familiarity gave her courage to say, "I thought you were to take us to the bus terminus, to board a bus home."

Eyes still fixed on the road ahead, Elvin responded. "As per instructions, this was your ride home. Richie asked for a lift in your transport."

Sophia, as keen as ever, caught the word "your" and wanted to object, that she did not book transport to be driven to the village.

Before she could object, she considered the type of scene Joy might witness, if Elvin, to explain himself, ended up revealing that Richie or someone else made the decision without consulting Sophia.

Sophia kept quiet as Elvin spoke again. "Madam, it would be hard for me to change the instructions. I will drive you home and pick you up tomorrow at midday, for the return journey."

His words were uttered with a tone of finality.

"Thank you, sounds good," Sophia said.

Joy and Sophia spent time chatting on a variety of topics, including the latest clothing fashion, shoes, food, and books, but nothing about the main reason for their trip to the village.

About one hundred kilometers from Nakuru, there was silence in the vehicle. Sophia, head in a sleeping position and covered by her sweater, was in deep thought. She reflected on the turn of events, especially the drive home, which she concluded was a bad sign of things to come in the village. She worried about how the conversation with her parents would go, about her marriage, which was the main reason for her travel home.

Sophia felt the skin on her face tighten, as she thought of how annoying men could be. She thought of her father who commanded her mother to summon them to the village. Then of the unknown man who organized for the transport, and another man who knew about the plan and had just alighted in Nakuru. And even the man driving the car, and following instructions given, to cover up a plan he must be privy to.

Immediately, Sophia corrected herself, and removed Elvin from her list of annoying men.

She wondered why men gave themselves the title of decision-maker, by not consulting with others, especially the ones at the center, like her right now.

Sophia resolved to gather her courage and confront her father in the village, and Richie too, when she got back to the city.

Realizing that they were at about ninety minutes away from their destination, Sophia decided she would spend the time well, rehearse how to approach her father.

First, she would thank Mariko for all he had given her throughout her life. The life, love and sacrifices he made to see her through school, under conditions that would have made many others give up.

For a moment, Sophia wondered if people like Richie, Michael and the rest of their family members ever knew what it meant to lack necessities.

She then considered her dilemma, how to confront her father while in the village. She needed to have a clear plan, otherwise she might find herself lost in her usual tears.

After the word of thanks to her father, Sophia planned how she would transition to the next stage. She would beg him to desist from interfering with her life, which she could now handle by herself.

Sophia jerked on her seat, an involuntary response to her thought of cutting her father out of the remaining part of her life. Impossible. She thought, as she composed herself, grateful that her head and face were covered. She then questioned herself, "Is she not the love of her father, the girl who transformed the man from being Mariko, to Baba Sophia?"

She wondered what would happen to her family, if she asked her father to leave her alone. Would that mean her father will change his name, from Baba Sophia, back to Mariko? What would it take, maybe a village meeting to make the announcement?

She smiled, visualizing a village meeting made up of hundreds of men, women, and children. All receiving a stern warning, that henceforth they should call him Mariko, not Baba Sophia, as most of them knew him, especially her age mates and those younger.

She changed her thoughts, promising to inform her father that she would continue to work hard and support her siblings through school. Then she would beg him to let her continue to work at her job in the city.

Next, Sophia planned to ask her father to inform the teacher, the businessmen in town and all the others wanting to marry her, to leave her alone. Another smile engulfed her face, a smile of confidence, that she had a well-laid out plan on what to tell her father once they arrived home.

In the strategy, Sophia also planned to inform her mother that she was usually busy at work, the reason she preferred telephone calls in the evening.

Satisfied with her plan on how to handle her parents, Sophia shifted her thinking to what she would do when back to the city.

Before she could go any further, she dropped the idea, lest her thoughts on the city inter-fere with her plan on how to face her parents in the village.

Sophia uncovered her head and face as Elvin made a right turn, off the main road, onto the local road to their village. She questioned herself, if she missed a chat between Joy and Elvin, on the place to turn to her home. Otherwise, how did Elvin know where to turn off the main road, without asking her for directions?

A new fear gripped Sophia, though she could not tell if the fear was from their approaching home, or that someone in Akoth Towers had too much information about her family.

Chapter 30

On the two-kilometer drive to the village, pedestrians stopped to let the vehicle pass. Others stopped to wave at the dark green Prado. Some kids ran after the vehicle, until it slowed down and turned left, into Mariko's homestead.

People walking past on the local road, paused to look at the vehicle. One thing the people were sure of, was that the owners of that homestead did not own a car, though some home improvements had been made recently.

Some of the changes included Mariko transitioning from his tedious business at the live-stock market, to running a shop near the main road. Then some months back, the main house was plastered, and the interior floor and walls completed with cement. The grass thatched roof of the kitchen was replaced with corrugated iron sheets.

For those who visited the family often, they would have noticed that the children were rarely sent home from school for lack of fees or textbooks, as before.

And now, a Prado had just been driven into the home, attracting several villagers to wait by the roadside and see who the visitors were.

While the onlookers waited, they exchanged loud whispers of what they had heard. A girl from that home went to university in the city, and the vehicle belonged to a suitor, who had come to ask for her hand in marriage. That information was rejected by other onlookers who explained that from what they had heard, the girl was already promised to some teacher at the secondary school.

The people by the roadside watched, as Elvin parked the vehicle, stepped out, opened the back door, and two ladies, daughters of the homestead, appeared.

As Joy's feet hit the ground, Charlie and Babu, who had all along been watching the strange vehicle approach from afar, ran back to the house shouting, "Mama, Mama. Sophia and Joy have arrived early, in a new car."

Stella walked out of the kitchen, wiping hands on the *leso*, cotton one-piece fabric women tie around the waist. Stella had tied a *leso* top of her green flowered dress. She slipped her feet into a pair of canvas shoes lying near the main house and walked towards the vehicle.

She extended a hand and greeted Elvin, then her daughters with hugs. "Welcome back home, sorry for the long journey from the city, you must be tired."

Sophia smiled while Joy responded. "Mama, there you are mistaken." Stella turned and looked at Joy as Joy completed the sentence, "No one can get tired in such a comfortable car, and Elvin is a very good, careful driver."

There was a broad smile on Elvin's face.

Joy and Sophia picked their bags and walked into the main house as Stella invited Elvin into the house, to which he objected, and asked, "Is Mzee in?" Mzee is a

Swahili term of respect used to refer to a male head of a household.

Stella informed Elvin that Mariko was at work. They were not expecting Sophia and Joy until after four, the usual time the busses arrived from the city.

Elvin informed Stella that he was sent by Chairman, the owner of the company where Sophia worked, to drive Sophia and Joy home for the weekend. He would pick them up at midday the next day.

Stella requested Elvin at least have a drink of water before leaving. She called, and Joy came carrying a tray with two glasses and a glass jug full of water. Stella removed the white net covering the jug, filled one glass with water and handed it to Elvin.

He thanked her, finished the water, and placed the glass on the tray.

Elvin said goodbye and drove off as the onlookers by the road dispersed.

~ ~ ~ ~ ~ ~

"Ooh, ooh, my girls. You arrived so early without calling. I had assumed you would arrive at the usual time." Stella called out as she approached the main house, where Sophia and Joy were busy opening their travel bags, while Charlie and Babu watched, waiting to receive gifts from the city.

Joy glanced at Sophia before saying, "Mama, these small cars are not like the bus. They move amazingly fast, though when inside, it's hard to tell that the car is moving at a high speed."

Without any prompting, Joy added. "The other person who left the city with us was going to Nakuru, where they alighted, and we proceeded here."

Sophia looked down at her feet, in prayer, fearing that Stella would ask about the person whom they left in Nakuru, and Joy would carry the conversation through.

Stella must have been overjoyed from seeing her daughters, and confused by their arrival in a chauffeured vehicle, that she did not digest the response from Joy. She turned to Charlie and Babu, asked them to run to the shop and inform their father, that their sisters had arrived, and the visitor did not stay.

Mariko was confused by the message from his sons. He decided to stay at the shop until his usual time at the end of the business.

When Mariko arrived home in the evening, supper was ready, and the rest of the family were waiting for him, so that they could eat together.

Charlie and Babu had by now recovered from their excitement of seeing their sisters, especially Joy, after almost three years. The new clothes, shoes, and bed sheets they received as gifts, excited them.

Stella received two new dresses, a handbag, and new shoes. Mariko was very touched by the suit he was given. Being his first ever new suit, complete with a shirt, necktie, and shoes, all bought by Sophia during her travel to India.

Over dinner the family shared information on a range of issues, including work and studies. Joy was happy to answer most of the questions directed at her. "I am still working hard. What else would you expect when I have a genius for an older sister?"

The response surprised Sophia, as Charlie and Babu laughed.

"At first, I thought you said genie," Charlie said after he stopped laughing.

Mariko looked at Joy. "But you have always worked hard at school. You need to learn to work harder, whether with Sophia or not."

Sophia gave thumbs up before she turned to her mother who had called her name. "How is work? I see the job has taken you places. Who knew that I Stella, would ever wear a new dress bought by my daughter traveling in a plane?" She chuckled as she lifted both arms and embraced her shoulders.

Sophia, with eyes fixed on the family photos on the wall of the living room, responded without looking at her mother. "Ooh, work is good. A lot of tasks to perform, but I like it that way. If Silas and Kevin were home, all of you could wear your new clothes for a family photo. Will be good to add a third one to those two," She pointed to framed family photos, hung on the wall facing the sofa she sat on.

Mariko turned and looked at the family photos on the wall behind him, more to his right-hand side, as he spoke. "Kevin is fine at school, struggling with his

English class, but working hard to join Silas at university too."

He then turned back to the dining table, faced his two youngest sons, seated to his left, and addressed them. "That means these two boys have no excuse, other than to follow in the footsteps of their older siblings. There is no other route, except the one that leads to the university in the big city." Mariko said while pointing from one boy to the next.

Mention of the city brought smiles to the faces of the eight and eleven-year-olds. Of late they had been asking when they would visit their siblings in the city, and their parents' response remained the same. "When you qualify to go to university in the city."

Joy talked about her soon to be completed university study program before she turned and looked at Babu and Charlie. "If you behave well, you will attend my graduation at the end of the year."

Sophia joined in the conversation by addressing Joy. "Go on, tell Mum and Dad that you will soon complete your study program at university." Joy smiled, then frowned as Sophia completed her sentence. "Then join the job market, or the lengthy list of graduates without jobs."

Mariko and Stella turned to Joy at the same time, expectantly. Joy laughed aloud. "How can I miss getting a job, when my sister works in the tallest building in the city? How?"

The conversation shifted to Sophia's busy work-schedule. Sophia was happy and talked about the job she loved, explaining in detail. "I love that job, my PA duties…"

Stella's lips parted, like she wanted to say something, but did not, as Sophia continued. "I work for a big boss, the one whose father provided the vehicle that brought us home."

Mariko listened to the story of work, boss, and father's car with keen interest, indicated by his swift glance at Stella.

Sophia was too excited to realize the information she shared was revealing. Mariko could interpret it as his daughter must be having a special relationship with her boss. That would be the only reason the father of her boss gave a vehicle for their journey to the village, a round trip of a thousand kilometers.

Oblivious to the reaction from her father, Sophia continued. "My office duties involve a lot of paperwork. That, combined with going with my boss to all his official meetings, local and overseas, leaves me no time, except for sleeping at night.

Babu marveled aloud. "The next time I see a plane in the sky, I will not run into the house. I will look up and stare, it could be carrying my sister."

There was laughter in the room, but not from Mariko.

Stella saw the irritation on Mariko's face. After twenty-five years of marriage, Stella could easily interpret his facial expressions and other non-verbal clues. She could tell that Mariko was seething with anger. Maybe he was thinking about his good daughter. The daughter he had been waiting for, to return home and settle down with a good man, Cleophas, the teacher.

Mariko could also be thinking of common stories, on how some bosses in cities, employed young women for their own gratification. Mariko stomped his right foot on the floor, hard, without realizing it.

Sophia took one look at her father's face, and immediately shifted her narration. She commented on the many improvements made to their house and compound.

To which Mariko said, "Since I completed repaying the loan from the Cooperative society, I have made some savings from the shop business. I used the money to plaster the outside and inside of the house. As you can see."

Mariko scanned his eyes along the walls of the room, which served as a sitting and eating space. There were doors on both ends of the room. One from the sitting space led to the parents' bedroom, while the door near the dining table led to the girls' sleeping room. The boys had a separate hut, located on the right side of the kitchen.

Joy turned to her father. "Good. Once your son becomes an engineer, and another an architect, they will come and construct a house for you. All you need do is invite me to come decorate the inside, with the best furniture, like the ones seen in magazines."

Everyone laughed aloud. Mariko lifted his left hand and looked at his wrist. A new watch Sophia bought for him. He looked at his wrist again, and back at his family.

Charlie must have his father's non-verbal communication. He picked a torch and a key he had stored under his chair, bid all to a goodnight, and together with Babu, walked out of the living room to their hut.

Joy and Sophia removed the dishes from the table before retiring to the girl's bedroom.

~ ~ ~ ~ ~ ~

Once in the bedroom, Sophia and Joy talked about how different their parents acted and looked.

Joy, who had been gone for almost three years, explained the differences that struck her most. "I almost did not recognize Dad when he appeared at the door. His previously sunken cheeks are now filled out, a sign of eating enough food, a balanced diet."

Sophia smiled. "What about Mum? Someone should talk with her. She needs to watch her diet, otherwise we will soon need a new budget to replace her wardrobe."

Both laughed, before Joy added "Once I receive a letter of employment from my cur-rent employer, changing my status from student casual to employee, I will purchase a cross-breed cow for the family, for milk."

Sophia turned and looked at her sister, smiled and patted her on the shoulder. "Then our younger brothers can grow up like other children, drinking tea with milk, and even fresh milk if they desire that."

Each girl pulled a sheet over their heads, just in case of a mosquito, and the room fell silent, though not for long.

Joy pulled more of the shared blanket to her side as she asked, "Any plans to mention the name Richie in this village?"

There was no response. Sophia would not have fallen asleep that fast, especially on their bed where one could feel all the contours of the mattress, through to the metal bars of the bed frame beneath. The bed they were on was not that comfortable, nothing close to their beds and mattresses in the city.

Right next to Joy, Sophia was awake and in deep thought. To Sophia, her parents had behaved all right so far. She wondered if the atmosphere tomorrow, Sunday, would match today's, before they left for the city.

Sophia made a promise to herself, that if her parents did not mention the topic of marriage, she would. She was ready to agonize for three hours, pour out her frustrations, and empty her mind of all the words she had planned on their drive from Nakuru. She did not want to go back to the city without her parents knowing her thoughts on marriage, and the impractical idea of her leaving the city.

~ ~ ~ ~ ~ ~

Mariko and Stella did not sleep until early morning.

Immediately Stella had entered the bedroom, Mariko had asked. "Did you talk with your daughter about her marriage?"

The question irritated Stella. "Sophia has now become my daughter, not our beloved daughter, the graduate, as before."

Stella explained that she never found an opportunity to chat with the Sophia and Joy, for their brothers had not left their side since arrival.

"What about the vehicle that brought them home? A car that everyone was talking about along the road and at the shops."

Mariko did not receive a response, so he continued. "How sure are you that your daughter has not joined the list of lost girls in the city? Educated women who forget where they come from?"

Stella's eyes filled with tears when she heard what Mariko said next. "You heard it well when your daughter said she works and travels all over the world with some man. A man whose father owns the company, the father who gave the car that brought them home.

I do not want to see that car again at this home, cars from old men. Yet the message they had sent had tried to convince me otherwise, by saying the man was Sophia's age mate. Shameful."

"How do you expect me to know?" said Stella faintly.

"Because they are your daughters. Who else would know such things about your daughters, if not you?"

Before Mariko eventually retired to bed, just before the first cock crow at three in the morning, he told Stella to wake the girls up early. He needed to have a meeting with them at 8:00am, before leaving to open the shop, two hours later than usual.

Chapter 31

Sophia and Joy joined their parents for breakfast as instructed by Stella.

They exchanged morning greetings with their parents as they sat down at the dining table.

Mariko looked sternly at Joy. "I called you here, not because you have done anything wrong, but so you do not repeat the mistakes of your sister."

Joy looked at her father to hear more about the mistakes, but Mariko did not ex-pound.

On hearing the words referencing her, Sophia's face became warm, she was anxious, feared what to expect next. Her thoughts were interrupted when Stella spoke.

"What are your plans now that you have an excellent job. Do you have any other plans for your future, like getting married at the right age, settling down?"

Sophia and Joy turned at the same time, and found themselves facing one another, then looked away just as fast.

Sophia turned to Mariko, and not Stella who asked the question. "Papa, I have not stopped being your daughter, I cannot even imagine such a thought. I have not become a bad girl, unless working hard at my job makes me a bad girl, what you call mistakes."

Though it was a chilly early morning in July, a cold month when temperatures go as low as eighteen degrees Celsius, Sophia felt droplets of warm water drip down her back. She squeezed her hands together, to stop herself from trembling too much.

Sophia looked up and could tell that her parents were either digesting what she had said or waiting to hear her response to the question from her mother, of settling down.

To break the silence, she decided to continue. "I love my job and I work with and for good people. People who recognize my efforts and have rewarded me accordingly."

Now her hands were flat on the table, to steady her trembling body. "The frequent travels I go on with my boss, are a blessing in disguise, otherwise I would not have managed to save money and provide the support I have given this far."

In a shaky voice, she added. "They give us money for food whenever we travel, and I put every cent into my savings account." She said, looking down at her untouched cup of tea on the table.

Mariko cleared his throat but did not talk. He appeared irritated and in deep thought.

Sophia jerked on her seat when Mariko turned her direction and said, "Aaah, I see. How do you eat and sleep if you save all the money? Does the same boss pay for your expenses?"

Sophia looked at her father, eyes filled with tears. "Papa. For once you are wrong. If you think I travel with my boss for things other than work. You are wrong." Putting heavy emphasis on the word wrong.

Stella raised her hand, as students do at school. A sign that she wanted to say something. She lowered her hand when Sophia spoke.

"I got a promotion at work, not too long ago, in the form of a salary increase. The promotion also covers my transport, to and from work."

Joy, holding her cup of tea with both hands, turned to Sophia, and smiled, as Sophia continued. "The driver who brought us here is one of the company drivers who picks me up from the house in the morning and drives me back home after work.

The same driver asks me each weekend if there are places I need to visit, such as to the shops, so he can pick and drop me back home. Papa, the company values my work very highly. I hope you understand."

The room fell into silence. Joy prodded Sophia on her arm. A kick Sophia could not interpret well, was it to congratulate her, or urge her to continue talking and maybe mention Richie?

Sophia broke the silence again. "Papa. Please note that I am not being disrespectful. I… just… want you to know about my work life."

She turned the direction of her mother. "And Mama, you are still my loving mother. Always remember that when I do not answer your telephone calls, I am either busy at my computer, completing an urgent task, or away at meetings, with my boss.

If I miss your call during working hours, I will call you back between 7:00pm and 9:00pm. I hope that is okay with you."

The room went quiet again. The tight expression on Mariko's face had loosened up, into a smile.

Sophia stunned everyone when she smiled and then sighed. "Work and being busy is the way of life in cities. The best part is that, if one likes their job, as I do, they will enjoy their life."

Joy giggled, and Mariko turned and looked at her. She picked her cup and sipped tea, placed the cup on the table, picked a mandazi from a nearby plate and started to nibble, avoiding the annoyed look on Mariko's face.

Joy looked at her mother, then turned away and looked down to the floor as Stella spoke. "And how are you enjoying your life? Have you ever slowed down to think about your age? By the time I was twenty-five, I had three babies. When are yours coming?" The pitch of Stella's voice was raised as she uttered the last two words.

Sophia put back the mandazi she had picked and looked at her mother. "Maybe, one day. After my siblings get an education and can take care of themselves." Sophia said, while involuntarily holding the engagement ring, turning it round and round her finger.

The expression on her mother's face showed that she had taken note of the ring.

Mariko talked, in a voice different from the last one. This time round he did not sound quarrelsome. "Have you considered the proposal from Teacher Cleophas? He is not a bad man. A teacher, sure to provide stability, as always."

Joy smiled, lifted her cup of tea, and held it to her mouth, longer than needed to take a sip.

Mariko continued. "And with a teacher, comes a lot of reassurance, that your children will get an education, and some extra coaching from home. Have you considered that?"

Stella, who had been busy staring down at her feet looked up, as Joy looked at Sophia, seated on her immediate right.

Sophia kept a neutral expression on her face as Mariko spoke. "But if the teacher is no longer part of your new elevated life, I will go apologize to Onono, then you can voluntarily join their home and business."

Sophia jerked her head from side to side, to show a no, while looking at her father, in the eye, something she never imagined she could ever do.

Mariko continued. "Or, if you love the life of flying in those planes, Ndugu's son is in town from the US. I am told he came over to look for a good girl, like you, to marry."

Joy giggled. Stella stepped on her right foot, as Mariko added, "Though that one should not enter your head, the US must be a faraway place. Stick with the teacher."

The sisters exhaled at the same time, like they had been holding their breath for an awfully long time.

Sophia, still toying with the ring on her finger, said. "Papa, no offence meant, but I have already moved out of the village, and out of our town, into the city, where I now belong."

Mariko held up his open right hand, to the side of Sophia, a sign that she should not say more, but she spoke. "That city has done us wonders, my job."

Sophia bit her tongue, on realizing that her words came out wrong, not as she had intended. She had wanted to put emphasis on the job that had lifted her family from below the poverty line.

Mariko cleared his throat and asked, "So, when are you telling me about your city boy-friend?"

Sophia turned and looked at Joy, and back at her father. Her lips parted, like she wanted to say something, but stopped when she saw Mariko looking at his wrist-watch, then he stood up. He reached out and shook hands with Sophia and then Joy. "Have a safe journey back to the city."

He picked a small bag which had been by his feet and left the house and compound, to open his grocery store.

Stella followed by vacating her seat. "I am going to harvest a banana for you to take back to the city."

"Make them two or three, please." Joy said.

Stella looked at Joy while Joy continued to speak. "Assume you are taking two of the three bananas to the market. I will pay for the two, to give to friends in the city."

Elvin arrived just before midday.

Sophia and Joy were ready. Their luggage was arranged outside the house: three bananas, vegetables, and maize flour.

Joy and Sophia hugged their mother goodbye before their younger brothers. Joy's eyes, just like Charlie and Babu's, were full of tears as they hugged one another, Joy promising to be back home soon.

On their drive out of the homestead, Sophia asked Elvin to stop by their family shop, for them to say bye to their father.

~ ~ ~ ~ ~ ~

Their next stop was Nakuru.

Richie appeared from the building where they had left him the day before. They shared pleasant greetings, before Elvin parked and went into the building.

Richie asked Joy and Sophia to get out, exercise their feet, before the two-hour drive to the city.

Once they were outside the vehicle, he looked at Joy "I have a request. Do me a favour."

Joy looked at him, as he implored her to say yes before he could mention the request.

"So long as you do not ask me to stay in this strange town."

"Nothing close to that. I want to upgrade you to first class." He pointed to the vehicle. "Take the co-driver's seat while I languish in the back seat."

Joy jumped on her toes, and hugged Sophia as Elvin returned and occupied the driver's seat.

Joy opened the front door and gave Elvin a smile as she made herself comfortable in the co-driver's seat.

Richie opened the back door for Sophia before he walked around the vehicle and sat behind Joy.

As Elvin drove on and joined the main highway to Nairobi, Richie placed his right hand on Sophia's shoulder.

Sophia, not wanting to engage in conversation, especially about her visit home, pulled a *kikoy* over her head, down to her knees. She then rested her head on the headrest, trying to find a comfortable position to fall sleep.

The journey was occupied by chatting between Richie and Joy, about the weather and crops in the village.

One hour into the journey, Richie drifted off to sleep. Joy conversed with Elvin until he stopped the vehicle in front of their apartment.

Joy pointed out how the three bananas would be shared. "This one is for us, the second one is for Chairman and the third one is for Elvin."

As Elvin tried to object, Joy cut in. "Richie will eat bananas either at his parents' house, or our house," to laughter from all.

Back in their apartment, Joy called her parents to let them know they traveled well and were now in their house in the city.

After the phone calls, Joy patted Sophia on the back. "Well done sister, everything well said. At some point, I had to pinch myself, to be sure that I was not dreaming." She chuckled. "Wherever you found that courage, please keep it up, for your own good. Otherwise, the world will walk on you without looking back."

Sophia gave Joy a weary smile, wishing she could be as happy with life as Joy.

Joy strode to the bathroom for a shower, then went to the kitchen to prepare supper.

Sophia entered her bedroom and sat on the dresser chair. She opened her phone and typed a message to Richie. "Thanks for the ride in the pricy comfortable vehicle. It brought our village to a standstill."

She pressed the send button and put the phone on the bedside table as it started to ring. She checked and decided that she was not in a mood to chat with Richie or anyone else. Telling herself that she needed time to digest what had happened that morning, with her parents.

After a count to six, the phone stopped ringing, and a message dropped in. "Hi my Sun-shine. My pleasure. Did you pass my message to your Mum as asked? Did you mention my existence?"

Sophia thanked herself for not answering the phone call. She still had no energy to revisit any of the events with her parents. She decided that what she needed most was to hear from her mother on how her father took the information she shared with them.

From the way Mariko left the meeting, abruptly, Sophia had no way of knowing if that was a sign of protest, or acceptance, that his daughter was old enough to make some decisions. Which meant that she had no answer for Richie. Yes, she did allude to his existence in her life, without telling her parents who he was.

Sophia reckoned that if she told that to Richie, that she never mentioned his name to her parents, he might ask her why. And, there was no way she was going to tell him that his mention was in the middle of an intense argument with her parents.

Sophia typed a response to Richie. "I mentioned only a half of your existence to my parents, the rest is your homework."

~ ~ ~ ~ ~ ~

On Thursday, Stella called to know how Sophia and Joy were getting on.

Later in the evening, Joy stood next to Sophia. "Guess what, you lucky thing," prompting Sophia to turn and look at her.

"When Mum called today, she sounded happier, compared to before."

Joy moved closer to Sophia, folded four fingers, and extended out her pinkie. Sophia did likewise, and they locked their two fingers, a sign of a promise made, to stay mum, about whatever information was forthcoming. "Mum whispered to me that Dad has cooled down."

Sophia's eyes bulged out as her eyebrows rose.

Joy continued, "On Sunday, when he got back home from the shop, he was still annoyed. Guess what was annoying him?"

Sophia's lips parted, but nothing came out. While she thought of what to say next, Joy continued. "That, his daughter had gained courage from her city life, the courage to answer him back."

Sophia smiled, wishing she could reveal to Joy the amount of time and energy she had spent, strategizing on what to say and how. Or, what it took, including sweat down her back, during the Sunday talk with her parents.

Since Sophia remained silent, Joy went ahead to talk. "You know what, Mum was glad that you stood your ground. Mum is tired of being the only one who gets direct bashing from Dad.

Though, at the end of it all, he blamed her for your responses. Mum is happy that you talked. She said he is learning to avoid the schoolteacher and his father. Though in my opinion, Dad needs to face them with the truth. Of course, unless you have not made up your mind."

Sophia ignored how Joy completed the sentence. Instead, she said, "Richie asked me for your cell phone number, heard any word from him?"

Joy smiled, lifting her left hand to cover her mouth. "Ooh yes, we had tea on…, many days ago. Though I was disappointed he did not take me to one of those exclusive clubs."

Joy completed the sentence as she walked away, a sign that she was not ready to divulge details of her meeting with Richie.

Sophia wondered, if Joy had mentioned the many families wanting their sons to marry her. She smiled, knowing that it would not be long before Joy disclosed the details.

Chapter 32

One Friday evening, Richie arrived at Sophia's office at exactly 5:30pm. "Hi Sunshine," he greeted her as he sat on the edge of her desk.

Sophia looked at him and back to the desk, prompting Richie to say, "I am not as heavy as you imagine."

She locked eyes with Richie as she changed the topic. "Another week gone by, how was the money market?"

Sophia knew that Richie loved to talk and hear about local and global money markets, so she used that to distract him from talk about his weight.

There had been a few times when Richie went to her office just to talk about global markets without end. Once when Sophia informed him that she had enough PA tasks to keep her busy, he had resorted to forwarding articles on the stock market to her company email account. Occasionally she shared her opinion on some of the articles. A mention of such articles always excited Richie, that she had read the articles, and she was ready to engage in a discussion.

Sophia was surprised when Richie avoided the money market topic, and instead said, "Mum has her weekly family dinner, and you are invited."

"Since when did I become family?" The words escaped before Sophia could bite her tongue.

Richie ignored her response and instead gave her options to choose from: "Choose one, and work late then proceed home, or I pick you from your place at 6:30, 7:00 latest."

Sophia looked at her work suit. "I will go home."

She switched off the computer, locked her drawer, picked her handbag, and walked out, into the elevator and down to the car park for her ride home.

More than a change of clothes, Sophia needed time to reflect on what the invitation to dinner with Richie's family meant. She finally convinced herself, that going for the dinner did not mean much, and she would have a chance to visit and see where and how rich people live.

After a shower, Sophia spent time at her over-flowing wardrobe, in search of something to wear.

When she finally walked out of her bedroom, she had changed clothes three times.

Due to the ticking clock, she settled on a recent impulse purchase, a patterned teal Maki Oh jacket and trouser combination.

On arrival, Patience welcomed Sophia with a hug.

Beauta looked at Sophia from head to toe with a smile and a "hi" wave, while Georgina, Bill's wife acknowledged Sophia with a handshake. Bill surprised everyone when he embraced Sophia.

Nick, Richie's younger brother looked up at Sophia and smiled. "Finally, I get to see you, the owner of the flowers. Welcome."

Sophia smiled at the mention of flowers, while hoping that the topic would not arise again, though she would have liked to hear how Nick knew about the flowers she received from Richie. She wondered if the flowers were an open topic of discussion within the Mwasimba family.

Nick, though nine years' Richie's junior, seemed to have a lot in common with Richie, exchanging jokes and chats on shared topics throughout the evening.

Mwasimba did not appear until everyone was seated at the large family dining room, a sixteen-seat rectangular table.

He entered, greeted everyone, acknowledging Sophia's presence by turning in her direction as he spoke. He said grace for the food, before the silver cutlery started to click on plates.

While eating, the family shared common stories other than work. The one hour three-course meal was filled with chatting, sometimes at different sides of the table. Beauta appeared to be the second in charge at the table, after Patience.

After dinner, Mwasimba and Patience moved to the smaller dining room as the rest of the family shifted into the living room to watch a movie.

On their way to the living room, Richie held Sophia by the hand and asked her to join him for a walk outside the house, in the expansive but well-lit compound.

After a short walk, for about five minutes, they turned back as the dogs, already unleashed for the night, were bothering Sophia, being new in the compound.

Richie and Sophia went and sat on the veranda next to the living room. As they began to chat, Patience approached carrying a kettle of tea. A house staff brought three cups on a tray, placed them on a side table and left.

Patience served tea without asking Sophia or Richie if they would have some. Sophia decided quickly that she would drink the tea, though she knew very well that the caffeine would keep her awake for most of the night.

The trio had a brief chat before Richie excused himself. "I need to stretch my legs. I will be back with information on why everyone in the house is happy and loud."

Sophia looked at Richie and wished she could utter the words in her mind. "Good excuse, you leave me with your mother," as Richie walked away and into the house, through the back door.

Now Sophia needed all her courage to handle her new situation. She wondered if she would be able to carry on with small talk until Richie returned. She decided that the best was to bite her tongue as many times as possible, talk only when she had to.

Patience and Sophia discussed a variety of issues, ranging from life in the city in general, how she liked her PA work and travel. Then, when Sophia was relaxed enough, busy talking, Patience said. "My son informs me that he would like to formalize your relationship next year, when would you like us to meet with your family?"

Sophia felt sweat drip down her back and wished Richie had stayed around. She was reflective, wondering if the question originated from Patience, or had she had been sent by Mr. Mwasimba, just the way her father sent her mother to her. Sophia noticed the silence, took a quick glance at Patience, and all she received was a smile. She heard herself say. "I will call my Mum, to find out."

As soon as Sophia completed the sentence, she wondered if she just lied, or did she give in without knowing? She held her tongue between her teeth, lest she said something else that would draw more questions from Patience.

The next question from Patience came, faster than Sophia expected. "Have you discussed with Richie whether you will continue to work or not, after marriage?"

To Sophia, that was the million-dollar question. If she said she preferred to continue working for the company, would Patience, being one of the directors, recite rule c251 which stated that if there was a romantic relationship between two employees, one of them must resign from employment? If she said no, was she going to clarify by adding that she would find a job with a different company?

More fear gripped Sophia, especially when she heard herself say, in a whisper. "We have not discussed that"

Patience refilled her teacup as she spoke. "These issues are yours to decide upon. My guess is that you have discussed the issue of having children, when and how many. That would guide your decision to work or not work."

Sophia lifted her left hand and wiped her forehead. She wondered what else she could say to the company director seated right in front of her. A director of the company that gave her a job.

As she pondered the issue of her employment, she heard Patience say, "Though from what I saw at the last directors' meeting, you have a good grip on your work. Would you stop doing that to stay home? Curious."

Sophia looked at Patience, like she was ready to beg for something important. Then she heard Patience say, "Whatever decision you make, count on me," as Richie walked back and sat on a chair next to Patience.

"Hey Mum, what decision will be okay?" as he gave her a soft pat on the shoulder.

Sophia registered the shoulder touch as a family trait. A pat like the ones Michael likes to give her and other employees at Akoth Towers.

Patience looked at Richie as her face brightened up with a smile. "Nothing son. Women talk. My daughter here was about to tell me the number of children the two of you plan to have."

Sophia looked down on the floor and realized that she liked her shoes. In the process, she bit her tongue, a little too hard. She lifted her cup and sipped tea just in case there was blood in her mouth. More importantly, to protect her from saying anything, for no one can talk with a mouthful of tea. She sipped more tea, holding the tea-cup with both hands, tightly.

To her relief, Richie broke the prolonged silence. "Ooh mother, I should not have left the two of you to enjoy such a nice topic without me. To answer your question, six kids."

His response brought an involuntary wide opening of Sophia's eyes. She looked at him, as he continued. "That makes it twelve feet. Two more than the feet of all your boys together."

Sophia giggled, though she could not tell if that was in place of anger. Before she could put more thought into her reaction, she heard Richie say. "You know what Mum?"

Patience turned and faced her son. Sophia looked to her left side and touched a nearby potted flower, as Richie continued to talk, oblivious to Sophia's discomfort with the topic.

"I have a new idea. We can make them fourteen small feet. That way, Sophia and I can boast of having beaten our two mothers at the numbers."

The threesome burst out with laughter, and Sophia noticed something, Patience made a sign of the cross as Sophia wondered if that was a prayer.

On the drive back to Sophia's house, she was quiet, considering some of the questions that Patience had asked her. Before she could generate her own explanation, Richie asked.

"Did you hear what I told our mother about the feet. Please keep that in mind. I hope it sounded as interesting to your heart, as it did to mine."

Sophia did not respond. She remained quiet, wondering what it was with women, older women, and children.

Not too long ago, her mother had alluded to when she would get married and bring forth grandchildren. Now, Patience too was excited about children, an issue that Sophia had not given much thought. To Sophia, thoughts about children would have to wait until she was done paying for the education of her siblings.

Chapter 33

On Sunday, Sophia and Richie went out for dinner. Going back to the exclusive members' club uncorked unpleasant feelings in her heart.

Though she found the club an okay place to be, the fresh air, the delicious food, and laughter from the many patrons, Sophia did not look forward to seeing the many ladies at the club. She considered them to be shameless, with the courage to leave red lipstick marks on Richie's face. As they did during their last visit.

Sophia found her own comfort though, that on that Sunday the socialites would have little to say about her appearance. She wore one of the gift dresses from Beauta when they were in China, and Richie had not stopped telling her how gorgeous she was.

The other comfort was from his hand, ever on her back. Whenever his hand left the small of her back, it wrapped around her waist or held her hand.

Sophia noticed that whenever a lady greeted Richie by kissing him on the cheek, he would wipe his face using a handkerchief.

At one-point Sophia entertained a thought to ask if the ladies were his girlfriends, former lovers, or admirers. But she shelved the question for another day.

Some elderly women at the club, about the age of Richie's mother, were interested to know who the elegant lady was, ever guarded by Richie's arm. Many uttered the question, "Whose daughter?"

The questions gave Sophia another reason to bite her tongue, though not so hard this time. She would have liked to let the women know that, yes, she was a daughter of Mariko, a man known in the village as Baba Sophia.

To some women, Richie introduced Sophia as his girlfriend, to others as his fiancée and to one group, all he said was, "The invitation cards are coming, soon." To which one woman responded, "I will not attend, unless my daughter is the bride."

On their drive from the club, Sophia turned to Richie with a smile and a question. "Want to talk money markets or dinner at your home?"

Richie, still focused on the line of cars ahead, smiled. "Money and markets jog my mind, but dinner at my home warms my heart. Please choose dinner."

Sophia chuckled. "Your club just fed me well. I wanted to hear more from you, on where your dear Mom got the idea of marriage and babies, with me in between?"

He smiled, lifted his left hand, and touched her arm. "Well said, though you forgot to mention me in that entanglement."

Sophia did not respond, so Richie added. "Ever considered a life alone? Not me! I need you, to jog my mind and warm my heart."

Though she did not reply, Sophia told herself that she could not imagine a life where she walked all over by herself or went for dinner or lunch alone. The thought of eating out alone brought back memories of her kidnapping. She suspected that would not have happened, had she been with a friend, or Richie.

She lifted his hand from her arm and guided it back to the steering wheel. "I asked about the talk between you and your Mom, about babies, baby feet, whatever."

"Just look at you and me..."

Sophia turned and looked at him, then turned away when he began to speak.

"Products of our parents. I guess it will be nice for us to have our own original products. The many feet you referred to as whatever."

Sophia involuntarily looked down at her shoes, while scratching her head. Richie added, "Do you know what the best part of our entanglement will be?"

"No." She said and looked up and saw that Richie was focused on the road ahead, overtaking a stalled car. When he merged back into the correct lane, he said. "You will prove to many that a smart lady can go to work, talk money and global markets, and arrive home to embrace and love her children, and her man."

Sophia turned to wave back to the guards at the gate, as Richie drove into her residential area. She had decided that asking Richie further questions would get him more excited to talk about children even before they agreed on marriage. She hoped he had not assumed that she would get married.

Chapter 34

When Sophia called to inform her mother about her forthcoming trip, Stella asked. "How long will you be away, when your visitors from the city are expected in the village the weekend after next?"

"What visitors?" Sophia panicked. How had her parents agreed to the request from Richie's parents so fast? She had presumed that her father would dismiss or delay the date, giving her more time to work as a PA at Akoth Towers.

Sophia got up from her work chair and stood by the window facing outside. Though her mind did not register what was beyond the window. She faced a larger challenge, her parents being ready to receive a delegation from Richie's home.

A myriad of questions dashed through her mind. Who was Richie? What did she really know about him, aside from their shared study program at university, and now as a co-worker?

Yes, he was also very fond of her, he liked to come to her office to discuss finance and global markets. He brought her flowers, every day, and had introduced her to exclusive clubs in the city. And he always told her that he loved her.

For a moment, Sophia worried how dull her life at Akoth Towers would be without Richie. She dismissed the thought, reminding herself of her role at the company, to perform her duties as PA, so her life would be okay.

Then, she remembered that she would still have Patty as a friend. And over time, she had reconnected with some of her friends from university and high school.

Sophia walked back to her desk and read more email messages from Michael as they dropped in. The biggest surprise was when she learnt that Michael had pulled out of the trip to Italy, due to illness. That meant Sophia and Richie would attend meetings with the supplier of the Company's investment and financial instruments, including a visit with some of the computer program developers.

She had a brief panic attack, before she read the next message, explaining that their role was to only meet with the supplier. The technical team from the Mwasimba Company was already on the ground, inspecting and consulting on details of the financial instruments. She released a loud sigh of relief.

Sophia comforted herself, having been fully involved in all preparations for Michael's official endeavors, therefore she was well informed on the procedures.

Deep down in her heart, Sophia knew that, with a little guidance, she had enough knowledge and in-house details to rescue any situation. It was a skill she rarely revealed, afraid to compete with her boss. She preferred to limit her role to her PA duties.

Her mind drifted to Richie. She was surprised and annoyed at the same time. That for two days, Richie had started and ended his visits at Michael's office.

Sophia smiled, remembering that work came first for Richie, the same as for her. A new worry set in. Could it be that Richie's new behaviour was sending a message to her, on the distance they needed to keep while on the official trip? Sophia was apprehensive at the thought. Would she be content with Richie for a week without the flowers, without his hand on her back?

In the South wing of the 52nd floor of Akoth Towers, Richie was terrified, and overjoyed at the same time. His alarm came from realizing this would be his first chance to prove his professional worth to his father. Richie knew his handling the assignment well would influence his career plan, which included initiating and heading a new department within the Company.

Richie spent long hours in Michael's office, to get every detail on the meetings right. They summoned Sophia now and then for a document, details on some issue, or more information to add to the all-important PowerPoint presentations.

~ ~ ~ ~ ~ ~

Saturday came, and Sophia now accustomed to long-haul flights in business class, was ready for the overnight flight, her first trip to Italy. To her, the trip meant more than enjoying the flight, she would save money for school and university fees.

Smiling, she thought of how her job had brought comfort to her family. Silas, now in university, did not need to hassle with a side job. She had already paid his tuition. She had also made him comfortable in the third bedroom in her apartment. With the thought of a bedroom, it dawned on her, that, in less than sixteen months, Kevin would enroll at the university, if he passed his national exams. She would need to find an even bigger house to accommodate all of them.

Sophia took comfort, that from the look of her ever-increasing responsibilities as PA, and now that she was traveling without Michael, almost being his representative at the Company's meetings, she would soon receive another salary raise. After that, they would find a bigger house to rent.

Arrival at the airport and check-in process was flawless, with the adept help from Janet, the Company travel agent.

As Sophia and Richie walked down the long corridor to enter the plane, she was so excited by Richie's renewed closeness, that she did not look at the travel documents Janet handed to her.

At the entrance to the plane, the usual courtesies and an airline hostess guided them to their seats. When the hostess stopped and pointed to Sophia's seat, Sophia swallowed hard and almost corrected her on the location of her seat, in business class.

Richie, with his left hand extended, showed to Sophia to take the window seat before he sat on the aisle seat.

Sophia, still in shock that she was in first class, heard the air hostess ask if she could help with her handbag.

"No thanks. I will keep it under the seat in front of me." Sophia said, before she realized that the said seat was located too far to the front.

She fastened her seat belt, removed her boarding pass from her handbag, looked at it and then put it back. A smile broke on her face on confirming that she was booked to travel first class, another of her many firsts.

Sophia found a friend in the window through which she could blankly stare outside, while her brain raced. She wondered how their travel would be, with her seated right next to Richie.

Richie touched her arm, to alert her to make a choice from the many drinks the air hostess had brought. Sophia took a glance at the glass of wine in Richie's hand before she chose orange juice. She took a sip, placed the glass in the side holder and turned to stare outside.

Lost in thought, she suddenly noticed tarmac, grass, then scattered buildings below. The view returned her to reality. She had been too deep in thought to notice that the plane had taken off and was already in the sky. She turned to her left and mumbled. "We are in first class, where well-paying passengers travel in comfort, no blocked ears at take-off."

Richie, with headphones on, turned, grinned at her before he returned to the movie he was watching.

She looked around the cabin, for a quick count of the lucky people in first class. Richie turned and looked at her, and their eyes locked, which Richie broke with a smile.

"Geez! Why did I assume you have flown enough times not to tense up so much? Join me in watching this," he said, pointing to his TV screen.

Sophia gave him a soft elbow nudge. He held her hand in his and turned back to his movie.

The next time Sophia came to, she heard a soft whisper in her ear, "Sunshine, time to eat some food."

She grumbled inaudibly as she opened her eyes while squeezing them for a clearer view. Richie pointed to a sachet beside her food tray.

Grateful, she gracefully opened the wrapper, pulled out the immaculate white towel and wiped her hands and face as she yawned. "How far are we from our destination?"

With a full mouth, Richie turned her direction, his Adam's-apple bulged, then retracted before he spoke. "Very far. The closest things to you are the food right in front of your eyes, and me."

She smiled as she lifted the cover from her food. "Totally. You are right about the food." Without looking up, she could sense his eyes all over her.

She turned and looked at him, "I forgot to make my choice of food from the menu they gave me."

"You appeared too comfortable to be woke up, so I marked food items on the menu for you. Bon appetite," then pushed a forkful of food into his mouth.

Uneasy with him staring when she began to eat, she asked a question, sure to divert him. "So, how is the stock exchange today?"

Richie covered his food, picked up the Financial Today from his seat pocket and opened to page three before lowering the paper to Sophia's view. "Pity that we are on our way to the West, leaving Africa rising behind us. This paper is full of articles on future investment opportunities in Africa."

She pushed the paper away, from blocking her food, as he added, "I cannot wait to get back and share this with Chairman. He needs convincing to let me start a new department, to monitor global markets, for the benefit of the Company."

Sensing that Richie was getting into a monologue, she said, "That's a promising idea, particularly since you will get a whole floor for your offices, or even a tower."

"And you will find me an excellent PA, like you, if not yourself."

Sophia took the paper from Richie's hand, folded, and placed it in the seat pocket. "Just imagine, you and I working together. All I see are days starting and ending with discussions on the global money markets. Not good for the Company."

Richie smiled as he uncovered his food. "Money market discussions between you and I will be held at our breakfast table. That way I will leave for the office already happy."

She unconsciously looked at the ring on her finger, then turned back to her food and ate without looking at him. She crowned her enjoyment of the food by eating all the chocolate mousse dessert, then turned and asked, "What time is it?"

"It is nighttime all over."

"Good," she said, unfolding a blanket, and covering herself, head to toe.

The next time Sophia uncovered her head, she was surprised to find her seat reclined.

Richie, with headphones on, smiled as she rolled the seat back to sitting position. She got up and walked to the washroom.

Immediately she returned and made herself comfortable in her seat, Richie looked at her intensely.

"What now?" She asked.

He extended his left hand to her, bearing a single red rose. "Good morning Sunshine, I brought you a flower."

She looked at him, as thoughts drifted through her mind. She wondered what effect it would have on their trip if she declined the flower. After a moment, she decided that it was not the first flower he gave her on a plane and accepted the rose, held it close to her nose and inhaled, before exhaling, loud enough for Richie to hear. Ignoring his gawking, she held the flower in front of her eyes, turned it round twice, then looked at him, grinning. "Nice. Smells so fresh, I love it. No, I like it."

Richie placed his right hand on his heart, "I am offended. How can you love a rose?"

She inhaled the flower again. "You misunderstood me. I said I liked the rose, and maybe love the hand that gave it to me." She put on headphones and turned to watch cartoons on her TV screen. In the process, she missed hearing what Richie said, all she saw was his mouth move.

After about ten minutes of watching TV, Sophia took a quick glance at passengers in their compartment. She noticed that many were busy working on laptops or paperwork, then she wondered if that was what they too should be doing, instead of watching TV.

She contemplated, if the people who flew first class did so out of need, to continue with office tasks while on travel. The idea made sense to her. For some well-paid people, putting in six to eight hours of office work in-flight would easily pay for their ticket in first class.

Sophia smiled, acknowledging that the rich do their arithmetic well. Instead of sitting, crammed in tight spaces in economy class, where one could not do much, except watch something on the television for comfort, they paid for first class.

To Sophia, the rich must have calculated the prohibitive costs of arriving tired for a business meeting. With the thought on leg space, she involuntarily lifted her head for a peek at Richie's long legs. His eyes followed her to his legs.

From what Sophia saw of Richie's long legs, she concluded that there was no way he could travel in economy, then be able to walk out of the plane on arrival. It was fair for Richie, and tall men like him to travel first class. Arrival at the other end meant work. They rarely had time to stretch legs and cry about back-aches.

Richie squeezed her fingers tight, and then loosened his grip before turning the ring on her finger. Sophia pulled her hand away, retrieved a book from her bag, The History of Family Businesses 1850-2000, and continued from where she'd stopped reading.

Chapter 35

The drive from Fiumicino International Airport to the hotel was uneventful, until the door to Sophia's room was opened and the hotel staff stepped aside to let them in.

Sophia received the door key card as Richie followed her before she could close the door. She assumed that since it was late Sunday morning, he was stopping by her room before continuing to his.

She went to the bedroom side and returned to the living room, laughing. "The hotel people made a mistake. They delivered all your luggage to my room, that means you will be in your travel clothes until we return."

"No" Richie replied from the comfort of his seat in the living room, the TV remote in his hand as he explained. "Why stay in two rooms, when one will do?"

Sophia looked at him, then turned and went back to the bedroom and into the bathroom and closed the door behind her. She took one look in the mirror and went back to the bedroom and sat at the edge of the expansive king-size bed. She mumbled a promise to herself.

"I must remain calm, and that includes no shedding of tears. I traveled in first class to participate in important meetings that Michael was to attend."

She decided it was time to remind Richie that they were on an official visit, and they had two choices; to fight and adversely affect the meeting outcomes, or manage the situation amicably, and travel back to the office with impressive feedback.

The trip was her one chance to make an impression back in the office, that she could be trusted with important company assignments. Her hope was that she would receive another promotion, a salary increase.

Sophia walked back to the sitting room where Richie was, watching an English League football game. She cleared her throat to attract his attention before she went and sat by his side on the two-seater sofa. She snuggled closer than she had ever gathered courage to do.

Her action prompted a broad smile and his hand on her shoulders, after switching off the TV.

She turned and faced him with a broad smile, revealing her deep dimples. He cuddled her to his side, maybe expecting a kiss and praise on his choice of room and bed.

Sophia said. "We will do this official visit in a very cordial way, at least until Thursday. Ok? You move into a different room, and that will allow you and me to stay alert at all the official meetings. Thank you."

She stood up swiftly, went and sat on the single chair opposite the two-seater, from where Richie had not stopped staring at her.

Richie stood up without uttering a word.

She watched as he walked past the bedroom into the bathroom without closing any door behind him. He re-emerged a few minutes later, in a loud monologue.

"We got a fantastic room. It would be so nice to spend the night here which will make me very attentive at each meeting. These hotel people have a truly clear idea on the size of bed best for two people, though we would not require all that space to sleep well."

He returned to the sitting room with a smile on his face, knowing that his words about the bedroom contradicted what he knew. In the depth of his mind, he had seen the sense in Sophia's reasoning that they had traveled for company duties, so, sleeping well before each meeting was top priority.

Though he supported her suggestion to stay in separate rooms, there was no way he would admit that to her. To him, a voiced acknowledgement of the wisdom in her argument, would kill the intrigue she brought to him every time she objected to his reasoning. It was one of the reasons that he needed her in his life; to keep challenging him, in his private and professional life.

He walked to the study table nearby, picked the room phone, dialed the reception desk, and talked briefly.

After some minutes, he answered a knock on the door. A hotel staff walked into the bedroom and a moment later, left with Richie's luggage.

Sophia was watching TV when Richie made the phone call. She looked up with surprise on seeing the hotel staff leave with Richie's luggage.

Richie sat on the arm of the chair Sophia sat on. He took the remote and changed the TV channel to cartoons.

There was another knock on the door. Richie opened and accepted a key card, walked back, and dropped the card on the coffee table before going back to the arm of the chair.

"Sunshine, do not get lost in here. It's time for some lunch, though I prefer room service." The smile she gave him confirmed she was in agreement.

After lunch, they sat outside on the balcony and watched birds and brown leaves drop off tree branches. It was October, the Fall season.

They retreated to the room when the outside got too cold for their liking.

While in the room, they revisited their PowerPoint presentations and perused other documents for tomorrow's meetings. After, before Richie watched a football game, while Sophia read a book.

At 5:30pm, Richie switched off the TV. "What is the time? We have an early morning to-morrow with the Mwasimba staff who have been here. Time to go look for food."

Sophia went to the bedroom as Richie called out, "See you in sixty." He waved a key card to her. "I have your key as I will be ready before you."

After about fifty-minutes, Sophia appeared from the bedroom, dressed in a pleated Issay Miyake dress and a broad smile, prompting Richie, who had returned to her room earlier, to walk towards her. "Oh Sunshine, you look very elegant," as he kissed her.

Richie held her right hand and they walked out of the room as a door across the corridor opened, and two men in black suits followed them. The four walked to the elevator and into the hotel restaurant.

They all sat at one table and ate dinner from a buffet setup. Sophia was amazed how easily Richie conversed with the two men. A stranger, not aware of the arrangement, would assume that the four were colleagues who shared an office.

Then it hit Sophia, that she could be the stranger at the dinner table. From what she had observed, staff turnover at the Mwasimba Company was incredibly low, which meant that the two security men have probably watched Richie grow from a boy, into the man he was now.

After dinner, the four arrived traveled back to the hotel and stopped by the door to Sophia's room. Richie still holding onto her back, he cuddled her closer, right in front of the two men, and kissed her to a good night, before freeing her. "Sleep tight and see you tomorrow."

She smiled, though embarrassed that the other men were present. She entered her room and closed the door, remembering as always to secure the latch before she retired to bed for the night.

Sophia woke up to the familiar ring of her alarm clock. She was happy with the way she felt, relaxed, and she could smell the flowers in the living room.

As soon as she opened her door to leave for breakfast, the door across the corridor opened. She wished she had been given a room on a different floor, away from Richie.

This life of being guarded scared her, made her imagine there was danger nearby, lying low and waiting to jump on her.

The man exchanged morning greetings with Sophia, looked at his watch and asked if she was okay to wait ten minutes before going for breakfast. She nodded and re-entered her room while thinking, "I was all set for breakfast, now I have ten minutes of idleness."

She picked her book and read two pages, closed it, and walked outside, to the balcony of her room.

A knock on the door interrupted her admiration of the scenery outside. She left her room and joined Richie and the two men.

Sophia noticed that Richie was not dressed in clothes for official meetings and wondered why, though she did not ask.

At the elevator, one of the men pressed the up button. Sophia held her breath, thoughtful. "If I mention that the breakfast room is down, on the second floor, I will be attracting attention, that a security person, expected to be alert and informed has pressed the up instead of down button on the elevator.

She kept her mouth shut, while listening to Richie complain, why the need to wake up early, just for breakfast.

They got off the elevator three floors up and walked to the left where one of the men scanned a card and a door opened, revealing an expansive breakfast room. There were a few patrons eating breakfast. The foursome served themselves from a buffet and sat down at a table by one corner of the room.

After breakfast, they returned to their rooms.

Sophia thought of how easy men have it, when it comes to dressing. When it was time for them to go downstairs, ten minutes after getting back to their rooms, Richie showed up, clad in a black pinstripe suit, white shirt, floral necktie, and shiny black leather shoes. Yet, all that she had managed to do was brush her teeth and check her navy-blue skirt suit one more time.

Chapter 36

Four days passed extremely fast. By Thursday evening, Sophia could not wait for the official dinner to end, so she could retire to her room and sleep. The next day, Friday, was a free day. On Saturday they were to visit a production line of their computer hardware supplier.

Sophia knew she deserved to rest, after putting in many hours at official meetings, listening to presentations and technical discussions on marketing and financial investments.

On some days, she put in more than twelve hours, when one added the group dinners.

She now appreciated the work that Michael did at his many meetings, discussing intricacies of business collaborations, misunderstandings, and strategies.

At the meetings, Sophia saw how much effort Richie put into each presentation and discussion. His motivation gave her courage to respond to some of the questions asked, and she could tell that he appreciated her input. She was also appreciative that during the official sessions, Richie did not stare at her or hold her back or hand.

Though, by day three, she was in panic mode, fearing Richie may have lost interest in her. A worry she dismissed quickly. If the meetings were so strenuous on her, then it must be a triple burden for Richie.

Then a thought flashed through Sophia's head. The day was Thursday, not a day to collapse into her bed at the end of the dinner, but the day she had made a promise to Richie.

She involuntarily glanced at Richie at a nearby table. An unwise move, she thought, as their eyes met and locked.

Twenty minutes later, Richie, Sophia and the two security men were in the elevator, on their way to the eighth floor, their rooms. Sophia did not even feel the hand holding onto the small of her back, for she was in deep thought, wishing she had shared details of the promise she had made to Richie on Sunday afternoon.

Her intended plan was to discuss what she perceived as Richie's way of making decisions without consulting her. One example was when he decided that they should share a room or that she had agreed to marry him and a delegation from his home would be visiting her parents in the village.

Sophia was surprised at how fast the elevator ride was. She opened the door to her room, and as expected, Richie followed her in.

Immediately they entered the room, he bolted the door, something he had not done before.

He walked to the living room, while loosening his necktie, removed his coat, and threw it on the study table, picked the remote and the television was on. Without caring to check the channel, he called out. "Sunshine. Time to know you better."

Sophia left the bedroom after securing the official documents in the safe. She entered the living room and stood in front of Richie.

He beckoned her to sit beside him. Instead of sitting, she turned and walked towards the bedroom, saying, "Sometimes comfort comes before watching TV."

After a few minutes, she was back, dressed in a cream sundress decorated with large brown butterflies. She sat next to Richie, who removed his necktie and tossed it on the coffee table.

Sophia was reflective, juggling words, how to explain what she had meant when she suggested that they stay in separate rooms until today, when the official meetings ended.

Tired from the four days of marathon meetings, she knew that she needed to draw deep into her diminishing energy and courage, to utter the words which weighed her heart down with fear. She hoped that she could explain herself, without breaking down into tears, or being rude.

Richie cleared his throat to attract Sophia's attention. She looked at him as fear gripped her on recalling, that for many days Richie had not held her by the waist or shoulders. Before she could think further, he kissed her and asked. "So, how has your evening been?"

"Good," she said, too nervous to say more. She worried that for once, they sat together, and Richie was not cuddling her.

Next, she feared that he would insist on sleeping with her, and not respect her reasoning, that he was not her husband, so she could not share a bed with him.

Richie interrupted her stream of thoughts. "Don't break my heart."

Sophia's head jerked up, then turned and faced Richie as he added. "Would you care to tell me about your other men?"

Before she could digest his request, she needed to calm her heart which was pounding in her chest and head. She had no energy left in her, so, all she managed to utter was a short question. "Which men?"

"The schoolteacher, the sons of the businessmen in your local town, and the poor guy who flew in from the USA."

Sophia's heart had never felt pierced that hard before. She touched her chest, just to be sure the warmth she felt was not blood oozing from the piercing.

She did not utter any of the hundreds of words in her head, because her throat and mouth were too dry to speak.

What was she expected to say? Was she to start from the beginning, narrate how the teacher was her father's idea and she had zero interest in that man? Or, that the las time she set her eyes on the man from the US must have been a decade ago, and that the Onono sons were just spoilt brats, known for their bad behaviour of harassing girls?

More fear gripped her, as she mused if Richie had information about her abduction case.

Richie stretched his left hand and touched her thigh. Unlike his earlier touching, that touch did not send any warm feelings into her body. "Eeeh, what does your silence tell me?" he asked as he pulled his hand away.

Sophia opened her mouth, but no word came out. Her plan was to ask him what he wanted to know that he did not already know. She changed her mind, deciding there was no need to say anything.

She was in distress, on recalling how Richie had arrived at her apartment without her giving him the address, and now, he seemed to know everything about her problems in her village and hometown.

She made one promise to herself, that no tear would drop out of her eyes, even if it meant resigning from her job and going back to the village to marry the teacher and make her father a happy man.

To make her parents happy in old age had been one of her long-held promises. To make up for the happiness they had missed all the years they lived in poverty, struggling to feed and educate their children.

She resolved that she would engage in the conversation, stick to the truth, and only the truth.

She stood and walked towards the bedroom. Halfway, she turned and went back to the living room and stared at Richie until he spoke again. "I am waiting for an answer."

Sophia held his eyes. "The answer you are waiting for should come from your source of information on what you call my men."

He signaled her to sit. "Are you denying there are no men interested in you?"

Her frown loosened. "Are you trying to tell me there are no women interested in you?"

He chuckled. "You are first my dear. But in summary, I have no heart for another. Only you."

Sophia, feeling very cornered, locked eyes with Richie. "Why not get full details on my so-called men, from your source. Though, as you are very aware of, I am not married to any of you."

The TV remote dropped out of Richie's hand as he stared at Sophia. He looked away, on realizing that by 'any of you,' she meant the four families chasing after her hand in marriage.

Secretly, Richie felt guilty that he was interrogating her about the other men. From his meeting with Joy, Richie knew that Sophia had no relationship with the men, nor did she want to marry any of them. But he wanted to hear Sophia confirm that to him.

To Richie, if Sophia confessed her innocence in the scheme of her parents, she would in-directly confirm that Richie was the only man she could consider for marriage. And there she was, refusing to acknowledge that.

The quietness in the room was deafening, though the television was on. Richie broke the silence. "I can help you out. Why do you want to disappoint your dear father?"

She looked at him as he completed the sentence. "By not marrying his choice of husband for you?"

Sophia sneered at him as her nose wrinkled in disgust.

Richie opened his mouth to say something, but Sophia cut him off. "Good, if my father has found me a man, why not let your father find you a woman, instead of chasing after me?"

He grabbed her by the shoulders, turned her face to his and kissed her. When he withdrew, he said, "Sunshine, that's another reason I love you. You are my father's choice."

Sophia looked at him, like she needed to hear more. He spoke again. "I love you, and, my father, Mr. Chairman of all things, has already put his seal of approval on my choice." He chuckled. "I have a strong feeling he would have still picked you, had he met you first."

"I pity you. What will you do with all those ladies who love you? Did I have to become a PA for you to notice my presence?"

He smiled. "Are you sure you want to go back in time? How rigid you behaved while at university, never willing to interact with any of us?"

She chuckled, then turned and looked at the television screen. She needed time to think of a new strategy, on how to counter what he just revealed, that she had no time for men while at university, which she knew was the truth.

Without looking at him, she said, "I had no idea people go to university to talk, talk. I was there to study."

She completed her sentence with a smile, which faded when Richie spoke. "I am surprised that you had time to notice the many ladies who followed me."

Sophia interpreted his words to mean either the end of their discussion, or, he was going to answer her question on the many ladies who liked him while at university, and of late at the many members' clubs.

She waited, and when she did not hear more from him, she stood and walked towards the balcony, while in a monologue. "So, the score is about even, many men following me, with the many women who follow you."

She looked back and noticed that Richie had a smile on his face, but he did not talk, so she continued.

"Tell me, what would be your problem with the man I choose to marry?"

Richie stared at the TV, though Sophia could tell he was thinking, then he spoke. "The problem will be with my heart if you do not choose me. Though I know you are a clever girl and will choose me, for I love you."

"Okay, I am not choosing any of you men, because marriage is not part of my plans."

Richie said in a faint voice. "Promise me one thing only." He noticed her attention, listening. "If I convince you on the goodness of marriage, I will be the only one in the competition."

She laughed aloud, giving him a chance to add, "Promise me, you will also let me know if the other men convince you, before I do."

With those words, Sophia unknowingly dropped her guard. "I have known one fact for long, men can derail a woman's focus, and as of now, my focus is on my job, and romance on company premises is against company rules."

"Why do you want me to repeat myself?" he asked her.

Sophia waited for Richie to explain himself. When he did not, she changed the topic. "You know what Richie, I have known you for almost six years now, and my guess is that you are a good person, unless you can hide it for that long."

The usual smile returned to his face, then disappeared as she completed the sentence. "As I said, my current life plan is for the next ten years, which is a long time. The best you can do for yourself, is marry one of the many ladies from the clubs."

Richie jerked out of the seat so suddenly that he scared Sophia.

He walked towards the study table, while unbuttoning the top of his shirt. His action prompted Sophia to stare at his muscular arms and hard chest, squeezed within his white shirt.

With both hands in his trouser pockets, he paced the room and off into the bathroom.

A few minutes later, he re-emerged and said, "Let me make one thing clear to you. Those ladies at the club and other parties, are like the schoolteacher, Onono and Ndugu's sons. If you can marry one of them, I too will marry one of the ladies. But I do not want them, I want you."

He completed the sentence in a high pitch, which he must have realized, picked the remote and increased the TV volume.

Sophia remained quiet, knowing it was time to bite her tongue while she reflected on what Richie just said. She acknowledged he could be right. Just the way the families in her town and village were after her hand in marriage because she was a well-behaved girl, it could be the same for Richie. That the ladies and their families in the city and at the clubs, were after him, because he was a reputable man.

The thought propelled her into a fear, that maybe she was trying too hard to run away from a decent man.

She involuntarily looked at Richie, while she pondered if she should give him a long hug, a sorry hug. She abandoned the thought, knowing that such an act would need too much courage. She decided that staying quiet would be the better choice. Or was she mistaken?

Richie edged closer to her, supporting his head between his hands.

Sophia, afraid to look at his face, picked the remote and changed the TV to the weather channel.

He reached her side, held her shoulders and guided her towards the two-seater sofa. As they sat down, he asked, "Am I putting too much pressure on you? Please tell me how much time you need, and I will respect that."

She did not answer. Her only wish was that Richie was not privy to the heart pounding in her chest.

She remained quiet, reflective, imagining how happy her life would be, once Richie gave her more time, as he had just indicated.

Sophia then asked herself, if, after the ten years, she would find another loving man like Richie. A man who would bring her flowers, even when she objected. A man who would say he loved her and wanted to spend the rest of his life with her. With that thought, her eyes turned to the bouquet of flowers on the coffee table.

She worried if she would ever find a man who would respect her word, whenever she said no to something, as Richie did. For example, the last time she objected to him joining her in bed, he slept on the couch. And on Sunday, when she opposed to sharing a room with him, he asked for a different room.

She questioned if there was another man out there in the city, one who would still hold onto her back, when so many socialites scorned her. "Richie, trust me when I say marriage is not yet part of my plans."

"Why?"

She felt the knot in her chest tighten. "First, I don't know how to explain. Second, you won't understand some things." She sighed.

"Mmhhh?"

"Since you seem to know so much about me, by now you must know that all I want is to perform my PA duties, see my brothers through school," she said in a shaky voice.

He cuddled her closer and held her tightly against his chest. He kissed her forehead as he stroked her hair, in silence.

Sophia did not move, she stayed quiet, knowing that if she moved or said more, the tears in her eyes would stream down her cheeks.

After what seemed like twenty minutes of quietness, Sophia assumed that Richie had dozed off. She freed herself from his hold but was surprised to see him wide awake. She went into the bedroom, pushing the door closed with her leg.

She flipped the beddings aside, climbed into bed and covered her body to the head. She stayed in bed and fought off sleep, waiting to hear Richie's next move, hoping that he would leave for his room.

Sophia awoke to Richie calling her, "Sophia, Sophia." She rubbed her eyes and looked at him. He kissed her on the cheek. "Good night my love. See you tomorrow at ten for our sightseeing trip. Please come lock the door."

He walked out of the bedroom and the room, pulling the door to close behind him before Sophia bolted the door and went back to bed. For the first time in a long time, since they vacated their one-roomed house, she slept without taking a bath.

~ ~ ~ ~ ~ ~

It was two in the morning as Richie opened the door to his room.

He left his shoes and socks behind the door, grabbed the remote and switched on the TV. He did not surf through channels as was his habit. Instead, he sat on the over-stuffed chair and stared at the TV screen.

Richie was reflective. He felt sorry for putting Sophia through a lot of challenging questions. He felt angry with himself, that he had put too much pressure on her, forcing her to utter what he already knew, that she worked hard to support her family.

He imagined what it must be like, for someone to work hard and wait for a pay cheque, then to see the money leave their bank account. Something he had never had to do in his life. His accommodation had always been there, and he had never paused to find out where his mother and the house workers sourced food.

Richie told himself that he needed to help Sophia, give her whatever amount of money she would need, even if it meant touching his legacy fund. But on further thought, he knew she would reject his offer. She was an independent woman who preferred to earn her own money.

Supporting his head between his hands, Richie told himself that he did not want his family's money to come between his love for Sophia.

What if Sophia was trying to run away from him because of his family background? The thought scared him. Or if she was intimidated by the ladies at the club, because of what they could freely afford?

For a moment, he entertained an idea that he needed to force himself to stop seeing Sophia, give her the liberty she needed to perform her PA duties.

After a short while, he rejected the idea, knowing that his personal and professional life would disintegrate. Sophia was more than a PA, she had become a particularly important part of his life, challenging him into more growth through the questions she asked and suggestions she provided.

How would he get the pride he felt, whenever he walked into a club with Sophia by his side?

Who would challenge him with questions about the stock exchange and global financial markets? Who would listen to his endless stories on how he loved his duties as a manager, and the dreams he had, to initiate and grow a new department within the Company?

A broad smile appeared on his face, on remembering how Sophia stood up to serve him food, whenever he visited her house. A courtesy that touched his heart, increased his appetite for food, something he looked forward to in marriage.

He switched off the TV and let the remote fall onto the floor. He stood and paced the room, concentrating on how to make Sophia believe that the ladies at the club were not his girlfriends, but just admirers.

As he pulled the bed sheet over his head, he did something he had not done for many years, he let tears stream down his face.

He then prayed and promised himself that he would take Sophia back to the various members' clubs and shield her from all the naughty ladies, envious men, and nosy mothers. He again prayed, that Sophia would one day change her mind about the ten-year waiting period. Would she ever agree to marry him?

Chapter 37

Sophia groaned when she woke up and saw a message on her phone. "Please call room service for two. I will come over at nine for breakfast."

She read the message again and her first thought was that Richie planned to continue with the difficult topic from last night.

She typed a response. "I have no appetite to eat in my room, I prefer the dining room."

She read the message again and clicked the delete button, then typed, "Okay," and clicked send. It pleased her that Richie had at least asked her to order the food, and not gone ahead to order from his room.

After a brief chat with the two security men along the corridor, Richie entered Sophia's room. He was surprised to see her looking happier than he expected. He made a silent promise to himself, to avoid any topic that would spoil her good mood.

They ate breakfast while checking out the city map for the location of sites they would vis-it.

Richie felt happier by the minute, seeing the expression on Sophia's face, as she called out names of places she had heard of before she summed it up. "Rome. How about, we live by the adage, when in Rome, do as the Romans do?"

"I am fully with you on that," Richie said as his hand smoothed down the side of her arm.

Though he had been with Sophia long enough to be used to her beauty, he could see that she improved day by day. He still marveled at her dimples, how perfectly they lined up with her oval-shaped eyes.

She ignored his stare and continued. "You promised a visit to the Vatican. We can do that on Sunday, before we leave for the airport. Today will be to the famous Colosseum, the Pantheon, cathedrals and many other historical sites."

Richie looked at his Rolex, stood and extended his right hand to Sophia. "I'm not being rude, but the tour bus will leave without us. Please carry the map and a sketchbook." He picked his leather jacket and hung a camera around his neck.

They walked out of the room, joined the security men at the elevator and headed to the vehicle waiting outside.

Sophia wondered if men were created to think alike. Otherwise, what a coincidence, that three men dressed in some sort of uniform. Except for different shirts, how did each decide to wear jeans, sports shoes, and a leather jacket? She glanced at her black trousers, cream blouse, and sweater, and was thankful that she did not pick jeans as earlier planned.

After a two-kilometer drive, they joined other sightseers waiting to board the tour bus. At the entrance to the bus, they showed tickets and were each given a map and red headphones. They followed Richie to the upper deck of the tour bus and found strategic seats.

Once they were comfortable, one of the men turned to Richie, "I am now with you on this, those small cars would not enable them such a view."

Richie gave thumbs up. "You see, for once I am right. Do me a favour, enjoy the day. We can even wander off in different directions and meet up later."

Sophia put on her headphones and listened to the tour guide-recording provided in the bus.

As the bus drove into the city, she turned to her group. "I have an idea. Since we are on an all-day bus pass, why don't we stay in the bus for the one-hour round trip, then decide on which stops to get off at on the second ride?"

She received no objection, so they stayed and admired several sites from the bus. Sophia opened her map and marked places as they drove past. Richie was busy taking pictures with his camera until she gave him a soft elbow nudge. "Any destinations of interest I mark for you on the map?"

"Everything appears new each time I have visited. I will follow your lead today."

It occurred to her, that this was not Richie's first visit to Rome.

On the second circuit of the bus, the group alighted to admire several water fountains with oversized human sculptures. The foursome stared at the Trevi Fountain at the piazza dei Trevi. Each consumed in internal thoughts, noticing the near naked sculpture of a man, not wanting to discuss the beauty of the fountain.

In line with the popular tradition, each turned and threw a coin over their shoulder, into the water.

By three o'clock, Sophia was overjoyed with the many historical places they had visited, including climbing the Spanish Steps. As they descended, Richie said. "I know you are still enjoying yourself, but allow me to be your tour guide for—"

"I do not see a problem with you taking over." She cut in. "You seem to know the place like the back of your hand."

When she paused, Richie completed his sentence. "I need one hour to show you a place you might like, before we hop back into the bus for the famous Colosseum."

He interpreted her smile as a yes, circled his hand around her waist, waved his phone at the two men as he guided her away. "Sunshine, it will be a shame to take you back without showing you some hidden shops in this city."

They walked in and out of designer clothing shops. The only advantage they had over their limited time was that the shops were situated next to each other, on the same street.

The expression on Sophia's face brought warmth to Richie's heart, a total transition from the sorry look she had the night before.

The other surprise was that Sophia tried on several outfits and bought some. While waiting to pay, she turned to Richie and said, "I hope Joy can one day find her way here. She will spend a week admiring those designer clothes, no imitations here."

"Let me know when you have time, we can come back as tourists."

She did not respond.

Richie struggled with the urge to offer to pay for some of her items but shelved the idea. He weighed the chances of triggering her thoughts about budgets and school fees. He decided it was not the right time to spoil her shopping mood.

What he appreciated most was seeing Sophia happier than he had ever seen her. It gave him renewed hope, that someday, once she overcame her financial burdens, he would have an intelligent and happy wife by his side.

At 4:30pm, the four sat in the tour bus to the Colosseum. After two hours of walking and taking photos of the different sections in the massive ruin of the ancient sports arena, Sophia's phone had many photos.

Each time Richie looked at Sophia, he resolved to find a way to convince her to come back with him for a holiday, paid entirely by him. From her day-long dimpled face, he knew that they would spend a week walking the streets of the city with few complaints.

~ ~ ~ ~ ~ ~

Richie kissed her bye at the door to her room. "I need a shower and a change of clothes before we step out to explore what the Romans eat in the night."

Sophia looked at him with begging eyes. "I hope you are not serious about that, I will trade-in dinner for a rest."

He followed her into the room. "It sounds like you did not do as the Romans when in Rome. You tired yourself out before dinner?"

Sophia placed her shopping bags on the table and sat on a nearby chair. "You know what, is it okay if you guys go eat while I sleep?"

"I am guessing that you are equally hungry. After using up all your energy walking the streets of Rome."

"The pizza we ate was good enough. And, I have a feeling you will bring me take-away food."

Richie guided her to the two-seater sofa and switched on the TV. "It will be my pleasure to bring you dinner, and even feed you if you allow me. The only problem is that you will miss eating at an Italian family-style restaurant. Nothing close to the formal dinners we have had all week."

Sophia leaned back on the sofa and yawned as she stretched out her arms. "What is the time? I need at least thirty, no, forty minutes to enjoy a long hot bath. That's the only way to bring me back to life."

Richie bit his lower lip, not wanting her to hear what was in his mind. He had wanted to offer her a bathroom massage, to help relax her body. He did not, preferring to see her smiley dimples the rest of the evening. No need to offer help he knew she would not accept.

He stood, pulling her along, embraced her for a long minute, only releasing her when he felt she was getting comfortable enough to doze off. "We'll share the extra ten minutes, please make it thirty-five instead of forty. I will leave with your key, as I will be ready before you."

He walked out as Sophia strolled to the bathroom where she ran a full bath of near hot water and poured in an overdose of bath salts and soothing lavender oils. After soaking for twenty minutes, she stepped out of the bathtub, revitalized.

She looked at the pair of jeans she had picked for the evening and decided she was too relaxed, relieved of her tiredness, to wear jeans.

At the wardrobe, she selected a knee-high bareback dress with straps meeting at the neck, forming a round necklace. Guessing that Richie was waiting for her, she could smell his fresh cologne, she picked a complimenting evening handbag and matching brown leather jacket and walked into the living room. "I hope there are no mosquitoes in this city. I want to feel the evening breeze."

Richie switched off the TV and walked to meet her. He had changed into formal black trousers, auburn coloured turtleneck, and a formal black jacket.

Sophia checked him out, head to toe. "I want to walk next to you. You look ready to protect me from the Roman lions. Do it more often."

"Thanks. You look charming. I hope your soak in the bathtub helped." He topped his compliment with a kiss on her cheek.

She edged closer to him and he encircled her waist, holding the small of her back, under her jacket. He guided her out the door while whispering into her ear. "Can you do me one favour?"

She turned to face him and almost hit his nose with her head, as he completed the sentence. "Please, may I have your jacket once we arrive at the eatery?"

The two security men had also changed into T-shirts and formal jackets. They joined them in the elevator and rode downstairs where they boarded a vehicle waiting outside.

The eatery was small, compared to the large hotels where they ate group meals during their meetings.

They were shown to their reserved table.

Richie seemed surprised when Sophia removed and handed her jacket to him. He held a chair for her, pushed her in before he hung the jacket on the back of her chair. He took the seat beside her and kept his hand on her back. He was glad when she did not react.

The waiter handed out menus before he sang out a list of drinks from which they could choose. As the rest struggled to read the Italian menu, Richie asked the waiter to suggest what would make a good Italian dining experience for them.

The meal was served uninterrupted, one course at a time. The group ate amid chatting and laughter. When they finished with dessert, Sophia looked at Richie and expressed her gratitude for his encouragement that got her to join them for the dinner. Saying she could now declare that she had eaten authentic Italian food.

She received more back rubs, with each of her words in praise of the food.

Back at their hotel, Richie followed Sophia to her room, and insisted they watch a movie together. An idea he soon regretted as she dozed off on the sofa.

Chapter 38

Their journey back to Nairobi went well, though Richie was unusually quiet. They arrived and shared company transport from the airport, dropping Sophia off first.

Richie walked her to the door where he wished her a nice evening. "Bye and see you soon."

Sophia assumed 'soon' meant on Wednesday, the day they would work together to pre-pare their travel report for Michael and other Company staff.

Joy and Silas were not home. Sophia took her time in the shower and dressed in clothes she considered would not constrict the hard thinking she planned to do. She needed to prepare for a phone call from her mother, any time soon.

Before her travel to Italy, Stella had said there would be Sophia's visitors from the city.

Sophia needed to reach a decision on marriage, and whom to marry. She had already decided that whatever the word love meant, it did not matter to her much.

What mattered was for two people to agree to live together and consult one another on decisions that would have an impact on both. Just the same way corporations thrive, whereby owners and employees have a contract with clear dos and don'ts, just like the company she worked for.

Sophia almost smiled to herself, on recalling how a mere signature on a contract had enabled her to work as a PA for Michael. She had arrived as a stranger, but because of the agreed upon contract concerning her duties and obligations, she had thrived, as a person and a professional.

The opening of the front door interrupted her thought process. Joy and Silas entered the house. They called out and walked to her bedroom where they shared hugs of welcome.

As she returned their greetings, Sophia looked at her brother and sister and wished she could be as happy as them. She tried to recall a time when she had been that happy. Certainly not while at university with all the money worries. Nor after graduation with all the anxiety about getting a job. On some days while at work, and of course, on Friday as she toured the City of Rome with Richie. Though she doubted if she ever looked as happy as Joy.

After about thirty minutes of updates, Silas excused himself, mentioning that it was his day in the kitchen. Immediately he walked out, Joy looked out of the bedroom, like to be sure he was out of earshot. She pushed the door closed and turned to Sophia. "They finally agreed on a date…," before she could complete the sentence, the doorbell rang, and she hurried out to get it.

After a moment, Joy called out. "Sophia, the other half of your heart is here."

All that Sophia heard were her own three words, "Ooh my God," as she collapsed onto her bed.

The next time she came to, she saw Richie seated on the bed by her side, holding her hand, and Joy was standing by the open door of the bedroom.

When Sophia turned to scan the room, Joy smiled and walked away.

~ ~ ~ ~ ~ ~

The next day, Richie woke up in the sleeping bag he had borrowed from Joy.

There was little conversation between Richie and Sophia at the breakfast table. He appeared worried as he told Sophia that it was good foresight, she had taken the day off from work to rest after travel. He would do the same.

Sophia did not respond. She had more pressing decisions to think about.

Silas left for school, wishing everyone a good day. Twenty minutes later, Joy walked to the main door, looked at her sister, then at Richie. "She is the only sister I have, keep her well and alive while I am gone." Joy winked as she closed the door behind her.

Richie smiled back and made a mental note, "This one has the right qualities to run a company, I will find her a decent job, soon."

Richie and Sophia spent the day chatting. At one point, Sophia said. "The trip must have exhausted all my energy, or maybe it was the shock of traveling first class." She laughed.

"Really? That would be strange." Richie said before he stood up and walked with Sophia to the three-sitter sofa. He switched on the TV before stretching himself out on the sofa and pulling her along. Both shared the sofa, facing the TV screen. "You know what, if you had a long cane in the house, I would ask you to punish me."

"Why?" she asked.

Realizing the underlying message in his words, he regretted them. "Sorry, that was my wrong choice of a metaphor. I do not recall ever being caned, nor would I ever lift my hand to anyone, unless I am forced to defend myself." He positioned a nearby chair cushion and rested his head on it. "What I was trying to say is that I am sorry for getting you so worried."

She snuggled, placing her left hand on his chest as he continued to talk. "I cannot explain why I have failed to understand your situation, especially when the people at your home have made your life difficult."

Richie paused, lifted his left hand, and smoothed Sophia's hair.

The room was quiet except for the sound from the TV. Richie assumed Sophia had fallen asleep on the comfort of his chest, so he called out, "Sophia"

"I am here with you."

He continued. "And I know that my interaction with the ladies at the club worries you. Would you believe me if I told you that most of them are like nagging sisters I never had?"

Sophia tried to sit up, but Richie's hand on her shoulder held her back to his chest as he continued to explain. "I have grown up with most of them—at school, clubs, birthday parties, home visits, church, and more. That is how our parents have raised us, together."

Sophia moved to make herself more comfortable, resting her head on Richie's shoulder.

Richie flipped the TV channel to the 10:00am money market report before he held Sophia's hand and entwined her fingers with his. "I hope you now understand how hard it would be for me to shame the ladies at the club."

She sat upright. "I have not asked you to shame anyone. And please, if you plan to do that, not when with me."

He helped her back to her previous position on his shoulder. "What I meant by shaming, is stopping them from coming to greet me, or rather to smooch my face. They have done that to many people before me, including my brothers. You will soon notice that their behaviour will change once we exchange our marriage vows."

He paused when he felt her body tense up. She was close enough for him to hear the throbbing of her heart. When he felt her body relax, he continued. "They do that to one another, often, in competition. They then turn around and give respect to whichever one of them gets married. And the round of competition starts all over again, with the next lady or man."

Sophia slid down to Richie's chest as she said, "You have missed a lot of news on your money markets."

Richie changed the channel to the weather station, saying, "I am now with you. The money markets will have to wait, until you have forgiven me." He felt the emptiness when she sat up, away from his chest. She kissed him on the lips, stood, and walked into the kitchen.

He strolled around the living room, admiring the decorative Maasai souvenirs on the wall before he followed her into the kitchen where she was washing dishes. He held her by the waist. "Sunshine, you make me happy, a more complete person. Thanks for agreeing to marry me."

She jerked her head to the side, so fast that it hurt. She lifted her left hand and touched her neck, to soothe the pain while she said, "Slow down, your words sound like my last evening, bad, bad. Who said I agreed to marry you?"

"Your good behaviour and your love for me, and most importantly, for setting December 18th as the day my parents will visit your home, to ask for your hand in marriage." He planted kisses on her cheeks.

Not wanting to hurt her neck again, Sophia slowly turned and faced Richie, staring into his eyes without uttering a word.

Thoughts jammed her mind. She remembered last evening, Joy mentioning something about a date. But then the doorbell rang, and Joy had gone to open the door, for none other than Richie. Then the fiasco of her fainting and sleep for the night, to be surprised in the morning, that Richie had spent the night, not only in their apartment, but on the floor of her bedroom.

She decided to wait to receive details of the date from Joy, later in the evening. She said, "Thank you."

Sophia recalled what she had casually said to Richie's mother, and her response when her own mother had asked why she was traveling when there were visitors coming to her home. Sophia acknowledged she'd played a part, given a go ahead for the parents' meeting.

After a prolonged silence, she decided to distract Richie, from further conversation about the meeting date and family visit. She loosened herself from his grip on her waist, kissed him on the cheek, and turned back to finish washing the dishes.

Richie stayed by her side. Halfway through, he held her waist and guided her to the living room. "Remember what joyful Joy said, I should not let you overwork. Come, you need a rest."

They watched TV and only stood to prepare lunch together before going back to the sofa. At 4:00pm, Richie stood and held his hand out to Sophia. "How I wish I could sit here with you forever. I know that is not part of your plan, tomorrow you must go back to your PA tasks."

Richie kissed her for long before he pulled away. "Let me leave, and see you tomorrow, to prepare our report. Whatever time you will be ready, I will be at your service."

Sophia held onto Richie's arm, walked with him to the door, said bye and watched him walk away. She closed the door and went to the kitchen, to occupy her mind, by preparing supper.

~ ~ ~ ~ ~ ~

After dinner, Joy followed Sophia into her bedroom and sat at the edge of the bed while Sophia sat on the chair by her dresser. They briefly talked about her travel and how her day in the house was before Sophia said. "I hear the parents have set a date, the 18th of December?"

Joy looked up from the new leather bag she was admiring, "Ooh yes, after a million calls from Mum. You know how she does it, calls and whenever you ask her a question, she says she will think about it. Which is her indirect way of saying, `let me consult with your father,' boss."

Sophia looked away from the mirror where she was admiring her hair. She turned to Joy and said, "Good. That will be after your graduation and before the Christmas holidays. This year we should go spend Christmas at home, all of us."

After a brief silence, with Joy admiring the designer clothes from Italy, Sophia asked, "Have you any idea where Richie found out details about my many admirers? We almost fought over that, in Italy."

Sophia was not prepared for the long lecture she received from Joy.

"I told him, and that was after careful consideration. You are my older sister, the eldest in our home, the pride of our parents. So, it pains me when you refuse to shine. I was surprised that you had not let Richie know that he is not the only one chasing after you."

Sophia shifted on the chair, turned her back to the mirror to give Joy her full attention while she added, "Sister, here is one reason I revealed the information on your behalf. Never let Richie imagine that he is the only man in your life, currently. You will later hate yourself for that.

He could be a good man, but he can change, and if that happens, you must be in a position to remind him of the favour you did him, abandoning all the other men chasing after you, for him.

Even if life stays good, and you never get a chance to scream the words back at him, he will have reason to love and respect you more. Because each time he looks at you, he will re-member that you had more than one to choose from, and you chose him."

Joy finished her lecture, stood, and looked at Sophia.

Sophia reacted by reaching out and touching Joy's arm, tenderly as she said, "Thank you for your very wise perspective."

"Good night and remember you are going back to work tomorrow." Joy giggled. "Lucky thing, whatever time you wake up, the driver will be at the car park, waiting for no one other than my sister."

Joy closed the door behind her and went to her bedroom.

~ ~ ~ ~ ~ ~

Everything appeared normal the next day. From the usual car that came for Sophia, to the fresh flowers on her office desk.

Michael was happy to have Sophia back in the office, welcoming her with a hug, which she partly attributed to the huge pile of PA tasks awaiting her.

It was a long day, filled with hours of working side by side with Richie before she started on her regular in-tray.

At the end of the day, 6:45pm to be exact, the door opened, and Richie strode into Sophia's office. "Who is overworking my love? Time to go home."

She turned in his direction. "Hear who's talking, like they are not in the office."

He chuckled. "Remember tomorrow is another long day, the day we present our travel report to Michael and a line of managers. And they will be busy digging their eyes into you."

Sophia smiled, logged out of the computer, while responding to Richie. "The best part is we have worked hard today. I know we will do an excellent job with the presentation."

Richie opened the connecting door and disappeared into Michael's office. Sophia took another look at the clock on the wall, pressed a key on the phone to alert her driver, before left her office.

Chapter 39

Sophia served two cups of tea and handed one to Richie before she paced the room.

He took a sip, looked at her and said, "The parents' meeting should be held at one of the clubs, they have meeting rooms available to members for a small fee."

"My parents are not coming to be tortured at those exclusive clubs." Sophia said in a firm voice.

She had been trying to convince Richie, that since his parents were initially to visit her parents in the village, she should be the one to choose the venue for their meeting in the city.

Joy was graduating from university in the second week of December. She had invited her parents to travel to the city for the graduation. Sophia's thinking was that instead of their parents hurrying back to the village after graduation, to be home for the visit from Richie's parents, it was more practical if the parents' meeting was held in the city.

Richie gave in on the venue, maybe after realizing that a meeting venue was not a big issue. The main issue was the discussion on their marriage.

After Sophia's discussion with Richie, she called to inform her parents that they needed to extend their upcoming visit to the city by a few days, to meet with Richie's parents.

Stella had no objection to Sophia's suggestion, until she heard what Mariko had to say. "I will not be cornered in the city for such an important matter, I have a home."

The parents traveled to the city where they attended Joy's graduation. As a present to Joy, Sophia hired a vehicle that drove the family to the graduation grounds. They used the same vehicle to travel to the city center to take graduation photos and to a hotel where they ate dinner, to celebrate Joy's big day.

Stella and Mariko were jovial throughout the graduation ceremony. Stella dressed in a cream dress and complimenting floral jacket and cream shoes. Joy had bought a wide cream cap that she insisted her mother wear, against her will. Mariko was clad in a grey suit, white shirt, and black necktie. He wore black leather shoes.

Mariko brought laughter to the crowd when he heard Joy's name called out, "Joyce Mari-ko," as was the tradition during graduation. On hearing `Mariko,' he stood up, looked around and sat down, sending the crowd into laughter, with some clapping for him.

Two days after the graduation ceremony, the family gathered to discuss the next event, meeting with Richie's parents.

Sophia, not wanting to argue with her father, which could spoil his joyous mood since Joy's graduation on

Friday, chose her words carefully. "Papa, I am sorry. If that is what you prefer, Richie's parents will come to the village. My idea was just a suggestion, to relieve you from the task of preparing for visitors, a week after your travel, and a week before Christmas."

Mariko did not hesitate. "Remember, you have very few relatives in the city. The visitors must come home, be received by my mother, my cousins, and other relatives. How else will they know that you come from a home, a family with many wonderful people?"

Sophia was convinced by her father's explanation. She knew that it would be fitting, for Richie's parents to arrive at her village, meet with more than fifty people, so she said. "I fully understand your point. Let them come to our family home as earlier planned."

She looked at her father, and when she did not notice any strained facial expression, she added, "I am open to any decision you make. If you want to meet with them, just to get to know one another before they officially come to our home, I will find a hotel for the meeting.

If you decide that you need your brother and some of your cousins to be present, we can ask Uncle Justus in the city, and two of your cousins from the village to travel to the city."

Joy left for the kitchen and returned with a thermal flask of tea and refilled everyone's cup without asking if they needed more tea.

The family engaged in general discussions as they drank afternoon tea. Later, Sophia cleared dishes from the table and joined Joy in the kitchen to prepare dinner.

While in the kitchen, Sophia sent an SMS to Joy, standing right next to her in the kitchen. "I am very anxious, pray that Dad gives in."

Joy read, smiled, and typed back. "You did very well, gave Dad all the power that he likes to have. I hear them talking, stay here. I have a feeling he will agree to a meeting in the city." Joy clicked send.

Sophia waited for three minutes before she moved to one side of the kitchen and read the message from Joy.

Sophia typed a message to Richie, "I will see your parents at my village on the 18th. Dad prefers to face Chairman with the support of his relatives." She clicked send, put her phone on top of the fridge and went to wash dishes while Joy prepared dinner.

After a short while, Joy moved closer to Sophia and asked, "I thought you sent me a message, did my phone refuse to receive it?"

Sophia, running more water than necessary to rinse a cup, said, "That was to the guy, to get him to panic with me."

Silas arrived home as Joy and Sophia set dinner on the dining table.

As the family ate, discussions centered on Silas' studies and Joy's plans now that she had completed her study program at university.

After they cleared the dining table, Joy picked up an envelope from the coffee table, announcing that her graduation photos were ready, handing the photos to her parents. She explained that the studio ones would be ready towards the end of the coming week, when her parents would have already left for the village.

Mariko vacated his chair, saying, "Maybe not," as he excused himself, saying he needed to go and chat with their good neighbour before retiring to bed.

Sophia had asked one of their neighbours with a spare bedroom to allow Mariko to sleep in their house. For cultural reasons, Mariko cannot sleep in the house of his daughter.

Stella waited for some minutes, to be sure that Mariko was out of earshot before she turned to Sophia with a smile. "He agreed. He will talk with two of his cousins to travel here. You need to arrange for Silas to send them money for transport. Not you. You hear that?"

Sophia grinned while nodding her head to yes. Stella wished them to a good night and went to her bedroom. Joy had vacated her bedroom for her mother. Joy would sleep in Sophia's bedroom.

After her mother had closed the bedroom door, Sophia went to the kitchen, picked her phone, and read a new message, which was in the form of an emoji, a sad face from Richie. She typed a response. "Please do not notify your parents yet, wait until tomorrow, or the day after."

She clicked send and left for her bedroom, as Silas entered the kitchen to wash dishes.

Chapter 40

Two days later, Sophia informed Richie that she secured the common room at her apartment building, as the venue for the parents' meeting.

She organized for a food caterer to deliver tea and African food for lunch, food items close to what her family would have served in the village.

Later in the evening, after the parents' meeting, Mwasimba called Richie into the living room, to update him on decisions made at the meeting. A session where Richie and Sophia did not attend, as their culture dictates.

Mwasimba looked at Richie. "They refused any compensation in exchange for their daughter…,"

Richie's forehead broke into a sweat. He saw the walls of the house spin round and round. The only thing that saved him was a nearby chair that he sank into. His father must have noticed the sweat and saw the need to rescue his son from a medical emergency, so he added, "But they agreed to give her to us."

Richie tried to collect himself, without much success. In his mind, how could they refuse dowry for Sophia, and then give her to them? The norm was that a family received dowry in exchange for their daughter.

Refusing to receive compensation was another way of saying they were unwilling to let Richie marry Sophia.

As Richie lifted his heavy head to face his father for further elucidations, his mother walked in with a food tray holding a tea flask, three cups, a sugar dish, and silver spoons. Patience placed the tray on a nearby coffee table and turned to Richie with a smile. "Congratulations son, for getting a wife. That family is honourable in their own way."

Richie turned in the direction of his mother as she served tea. He reconciled the words from his parents and felt a little bit better.

Unlike his father, who normally took time to explain things, using the boardroom style, his mother was straight to the point.

Mwasimba sat upright on his recliner massage chair, and looked at his wife, impatiently, as she continued. "Can you believe they are willing to give their daughter, that hard working girl, without any recompense?"

Richie picked a cup of tea, holding it with both hands to quell his shaky hands. He looked at his father and could tell that his father had seen the unsure expression on his son's face.

Mwasimba explained. "Mzee Mariko gave a reason, which at first appeared unconvincing, but now, on further reflection, it makes a lot of sense."

Patience chuckled, her lips parted, like she wanted to say something but did not. Her action confused Richie, who turned and looked at his father. He noticed the raised hand, Mwasimba's signal for Patience to stop interrupting.

Mwasimba took over the talking. "Aaah! I now see you have a tongue to talk, after you and your friends stayed mum at the meeting." He chuckled. "Let me give the information as received. You were noticeably quiet. Were you even listening to the conversation?"

Patience looked at her husband and laughed. "Surprise, surprise. I listened to every word and every thought at the meeting, while you and your cousins were busy getting worked up..."

"Mmhhh?" Mwasimba made the questioning sound, prompting Patience to say more. "How, an opportunity has been pulled from right under your nose. Another chance for you to prove to the world that Mwasimba reigns."

Mwasimba laughed loudly. "Ooh, you almost caught me there—" He stopped talking when the outside door to the living room opened and Michael and Bill walked in.

Michael walked right up to Richie. "Congratulations, man. They refused all the Mwasimba riches, means you will have some good change from Dad's budget."

Bill patted Richie on the shoulder. "Very close, almost joining our club of men," After which he took a few strides and sat on a chair next to his father.

Patience left and minutes later returned with another tea flask and cups for Michael and Bill.

The four men remained quiet, until Patience finished serving tea, took her seat and picked her cup of tea. Then Mwasimba spoke. "The explanation was from her father...," he paused, looked at Richie and continued. "My son, with that one you have no chance to play around. Once you say, 'I do,' just stick with her."

Richie massaged the back of his neck while his father spoke. "Otherwise, her father will be at your doorstep in no time."

Patience cut in. "To take away his beloved daughter from you. Wherever these people come from, they have strong family values."

Mwasimba explained the reasoning behind Mariko's decision on dowry. To Mariko, if he accepted the compensation, it would imply that he had sold his daughter to the Mwasimba family.

Mariko preferred that Sophia and Richie entered a marriage based on their defined agreement, rather than the parents receiving some dowry. Accepting any compensation would amount to blocking his daughter from ever helping her family.

Mwasimba turned to Richie. "Son, did you hear those words. Have they sunk into your head? Good to know what the words mean. Mariko prefers that his daughter continues to work and support them as she wishes. Just keep that in mind."

Richie nodded in agreement as Michael and Bill laughed, prompting Mwasimba to add. "I know, like your brothers here, you plan to talk her out of employment. Keep what I said in mind as you negotiate with her."

Patience, who seemed to have been waiting impatiently, said. "If I were you, I would avoid the chat about work, until after a baby is on the way. Babies will gently drive her out of an office, as they have done to many other women."

Patience saw one of the house staff by the door. She left to find out what the staff needed.

Michael stood, excused himself to leave, he had another function to attend. He looked at Richie. "If you continue with the same fortitude, next year will be even better. You have so far proved yourself under my mentorship."

Michael turned to his father, while addressing Richie. "Chairman should give you a pro-motion if you promise to stop the flower game." He patted Richie on the shoulder, before he walked out of the living room, to his car parked outside.

The rest of the family engaged in general talk as they ate supper. After dessert, Bill and Richie gave their excuses and left.

Mwasimba walked into the home library and Patience followed him. They drank wine while chatting about family related matters.

As the clock on the wall ticked to 11:00pm, Mwasimba cleared his throat and turned to his wife. "Never underestimate village people. That family is more complex and has stronger family values than what I had anticipated."

Patience sipped her wine, taking time to swallow before asking. "When would you have time for us to visit Mariko at his home, lest he changes his mind?"

Mwasimba, now standing up, looked at his wife. "I do not remember cancelling our appointment of December 18th, or did you? If you did, it means I will leave you in the city."

He walked out of the library, to the corridor leading to their bedroom.

Patience put away the half-full bottle of wine, switched off the lights and followed her husband.

Chapter 41

Mariko thanked his daughters for making him proud. But he did not explain if making him proud meant his oldest child would get married soon, or his second born just graduated from university, or both.

Whatever he meant, Sophia was grateful for the peace that had prevailed since her parents arrived in the city, two weeks back.

Sophia requested her parents to send her younger brothers to the city for Christmas. Mariko did not make any commitment. "I will think about your request, though the boys must assure me that this good life will not get into their heads and alter their determination towards university."

Mariko held one view, that if his younger sons stayed at Sophia's apartment, equipped with modern entertainment facilities, they might assume that life will always be that comfortable, and may stop working hard at school.

He addressed Sophia, "I see you have worked extremely hard and lifted yourself out of the poverty you were born into, your brothers should not come here and be con-fused by your achievements. They need to work hard for theirs."

Joy interrupted her father. "It could be the other way around. Once the boys see all the big buildings and good life in the city, they might work harder at school, to qualify and join the university in the city, as Silas did."

"As I said, I will think about the request," Mariko said.

Stella and Silas, engaged in a side conversation, stopped when Mariko called out, "Silas. I guess university will close before the 18th."

Silas raised thumbs up to his father, who then continued to talk. "I will need you and Joy to come home, some days before the visitors arrive. I hope you do not expect your mother to run up and down serving the city people."

Silas looked at Sophia. "Boys to serve food?" prompting Mariko to add. "Who said you would serve food? That has always been a role reserved for your aunts and many cousins. See you at home."

Joy smiled while looking at Sophia. "Count me in. I will come, for that means a new dress and shoes from my sister."

Stella looked at Joy, and as she opened her mouth to say something, Joy spoke, "None of my outfits are worthy enough for welcoming city people."

Mariko looked at Joy, shook his head and walked away, to talk with Silas.

Later in the evening, Stella called to inform her children that they traveled safely back to the village and were incredibly grateful for the fantastic reception they received while in the city. While talking with Joy, she cautioned her. "You must copy the good behaviour of your sister. Stop your behaviour of walking out of the house when the sun goes down and coming back as the sun readies to rise."

Joy shouted into the phone. "What?"

Stella continued. "You kept me awake throughout the night, on that Wednesday, before your graduation day."

While still on the phone, Joy turned and looked at Sophia and said, "Yes Mum."

Joy completed the telephone conversation then laughed out aloud. She went and stood right in front of Sophia. "I made a mistake. You owe me more than the bottle of wine you pro-vided at my graduation party."

"Wine? I thought you asked me to import a dress for you in the next few days."

"Now that Mum has turned her policing to me. Remember the day your fiancé took me to learn about members' clubs in the city?"

Sophia looked at Joy without blinking, hoping to hear more.

Silas looked at Joy, then Sophia before he chuckled and walked away, saying, "I need to go cry, for the entertainment I will miss when Sophia becomes Richie's wife, and Joy sneaks out for the night."

Joy ran after Silas as he scurried away and quickly closed his bedroom door behind him. Joy walked back to the living room, and finding Sophia gone, followed her to the bedroom.

Joy looked at her. "I have more news," as she walked to the wardrobe and started to sift through Sophia's clothes.

"I am not giving away my clothes, if that's what you are after." Sophia said.

Busy retrieving and hanging clothes back, Joy asked casually. "Have you heard from Mum, the report about that teacher, Cleophas, in the village?"

"What about the teacher, is he still waiting for me?" Sophia chuckled.

"You got me wrong, that is not what I wanted to say." Joy stood on her toes to place a folded skirt on the top shelf of the wardrobe. "Mum mentioned that the teacher is a father, of a three-year-old boy."

Sophia lifted both hands and held them across her chest.

Joy, busy admiring clothes, did not notice the expression on Sophia's face as Joy continued. "People can be mean. Imagine, Dad has been in touch with the father of the teacher, yet he never mentioned that his son already had a wife at home."

Joy clicked. "Was that man planning to make you his school wife, while he had a village wife? He better prays I don't cross paths with him when I travel home."

"Poor three-year-old child." Sophia lamented. "Imagine if I had given in to the pressure from Dad, just to make life unbearable for another woman, the teacher's wife."

Joy walked away from the wardrobe. She turned to Sophia and said, "Promise me, tonight you will take a careful look at your calendar and give Mum the best weekend for your wedding."

Could Sophia object?

Chapter 42

Richie waited by the elevator. He was leaning on the opposite wall, with hands crossed on his chest, and legs at the ankles.

He gawked at Sophia as she hurried to the elevator. He did not stop looking until she arrived, pressed the down arrow, and held his hand. "You look too relaxed for a Friday, where on earth do you get such energy?"

Richie had changed into casual black trousers and a woolen brown sweater, which he had unzipped to the second button, to reveal a matching shirt.

The elevator doors opened and the two stepped in as Richie said, "Do not tell me you have not seen that graph," prompting Sophia to tilt her head upwards, to see his face.

She paused and inhaled his fresh cologne, as he continued. "I will email you a copy, but here's a summary. Old people, like Chairman," he winked at her. "and your boss, fall on the extreme left of the graph. They are very energetic from Monday to Wednesday. Us, the younger ones, we tend to start on the right side of the graph; wide awake from Wednesday, and very tired on Mondays."

Sophia burst out with laughter before asking, "Headed home or following me as I go for drinks with my friends?"

The elevator chimed basement. Richie encircled his hand around Sophia's waist and guided her out while saying, "Please, meet your friends on Wednesdays, the reason it is called ladies night. I will follow you to your house. After, we will proceed to your place of choice for drinks and dinner." Her face brightened up, more from the thoughts in her head, and not the words from Richie.

When her eyes landed on Richie waiting for her near the elevator, he was stunning and captivated her into wanting to be by his side the whole evening. He was the reason she was ready to cancel her social meeting and disappoint her friends.

Sophia looked at Elvin, who was waiting for her by a nearby company car, and then back at Richie.

Richie got her non-verbal message and waved to Elvin. "Sophia just told me today is Friday, I will drive her home, if that is okay with you." He retrieved a car key out of the knee side pocket of his trousers.

Elvin smiled. "I can't interfere with that. I know she will be in safe hands." He got into the Mercedes Benz and drove off to a nearby parking spot.

Richie and Sophia walked to his car, the latest BMW model, with a sunroof. He had parked at the far end of the parking garage. He opened the passenger door for her before he walked around to the driver's side.

On their drive home, Sophia called three of her friends to excuse herself from their scheduled tea meeting and window-shopping.

She put the phone back into her handbag and turned to Richie. "When is your birthday? I need to buy you a special phone," prompting Richie to glance at her and back to the road, as she continued, "That way you will be able to call me, days in advance about tea and dinner."

While focused on the road ahead, Richie replied, "Thanks. Let me book you right away. Next week Wednesday, our dinner will be at my parents' house. While there I will ask Mum when I was born."

Sophia landed a soft slap on Richie's thigh. He chuckled as he negotiated through the Fri-day evening traffic.

On arrival at Sophia's house, Richie and Silas sat at the dining table and played cards until Sophia appeared from her bedroom. She had showered and changed into an evening dress. She had put on her favorite sexy but subtle Alai dress. It was white with a pleated skirt that shouted vivacity with every step of her lavender flat shoes.

Richie took one look at her and threw the cards in his hand on the table and said to Silas. "I was going to win, but now you win. I must leave before your sister changes her mind." He walked towards Sophia.

As they walked downstairs and into the car, Sophia was glad, that now she could go somewhere without worries of when her mother would call and ask her tough questions about marriage and her future.

There was still traffic on the road, so it was approaching seven in the evening when Richie turned into the Windsa Country Club parking as Sophia said, "You surprise me. Don't you know of any other place in this big city that serves drinks, other than these clubs?"

Richie switched off the engine and walked around. He opened her door and as she stepped out, he circled his hand round her waist. She tilted her head upwards and kissed him.

They walked towards the entrance to the building as he explained. "I know a lot of places in this city. Remember, you were to name a place of your choice, instead, you burdened me with the task." They stepped into the club.

Richie acknowledged the lady at the reception desk before scanning his membership card. Sophia took advantage of the release from Richie's grasp, turned, and liked what she saw in a nearby full-length mirror. There and then, she promised herself that she would not let anyone at the club spoil her evening.

Immediately they stepped inside one of the drinking sections of the club, eyes turned to Richie and Sophia by his arm.

Sophia felt like everyone was looking at her. She wondered if she would always be a stranger at the members' clubs, attracting attention whenever she arrived. She felt comforted by Richie's hand on the small of her back.

No sooner had they sat down, a group of ladies and men crowded their table. A few uttered in-audible greetings to Sophia, as one lady asked. "Richie, is she a foreigner, though her face says she originates from this country?"

On hearing the words, Sophia thanked herself for the outfit she had carefully selected for the evening, to give her the courage she needed, in case anyone confronted her, while she enjoyed her evening with Richie.

Sophia tried her best to join in the discussions of the ladies at their table, though she found the topics, talking about other club patrons, uninteresting.

After dinner, Richie extended his hand to Sophia. "Let us go greet some important people around here." Sophia used his hand as support to stand from her seat, as he addressed the people at their table, "We will be back for dessert."

They walked away, stopping at several tables where Richie introduced Sophia as his fiancée.

Sophia was keen during each introduction. Surprised by the many people Richie knew at the club as he introduced each person by name. He referred to some as auntie or uncle.

She kept a smile as she extended a hand to anyone who did the same, and she noted the displeasure from some of the women and men.

Doubt started to creep back into Sophia. She questioned if she had made the right decision, of letting Richie's parents travel to her home. A visit that she later learnt, had halted regular activities at the village, as relatives and friends asked to help with cooking or join in the celebration.

Sophia knew that it would be hard for her to withdraw from the on-going wedding preparations. Then she wondered why so many people, especially young women seemed to be annoyed that Richie had chosen her.

An idea came to her mind, and before she could consider if that was the right thing to do, she pulled away from Richie's grasp.

Before Richie could collect himself into what was happening, Sophia encircled her hands around his neck and kissed him for a long moment. Richie returned the kiss. She only pulled away after the handclapping by people in the club reduced.

Back at their table, Sophia ate all her dessert, a chocolate ganache. She remained overly excited and friendly throughout the evening. At one point, Richie left her and walked to a table at the far end of the room, where he sat down for a chat with an elderly couple.

Sophia looked each person in the eye whenever they directed questions at her. "Richie is such a fine man, where did he find you?" One lady asked, with a sneer.

"We found each other at the university and have never stopped loving one another," was how she answered the question.

"Ooh, you also attended the local university?"

Sophia chuckled. "We now work at the Mwasimba Group of Companies, as very competent employees."

An hour later, Richie returned to their table, placed a hand on Sophia's shoulder and kissed her on the mouth.

It was past 3:00am when Richie and Sophia drove out of the Club. As he walked her back to her apartment, she was happy, at peace with herself. Richie too appeared content, maybe because their visit to the club had ended on a happy note for Sophia, or because he would soon have her as his wife.

Chapter 43

The rich, or money can do wonders. Sophia was thoughtful as she looked at herself in the full-length mirror for the tenth time. And she liked her wedding gown, and herself in the dress even more.

Sophia was reflective. Unlike stories she had heard, of how the wedding couple took leave from work to organize their wedding–raise funds, fitting and refitting gowns, purchase flowers, book halls and caterers, and organize transport for relatives traveling from faraway places to the wedding. Her experience was different.

She hardly missed a day of work, except the four days of leave she took before her wed-ding day. Patty had insisted that, as the bride to be, she needed a rest, which Sophia quickly discovered meant spending time at places where specialized people reawakened her body.

Under the guidance of Patty, Joy and Tishia, her cousin and best bride's maid, Sophia found herself at different salons; for a massage, manicure, pedicure, exfoliation hair wash and set, and facials.

By Friday, Sophia felt like her twenty-five-year-old body had been replaced by a new one. Her only source of comfort was that inside, internally, she felt like the same old Sophia Mariko. Her soul and determination were intact.

She looked at herself in the mirror again. She had not come to terms with how easy it had been to find such a lovely gown. It was one afternoon in February while with Patty, Joy and Tishia.

They had driven out under the guidance of Patty, to a wedding boutique, hidden at one of the high-end stores in the city suburbs. That was after long arguments, Sophia wanting to visit boutique stores she knew within the city center, while Patty wanted them to start with boutiques in the suburbs. Patty and Joy won on the boutique to visit.

Sophia, knowing that Kevin, her brother would soon be in the city to start his degree program, had no plan to exceed her budget of two thousand dollars for the wedding gown. A figure she had increased after Beauta insisted that she would pay for the wedding cake, her personal gift to the bride.

Joy had made it hard for Sophia to argue about the cost of her wedding gown. Joy had insisted that Sophia should forget about tuition fees for now and make her once in a lifetime celebration, her best; unless she had plans of getting married again.

Recalling the last two words from Joy brought a sweat to Sophia's forehead. She wondered if that was the message she would be sending to guests at her wedding, if she had chosen the wedding gown she could afford.

Patty had added to Sophia's money worries, by taking her to a wedding boutique which stocked very likeable but expensive wedding gowns.

Sophia had spent the afternoon being pulled in and out of gowns by two boutique attendants, who appeared to know Patty well. Acknowledging how lively and friendly Patty had been to her since she arrived at Akoth Towers, Sophia had assumed that Patty's friendliness with the boutique staff to be her usual friendly nature.

The fitting took place in a large room, lacking in furniture, except for walls lined with mirrors, and one leather bench, for the bride to be, to see how she would appear in her dress when seated. The third item was the lengthy hanger rack holding what must have been twenty wedding dresses.

By the time Sophia had arrived back in her apartment, after 6:00pm, she was not only tired, but in debt. The boutique owner had insisted that she buy the dress she liked most, pay whatever money she had in her budget, and clear the remaining within twenty-four months. A deal that Sophia found so enticing that she accepted the expensive, but lovely gown.

When it was time to leave the boutique, Sophia had been troubled when told that she would leave the gown at the boutique. A staff from the boutique would visit her house once a week, to retake her measurements, until one day before the wedding day.

On the wedding day, two staff from the boutique would turn up to help Sophia dress. The wedding gown had to fit right, that way, the boutique would keep its reputation as the best, not only in the country, but the region.

A similar message was given to her line-up of bridesmaids and several children, chosen to balance the line of men: Sam as Richie's best man, Sophia's four brothers, Nick, Bill and their three cousins.

~ ~ ~ ~ ~ ~

"Sophia. Time for the bride to walk down the aisle." The words startled Sophia from her thoughts.

She felt her legs wobble. She looked up into the high ceiling of the dressing room of the church and inhaled three long puffs of air.

With tears brimming in her eyes, she looked at her parents, Stella to her right and Mariko on her left.

Sophia said an internal thank you, to whoever thought of the bride's walk-in strategy. She would need the extra support from her parents, each holding her by the elbow, to walk down the long church aisle, to the altar, where Richie was waiting for her.

One look at the large church, now without a single empty seat, Sophia understood the importance of the day. Seeing all those people who had come to be witnesses, as she made her wedding vows with Richie.

On her walk down the aisle, Sophia took a glance at the congregation. She noticed some familiar faces of family members, some people from the clubs, women, men, and children, dressed in beautiful attire, for her day.

She walked on, while in thought, almost accepting that the ladies from the club, many of them present in the church, would be part of her now extended family. Some would return to the clubs the next day, chastising one another, complaining, then importing dresses and turning up for another wedding, just as they had for hers.

She thought of how competitive the ladies and some men were. On further thought, she concluded that that was how their families managed to thrive in business, through competition. The thought on being competitive gave Sophia more courage to walk on, towards Richie, waiting for her at the altar.

Feeling the hands of her parents on her right and left arms, Sophia steadied her step. Encouraged by her new thought, that throughout her life, she had not let anyone down—her parents, her teachers, her boss, her friends, and her siblings. In no way was she going to let Richie down. She arrived by his side, and the wedding ceremony began. She was glad that for once everyone was waiting for her.

The groom smiled on hearing the words, `you may now kiss the bride.' After the kiss, which Richie extended, like he had no plans of stopping, Sophia opened her eyes and looked at the people seated past Richie's shoulder, on the front row. Her eyes met with very joyful faces. Beauta standing next to Michael, Georgina on the right side of Patience with Mwasimba on her left side. She saw Liz, Patty, and many colleagues from Akoth Towers. She felt two tears escape from her eyes, tears of happiness, on seeing her new family.

Sophia had a beaming smile as they walked out of church. Part of the delight was from remembering that everyone present was there to give her support, especially her parents when she nervously marched towards the altar, and now Richie, as they walked out as husband and wife.

The couple paused for photos. Many in attendance seeking to appear in one of the pictures. By that time, Sophia had forgotten about the fear that had weighed down her legs as she walked into church earlier on.

Chapter 44

On their drive to the wedding reception at the Windsa Country Club, Sophia was tempted to ask her husband, if other vehicles were diverted from the road, for their wedding entourage. But she did not ask, instead, she spent the time chatting with her bridal party, spaced out in the long limousine.

On arrival at the reception grounds, Sophia took a moment to take in the transformed fields of the club she had visited before. The fields now transformed into a new theme with tents, chairs, tables, and cake all matched her wedding colours.

As Sophia and Richie danced to the tent reserved for the bride, groom, and their wedding entourage, she asked Kevin to make sure her parents were comfortable, especially Sabrina their maternal grandmother.

From her elevated seat, Sophia watched her parents with satisfaction. Her mother and aunties were all smiles, though what Sophia valued most was the expression of satisfaction on her father's face.

Sophia appreciated that Mariko walked tall and sat upright. Within the few years Sophia had been in employment, her father's appearance had transformed, from one of poverty, into one to compete with any working-class man. She could now tell where her brothers got their handsome features from, and her eyes, and Joy's flat nose.

Her line of thought vanished when she felt Richie's hand on her chin, and before she could think of what he was up to, he planted a kiss on her lips, to loud applauding from the guests. He then voiced his reason. "Not the day to stare at your family. I am the one."

She whispered back. "Thanks. I was lost in thought, wondering what my father could be thinking about."

Richie squeezed her hand. "You want to hear a man's point of view, my father-in-law is beyond happiness and satisfaction. And you are the one who has brought it all to him."

She squeezed Richie's hand while thanking him for the reassurance.

As the guests enjoyed the sumptuous four course meal, Sophia beckoned Joy and asked her to talk Bibi, their seventy-five-year-old paternal grandmother, to eat some food.

Bibi sent Joy back with a song.

Bibi, who had received her culturally prescribed goats in December when Richie's parents visited Sophia's home, had not tired from dancing. To her, Sophia needed praises, not only for getting married the proper way by not eloping, but also looking incredibly beautiful in her wedding dress. Bibi instantly created a song, saying that she was satisfied from happiness and should be left to dance.

During the cutting of the cake, Sophia was surprised to hear Patty refer to Patience as auntie, and Patience's sister as Mum. Okay, she now got it, her best friend from the office was Richie's first cousin.

Richie gave the guests a reason to laugh aloud when he challenged Bibi to a dance. The crowd was very entertained and could not stop laughing and applauding.

After two songs, Bibi sent Richie away. "I see you have energy and are handsome, now go. I do not want to see you…"

The reception grounds went quiet, except for the few birds humming their happiness, as they pecked on food droplets from the expansive reception grounds.

The quietness did not last long, Bibi completed her sentence, "Until next year when you bring forth my first great grandchild."

The reception grounds vibrated with thunderous laughter.

Richie smiled, a knowing smile, that their fast-approaching honeymoon, an overnight flight away, was sanctified by an old wise woman.

Chapter 45

After ten days away, Sophia and Richie flew back from their honeymoon. They were blissful, after days and nights of endless discoveries of beaches in the Seychelles, their bodies, their shared likes, dislikes, jokes and more.

They also spent time marveling at the waterfront resort with its glass-covered floors, revealing hidden ocean features: a stream by the side of their bed, a Jacuzzi with marine life covered by a transparent glass base, white below the floor of their living room, and oceanic themes on walls.

Back in Nairobi, Richie informed Sophia that they would be living in the north wing of his parent's house.

"Woi woi. My dear husband. What are you telling me, that at your age, you have been residing at your parents' house?"

He cuddled her. "I doubt if you want to take up residence at the Akoth Towers. Anyway, my older brothers did the same, stayed at home with their wives for some time."

Sophia looked at Richie, confusion written all over her face, so he explained. "A family tradition. Once the

Mwasimba boys were in high school and tired of waking up early to be driven to school, Chairman allowed us to occupy his penthouse, at the very top of Akoth Towers."

"What? There is a house above the executive boardroom?"

"That top floor has been my weekday house for years, since high school. It will now re-main Nick's residence. Do you still want to reside at the source of your daily flowers?"

"You know what, residing in the city center sounds interesting." She chuckled, smoothing a hand down his arm. "It means I will be able to put in more hours on my PA tasks."

Richie cuddled her. "No way. Please relegate work and PA tasks to the bottom of your list of priorities."

The End

One last request

Book reviews help other readers to find books. If you enjoyed reading this novel, please go to your online book retailer and write a few sentences on what you liked about *The Girl who Left the Village.* Thank you for your support.

About the Author

K is for Kwamboka

Eileen K. Omosa, Ph.D., writes novels on change and adaptation. She applies knowledge and skills gained from over fifteen years of work experience in the natural re-sources management sector in Africa. She has facilitated projects on conflict management, forestry, and food security, mainstreaming gender into natural resources management, land tenure and access rights for sustainable livelihoods, among other topics.

Eileen grew up in rural Kenya until the day she packed that grey suitcase for the city to pursue university education, and she has never stopped traveling the world. On her way to the North Pole, she made a long stopover in Canada where she attained a PhD in Rural and Environmental Sociology.

Since 2016, she has published nine contemporary romance novels set in Africa. The novels will get you reflective on development-related issues, including, if education opens more doors or conflicts for the African woman, and if the women ever find a balance be-tween career and cultural expectations? She follows immigrants to their destinations and explores how they establish and maintain romantic relationships in their new country.

When Eileen is not at her writing desk, she will be found outdoors implementing re-search on household food security, the reason she cultivates vegetables in her city. Visit her online at EileenOmosa.com

Join my growing list of fans at EileenOmosa.com to be among the first to hear of my next title, or other information of interest.

Books by the Author

An African Woman's Journey Series

1. The Girl Who Left the Village
2. The Secret He Never Told Her
3. The Woman She Became
4. The House Girl Becoming Angela
5. Nyawira the Inheritor
6. Bonuke the Enemy's Daughter
7. An African Woman's Journey Boxset 1

An Immigrant's Marriage Series:

1. The Fear Within Us
2. The Family Between Us
3. The Love Within Us (2021)

Join my growing list of fans at EileenOmosa.com to be among the first to hear of my next title, or other information of interest.

Below is a preview of the novels

Book 2: The Secret he Never Told Her

His wife staying in employment will reflect negatively on his capability, but resigning will stall her career goals. Can they ever find a middle ground?

In less than two years, Sophia has hauled her family out of poverty. Satisfied with the outcome of her hard work, she's focused on building a career with a stable income when Richie asks her to resign from her job and become a stay-at-home-mom.

Richie cannot envision his wife struggling to balance the tasks of wife, mother, and employee. He asks Sophia to stay at home, provide the comfort he needs to work hard at his job, and earn enough money to cater for the financial needs of his family.

Sophia cannot imagine life without her job, the way to grow her career, realize her dreams.

How will Richie convince Sophia that he has enough wealth for his wife not to work a single day, yet Sophia is determined to prove that a woman can balance her professional and family life?

The Secret he Never told Her is book two in the Series, An African Woman's Journey. Sophia's story starts in The Girl who Left the Village and concludes in The Woman She Became. A trilogy where education, culture, ambition, and love intertwine.

Book 3: The Woman She Became

Can Sophia transition into her new family without sacrificing something personal

Sophia and Richie leave their baby behind and go for a holiday to celebrate Richie's promotion at work and to prepare for Sophia's imminent return to work. Little did she know the journey would transform her career and family life.

While in the USA, Richie reconnects with James, his long-gone brother, but fails to convince him to return home. Sophia steps in and persuades James, unaware of the momentous favour she's done Richie's family. Did she get too busy to mind her well-being?

Sophia becomes reflective on what it means to lead a happy and satisfactory life, the kind she envisioned. She finds the answer and realizes she's always had it on her long journey of searching for empowerment and social change.

Does she welcome the WOMAN she's become?

The Woman She Became is book three in the series, An African Woman's Journey. Sophia's story starts in The Girl who Left the Village, followed by The Secret he Never told Her. A trilogy where education, culture, ambition, and love intertwine.

Book 4: The House girl Becoming Angela

Angela cannot afford to lose this job of house girl to Ronny's children, no matter what his sister or mother-in-law say or do. But can she change her title to Wife?

Ronny Kipchoge's well-balanced domestic sphere tilts, rendering him a single parent to three young children. One year of residing with his parents gives him the child-care support he needs to perform his CEO tasks. But now he must leave for his house, give his mother time to care for his ailing father. Schools will reopen in two weeks; the reason Ronny has no patience when his sister interrupts him with her criteria on why he should not hire Angela as the nanny for his children.

Angela desperately needs a job to provide for her son and save for her lifelong dream of a university education. While Ronny fumbles through grief and work, Angela, his twenty-three-year-old nanny, "mothers" his children so well that he has ideas on how to make her stay forever. But the more Ronny tries, the more he draws Angela into a web of struggles at his house, as friends and family are eager to get Angela out of the picture.

Will Ronny and Angela let outsiders dampen the growing at-traction between them, or can they combine forces to over-come the challenges and live a HEA in this clean second chance romance?

Book 5: Nyawira the Inheritor

He's hesitant of women from wealthy families, she terrified of marrying to please her parents. But when their paths cross at a gym, can they resist their hearts' desires in this forbidden romance?

Odhiambo, a gym instructor, has sworn off women from affluent families after his fiancée was taken away to marry a well-off man. When he's hired to help Nyawira shape into a centerpiece at her unavoidable wedding, he senses trouble. The moment he extends a hand to welcome her into the gym, a warm tingle runs up his spine, only arrested by Cynthia's scowl. He dismisses the feeling—nothing can work between him and Redempta.

Nyawira is focused on her career when Cynthia reminds her, she's running out of time to get married. Turning down the wealthy men chosen for her is tough, but nothing compared to telling her mother she's in love with her gym trainer, and Odhiambo is in debt.

When Nyawira and Odhiambo dine at a location of the city Cynthia would not approve of, her body, mind, and taste buds awaken. She's in love with Odhiambo and he wants to take the risk, again. Now Odhiambo must decide if it's worth the trouble to marry a billionaire's daughter when he's in debt?

This book is for you if you've been looking for a clean con-temporary romance on what it takes to marry across the tracks.

Book 6: Bonuke the Enemy's Daughter

What if she returns home with the man she cannot live with-out, and her parents cannot live with?

Bonuke Kebaso has envisioned a career in the solar industry as the way to gain independence from her parents. Determined to complete her university study program, she forgoes her comfort in the city for field research at a solar farm in a re-mote area of Maasai Mara. Everything is going according to plan, until a helicopter lands and Jade, the son of her father's enemy, jogs down the ladder.

Jade Momina has lived his adult life driving flashy cars in Nairobi. But when he calls off his arranged marriage and be-comes the front-page story in the media, his father gives him one option—run, get busy at a family road construction project until the media find their next popular story. Bad press will crumble Momina's success as a politician and business owner. When the helicopter lands, Jade pauses long enough to rest a hand on his pounding heart, thankful. If the person he sees beyond the dusty airstrip is Bonuke, he's ready to forgive his father for banishing him to Maasai Mara.

The sensible action for Bonuke is to call her father to airlift her back to Nairobi. But she will not, completing the field study is her only means to financial freedom from her parents, and seeing Jade only reminds her of their stolen kiss nine years ago. Three months at a remote work site rekindles her feelings, and she falls into Jade's open arms.

Can the two lovebirds overpower the combined forces of their feuding families to live a HEA in this clean contemporary romance?

An Immigrant's Marriage Trilogy

Book 1: The Fear Within Us

She's fearful of strangers. He's focused on growing his business. But when a snowstorm delays their travel, will they open their hearts or resist, let fear control their destiny in this holiday romance?

Abikok never expected to go through another terrifying road trip since her family's escape from South Sudan. When a snowstorm diverts her plane to Saskatoon, she must put aside her fear of strangers and share a car with Omondi to Edmonton if she wants to make it home for Christmas.

Omondi has lived his adult life accumulating wealth as his means to happiness. He's now ready to marry, but his fear that women will interpret any proposition he makes as harassment stops him from approaching prospective partners. When he carpools with Abikok, he realizes she is the woman he's been in search of. But how will he overcome his fear of rejection? Dare he ask her to be more than just a friend?

Abikok and Omondi take a risk that could change their lives. When their six-hour trip to Edmonton turns into three days, they take their best option and pretend to be a couple while they shelter at the homes of strangers. Can they nurture the growing attraction between them into a lifelong relationship, or will they let fear control their destiny in this chance romance?

The Fear Within Us is the first book in Abikok and Omondi's trilogy. The story continues in *The Family Between Us* and concludes in *The Love Within Us*.

Book 2: The Family Between Us

He is determined to marry in the summer. She's excited to meet his parents. But when Omondi's father offers an alternative woman, will he tell Abikok or run, tug her along, away from the truth?

Tourism industry millionaire David Omondi is eager to present Abikok to his parents—they have never stopped asking when he will marry. Omondi is certain his father will organize a party to welcome his fiancée home. They will like Abikok, no one has ever contradicted his decisions and choices.

Abikok is excited to travel to Kenya and meet with Omondi's parents, though her father disapproves of her engagement. She has entertained the idea to abandon her family and become part of Omondi's. A fearful thought, as she loves her parents and siblings.

… until they arrive home.

Omondi's father has a "better" woman for him to marry, and he has organized for Omondi to meet with the father of the woman. Omondi attends the meeting to shame the two elderly men. Little did he know it would kick-start his running from his village, town, holiday resort, and Ken-ya. Will he find a safe place to pause? Should he tell Abikok why they are fleeing in this contemporary romance?

The Family Between Us is the second book in Omondi and Abikok's trilogy which starts with *The Fear Within Us* and concludes with *The Love Within Us*.

Manufactured by Amazon.ca
Bolton, ON

20908562R00213